Nate reminded himself he was the same bitter, resentful kid who'd been spirited out of town in a patrol car sixteen years ago.

And Katy Bates sure wasn't the same lively, optimistic teen beauty he'd left behind.

That thought diverted Nate from the townfolks' taunts.

Suddenly his return wasn't about proving something to himself and the citizens of Coyote Flats.

It was about bolstering the spirits of his first love.

Now was time to return the favor Katy had granted him sixteen years ago.

Nate made a pact with himself. Somehow, some way, he was going to put a smile back on Katy's lips, to return the sparkle to her hypnotic blue eyes.

And prove to this woman he never forgot that he could be worthy of her love.

Dear Reader,

With spring in the air, there's no better way to herald the season and continue to celebrate Silhouette's 20th Anniversary year than with an exhilarating month of romance from Special Edition!

Kicking off a great lineup is *Beginning with Baby,* a heartwarming THAT'S MY BABY! story by rising star Christie Ridgway. Longtime Special Edition favorite Susan Mallery turns up the heat in *The Sheik's Kidnapped Bride,* the first book in her new DESERT ROGUES series. And popular author Laurie Paige wraps up the SO MANY BABIES miniseries with *Make Way for Babies!,* a poignant reunion romance in which a set of newborn twins unwittingly plays Cupid!

Beloved author Gina Wilkins weaves a sensuous modern love story about two career-minded people who are unexpectedly swept away by desire in *Surprise Partners.* In *Her Wildest Wedding Dreams* from veteran author Celeste Hamilton, a sheltered woman finds the passion of a lifetime in a rugged rancher's arms. And finally, Carol Finch brings every woman's fantasy to life with an irresistible millionaire hero in her compelling novel *Soul Mates.*

It's a gripping month of reading in Special Edition. Enjoy!

All the best,

Karen Taylor Richman
Senior Editor

Please address questions and book requests to:
Silhouette Reader Service
U.S.: 3010 Walden Ave., P.O. Box 1325, Buffalo, NY 14269
Canadian: P.O. Box 609, Fort Erie, Ont. L2A 5X3

CAROL FINCH
SOUL MATES

Silhouette®

SPECIAL EDITION®

Published by Silhouette Books
America's Publisher of Contemporary Romance

This book is dedicated to my husband,
Ed, and our children—Christie, Jill, Kurt,
Jeff and Jon—with much love.
And to our grandchildren, Brooklynn,
Kennedy and Blake. Hugs and kisses!

 SILHOUETTE BOOKS

ISBN 0-373-24320-0

SOUL MATES

Copyright © 2000 by Connie Feddersen

This edition published by arrangement with Harlequin Books S.A.

® and TM are trademarks of Harlequin Books S.A., used under license. Trademarks indicated with ® are registered in the United States Patent and Trademark Office, the Canadian Trade Marks Office and in other countries.

Visit Silhouette at www.eHarlequin.com

Printed in U.S.A.

Books by Carol Finch

Silhouette Special Edition

Not Just Another Cowboy #1242
Soul Mates #1320

CAROL FINCH,

who also writes as Gina Robins, Debra Falcon, Connie Drake and Connie Feddersen, has penned fifty-four novels in the historical romance, contemporary romance, mystery and romantic suspense genres. A former tennis pro and high school biology instructor, Ms. Finch devotes her time to writing and working on the family's cattle ranch in Oklahoma.

Ms. Finch is a member of the Oklahoma Professional Writers' Hall of Fame. She has received seventeen nominations and seven career achievement awards from *Romantic Times Magazine* for Historical Love and Laughter, Historical Adventure, Best Contemporary Romance and Storyteller of the Year.

IT'S OUR 20th ANNIVERSARY!
We'll be celebrating all year,
Continuing with these fabulous titles,
On sale in April 2000.

Romance

#1438 Carried Away
Kasey Michaels/Joan Hohl

#1439 An Eligible Stranger
Tracy Sinclair

#1440 A Royal Marriage
Cara Colter

#1441 His Wild Young Bride
Donna Clayton

#1442 At the Billionaire's Bidding
Myrna Mackenzie

#1443 The Marriage Badge
Sharon De Vita

Desire

#1285 Last Dance
Cait London

#1286 Night Music
BJ James

#1287 Seduction, Cowboy Style
Anne Marie Winston

#1288 The Barons of Texas: Jill
Fayrene Preston

#1289 Her Baby's Father
Katherine Garbera

#1290 Callan's Proposition
Barbara McCauley

Intimate Moments

#997 The Wildes of Wyoming—Hazard
Ruth Langan

#998 Daddy by Choice
Paula Detmer Riggs

#999 The Harder They Fall
Merline Lovelace

#1000 Angel Meets the Badman
Maggie Shayne

#1001 Cinderella and the Spy
Sally Tyler Hayes

#1002 Safe in His Arms
Christine Scott

Special Edition

#1315 Beginning with Baby
Christie Ridgway

#1316 The Sheik's Kidnapped Bride
Susan Mallery

#1317 Make Way for Babies!
Laurie Paige

#1318 Surprise Partners
Gina Wilkins

#1319 Her Wildest Wedding Dreams
Celeste Hamilton

#1320 Soul Mates
Carol Finch

Prologue

You can do this, Nate. You've spent fifteen years planning and dreaming of this moment. Don't wimp out now.

Nate Channing hauled in a bracing breath and exhaled slowly. He stood face-to-face with his lowly beginnings, and he was determined to lay the bad memories to rest—here and now, once and for all.

Removing his sunglasses, he reached across the bucket seat of his car to pat his dog on the head. "Come on, Taz, let's get this done."

Nate got to his feet, then turned to confront his unpleasant past. The ramshackle farmhouse with its surrounding pastures, where he spent his misbegotten youth, had tumbled down on itself, like the bitter memories that avalanched over him. Nate stared at the dilapidated house that was silhouetted against the blazing orange-and-yellow sunset, where rolling hills flattened into gray, arid plains. This was the rugged landscape where Nate had grown up like a wild weed.

He flinched when the sights and sounds of that night—fifteen years ago to the day—erupted in his mind. He could almost see the flashing lights of the squad car, see the crowd of bystanders closing in around him while he was read his rights, cuffed by Sheriff Fuzz Havern and stuffed into the back seat. As if it happened only yesterday, voices exploded around Nate.

"'Bout time we got No-Account Nate out of our hair," someone had jeered at him.

"Yeah, all he does is raise hell and howl at the moon, like the rest of the prairie wolves that prowl around Coyote Flats," somebody else yelled smugly.

"Whaddya expect? The kid's daddy is a jailbird, and his mama boozes it up and runs around with any man who'll give her a second look."

"Good riddance, loser. Now you won't have to visit your worthless daddy in prison. You'll be right there with him!"

The sneering comments chased one another around Nate's head as he strode purposefully toward the run-down shack that was overgrown with weeds and sagebrush. He took one last look at the broken front steps, shattered windows and chipped paint on the wood-framed home, and he saw nothing that he was going to miss.

This was the best of his childhood memories, he thought with a snort. Hell of a childhood he'd had.

Nate reached into the pocket of his slacks to retrieve a lighter, then set the overgrown weeds aflame. The dry branches popped and crackled as orange flames consumed and devoured the shanty. A plume of dark smoke rose in the twilight, drifting down the rock-strewn hill in the light breeze.

Nate stood there, purging himself of his bad beginnings, watching his bitter memories burn to cinders. Now *he* owned the deed to this property that his family had rented all those years ago. Now this drafty, leaky shack was his to destroy—

and rebuild. He was going to make something from nothing, something worth remembering.

Nate continued to stand there for the longest time, listening to the forlorn howls of a pack of coyotes that trotted west across the tabletop flats that were skirted by deep, winding ravines. He felt intense heat radiating from the roaring blaze that engulfed the shack and the caved-in barn that had become little more than a pile of rotted wood through the years. Smoke rolled, and flames reached up with orange-tinged fingers to claw at the gathering night.

Nate blinked back the tears that welled up in his eyes, assuring himself that it was just the pungent whiffs of smoke that caused the watery reaction.

"It's done," he murmured, then glanced down at his faithful companion. "Come on, Taz. Let's get the hell out of here."

Chapter One

One year later

"Nate Channing is back in town." John Jessup plunked down in the front booth at the Coyote Café and stared grimly at the man across from him.

Lester Brown slumped against the red vinyl headrest, his jaw scraping his chest. "The hell you say!"

"The hell I *do* say. Saw him with my own eyes, Lester. He climbed out of a shiny black Lincoln, wearing one of them expensive Army suits, or whatever you call 'em. He swaggered into the post office. I was still in the barber shop when he walked out and headed for the bank."

Lester scratched his hairy chest and muttered under his breath. "Can't believe that hoodlum has the gumption to show his face in Coyote Flats after all these years. But he won't hang around here long, I guaran-damn-tee, not if I have anything to say about it."

"You might not have a say, Les." John stared grimly at

the leathery-faced rancher. "According to the gossip at the barber shop, Channing is the one who bought the property and built that fancy palace on the farm where he used to live."

Lester snorted sardonically. "Yeah, right. Like that no-account could afford that sprawling mansion that's been under construction for nine months. Pull my other leg, why don'tcha, John."

"No kiddin'," John insisted. "The news broke today, right there in the barber shop. Old Sheriff Havern is the one who made the announcement that the house and land belonged to Nate Channing."

"What!" Lester crowed as he bolted upright in his seat. "You swear?"

John bobbed his bushy gray head.

Lester swiveled his barrel-shaped body on the seat to address the other patrons in the café. "Y'all hear that? The terror of Coyote Flats is back in town. Nobody around here has to guess where he got the cash to build that ritzy house. Drug money. You can bet your bottom dollar on it. But no matter how fancy No-Account Nate dresses these days, you can't make silk from a sow's ear. That bad boy is bad news. Always was. Always will be."

While the pillars of Coyote Flats society—such as they were—speculated on Nate Channing's reasons for setting up a base of operation in his hometown, Katy Bates-Butler sat frozen in the corner booth of the café, listening to a half-dozen conversations taking place simultaneously. Memories she hadn't allowed herself to dwell on for more than a dozen years spiraled around her, smothering her with their intensity.

Nate Channing was back in town....

Apparently, Nate had returned to Coyote Flats the same way he'd left—in an uproar.

Forbidden and *doomed* were the first two words that popped into Katy's head. Lord, she thought she had adequately buried all those feelings and sensations attached to Nate Channing's name. Yet, emotions stirred and shifted inside her. Heartache, outrage, despair…and love. Those poignant feelings were still there, churning, threatening to crumble her carefully controlled composure.

Katy clasped her trembling hands around her coffee cup, as if it was her salvation, then squeezed her eyes shut. "Nate…" she whispered shakily.

To Katy, thoughts of Nate were synonymous with a time in her life that bubbled with dreams, promise, adventure, innocence—and torment. She could almost see Nate Channing leaning leisurely against his rattletrap car, wearing a dingy white T-shirt and faded jeans. She remembered how his shaggy hair shone like a raven's wing, how his midnight-black eyes twinkled down at her with that endearing hint of deviltry….

That boy has a heart as black as the devil's, and he has a soul to match. That's what Katy's father had said—repeatedly. *Stay away from that cocky juvenile delinquent. He's bad news, nothing but trouble.*

But Nate Channing hadn't looked like trouble to Katy. He had been her forbidden first love. In some ways he represented all those defiant, rebellious feelings that Katy had experienced when dealing with a domineering father who picked her dates and friends and demanded that she live up to his lofty expectations.

No one in this dried-up, windblown West Texas town had realized Katy and Nate were kindred spirits, even if they had been raised on opposite sides of the tracks. But Katy knew, remembered with vivid clarity, the kind of connection she'd felt to Nate. While he struggled to overcome his bad reputation and bad breeding, Katy had struggled for her independence. Nate fought back the way she'd wanted to when her father handed down his unreasonable dictates.

The night Nate was hauled off in the sheriff's squad car, ridiculed and scorned by the citizens of this rural town, Katy had stopped believing that standing up for herself and battling her father's high-handed decrees were worth the effort and frustration.

When Nate Channing left town he took the sunshine from Katy's life, and she plunged into endless nightmares. Those nightmares still ruled and dictated her life.

Willfully, Katy battled for composure as she polished off her coffee, then left a tip for her lunch. She felt the desperate need to scurry from the café and take refuge in her private sanctuary before Nate Channing showed up. She couldn't bear to have him see what had become of her after all these years. She was a shriveled mass of emotional and physical scars. Discovering what her father had done to Nate had been her unending torment. The life the dictatorial, judgmental Judge Dave Bates had imposed on Katy was nearly unbearable, but what he did to Nate was unforgivable!

Although Katy wanted to bolt to her feet and counter each one of Lester's snide insults, to defend Nate's honor, she had been taught the importance of not calling attention to herself, not arguing or debating, for fear of the painful consequences. A riptide of emotion bombarded Katy as she came to her feet.

With head downcast, Katy skulked toward the exit, trying to ignore the hidebound old fools who were verbally crucifying Nate Channing. She just wanted to scurry back to her office at the library and shut herself off from the world the way she usually did....

"Katy...? Kat?"

Oh, God, no! Kate froze in her tracks when his voice, like rich velvet, rolled over her. Katy reflexively shrank deeper into herself, feeling the spotlight of attention beam down on her. All conversation in the café died a quick death. Heads turned in synchronized rhythm to gape at the tall, darkly handsome man who blocked Katy's escape route.

"Katy Bates?" he murmured. "It is you, isn't it?"

Katy Bates was dead. Katy Bates-Butler merely existed, a

fuzzy shadow of herself, one so thoroughly crushed by her nightmarish past that she had become an *un*person. Lord, she would have given anything for Nate *not* to see her like this. Ah, if only he could have remembered her as she had once been, not as she was now!

"Remember me, Katy?"

As if she could ever forget!

It was only that gentle, caressing tone of voice that whispered from the distant past that gave her the will to look up, meet those cocoa-brown eyes and drink in the sight of olive skin and high cheekbones that denoted a mixture of Native American, Spanish and white heritage.

Mercy, he was breathtakingly attractive. He had matured magnificently, and he looked better than any man had the right to look. The tall, thin boy she remembered from the past now possessed a well-defined, athletic build. There was a dynamic aura of power and strength radiating around him. He had traded his hand-me-down clothes for an expensive three-piece suit, Italian loafers and gold Rolex watch. His lustrous black hair boasted a stylish cut that accentuated his rugged features. Everything about Nate Channing shouted wealth, prestige and success.

Wow! Could he possibly look any better?

Damn, could she possibly look any worse?

Katy stood there like a tongue-tied doofus, wearing her drab green feed-sack dress that drooped past her knees and effectively downplayed her femininity. Her mousy blond hair was shoved back in a severe knot at the nape of her neck, and several flyaway strands fell around her face. She only wore enough makeup to conceal the half-moon scar under her chin. In comparison, she resembled a lowly peasant eclipsed by a magnificent Roman god.

With all her heart—or rather what was left of it—Katy wished a hole would open beneath her feet so she could drop out of sight.

"Katy…"

She died a thousand times when his gaze flooded over her, taking in her flagpole figure and unflattering clothes. She knew what he was thinking, could almost hear him thinking it. He was thinking the same thing her deceased husband had voiced a trillion times, right to her face.

You're an unperson with no brains and no body. You're just a scrawny, homely nothing who takes up breathing space.

The hateful words tumbled over her, and Katy's shoulders slumped another notch as her gaze plunged to the floor. Her husband and father had humiliated her countless times, and she had endured, but having Nate see her like this cut all the way to her shattered soul.

Nate stood in the doorway, stunned clean to the bone, watching in astonishment as Katy zipped around him and limped away. Seeing her had been no small shock, because she was a startling contrast to the mental picture he had carried around with him for years.

My God, what in the hell had happened to Katy? He remembered her as the essence of spirit and beauty. He had lived for her dimpled smiles and ringing laughter. Now she refused to meet his gaze for more than five seconds before scuttling out the door, as if the hounds of hell were nipping at her heels. He had expected a rude reception from everyone else in Coyote Flats.

But not from Katy Bates.

"Well, well," Lester Brown mocked sarcastically. "Who are you supposed to be? The new drug lord in town, what with all your fancy duds and expensive car? You think that will impress us? Think again, No-Account Nate."

Very slowly, very deliberately, Nate pivoted on well-shod heels to confront the unsympathetic jury of citizens who had condemned him years earlier—and still condemned him now. A dozen disparaging glares horned in on him like laser beams, not the least insulting of which was Lester Brown's.

Nate made quick note of Lester's rotund physique, doughy face, full jowls and that protruding lower lip that gave the man the appearance that he was perpetually pouting. Lester looked just as Nate remembered him, though age and additional weight had not been particularly kind to him.

Nate could understand why Lester held a grudge. His son had been one of Nate's running buddies in the old days. When Nate had been arrested, Sonny Brown had been in the car with him. Lester had no intention whatsoever of forgiving Nate for soiling his son's reputation, refused to believe that it wasn't Nate's influence that had been Sonny's downfall.

Sonny hadn't needed an ounce of help to stray from the straight and narrow. All by himself, he had dreamed up the trouble that Nate hadn't even contemplated when he was a teenager. The kid had been every bit as worthless as his old man, as Nate recalled. And a weasely coward to boot.

Although Lester wouldn't admit it, not in a million years, *he* was responsible for the way his son had turned out. But that admission would force Lester to accept blame for all his shortcomings as a man, as a father. It was never going to happen because Lester couldn't see over, around or through his inflated ego.

Squelching his bitterness and resentment, Nate nodded at the burly farmer who was sprawled carelessly in the front booth. "Hello, Lester, nice to see you again." Head held high, Nate ambled toward the counter to order a Coke.

"Better get that drink to go," Lester sneered. "Folks around here don't take to fraternizing with pond scum. And that's all you are, no matter how fancy you wrap the package."

The self-esteem Nate had spent years cultivating wobbled on its foundations. He had convinced himself, promised himself, that he would stand firm against the anticipated ridicule. Unfortunately, his pride was taking a beating on the first official day of his return to his hometown.

"You hear what I said, *boy?*" Lester taunted unmercifully. "Get it to go, and don't come back. You aren't wanted here."

The teenage waitress glanced uneasily at Nate as she set the soft drink on the counter. "That'll be seventy-five cents, sir."

"Don't waste your breath calling him sir," John Jessup said. "Channing doesn't deserve consideration or respect. Just treat him like the mongrel he is."

Nate endured the insults without flinching. He tossed two dollar bills on the counter for an extra tip, then turned to face Lester and John's condescending glowers. He was not going to stoop to anybody's low expectations of him ever again, he promised himself resolutely.

Although he had been in and out of enough hot water as a teenager to pass as a load of laundry and had been picked up for assault, battery and destruction of personal property, Nate had spent his adult life working toward acceptance and respectability. He had surrounded himself with symbols of power and wealth to insulate himself against inferior feelings planted by men like Lester Brown and John Jessup. But damn, standing here, confronting the unwelcoming faces from his misguided youth resurrected all those unproductive feelings he thought he'd overcome.

Nate knew the folks in Coyote Flats were still seeing and judging him by his parentage and his past mistakes. They were not prepared to accept him for the solid citizen he had become, for the dramatic attitude adjustments he'd made. To these people, he was the same as he had been sixteen years ago, the same wayward youth who'd gone bad.

You can't go home again...

The negative thought skittered through his mind, but Nate rejected it, even while he was being judged and rejected. Somehow, he would earn the trust and respect of these dogmatic folks in this dying Texas town. He would not let them get the better of him, and he would give them no reason whatsoever to compare him to the troubled, hurt, neglected kid he had once been.

Clinging to his battered pride, Nate exited the café, feeling the condescending gazes stabbing him in the back. The minute he stepped outside, he realized he had been holding his breath. He exhaled slowly, congratulating himself for passing the first of what he predicted would be many tests of self-control and character. He hadn't lowered himself to Lester Brown and John Jessup's rude, disrespectful level. He had been polite, not belligerent. He had treated the men with courtesy, even though it hadn't been reciprocated.

Nate's tension ebbed and an amused smile pursed his lips when he noticed that Millie Kendrick was waddling toward him. Leaning on a grocery cart for support, Millie toddled across the town square, which was surrounded by shade trees. She circled around the fountain where a statue of a coyote sat on a rock, its concrete head thrown back in an eternal howl.

Millie and her shopping cart had logged many a mile on these streets, he recalled. The old woman looked exactly as Nate remembered her. Millie was dressed in her usual attire of a flowery cotton smock and tattered straw hat that was adorned with plastic bluebirds, cardinals and sunflowers she had glued to the floppy brim. Folks in Coyote Flats claimed Millie was touched in the head, that she blurted out the first thing that came to mind. But nonetheless, folks tolerated her presence in town.

Unfortunately, the citizens of Coyote Flats had zero tolerance for Nate Channing—the hoodlum who had bad blood pumping through his veins. Nate, they had concluded, would never overcome his lowly raising. He was destined for trouble.

Millie halted ten feet away from Nate, propped her elbows on her shopping cart, then angled her head to look him up and down—twice.

"Nate Channing, ain't it?" she panted, out of breath from her long hike.

"Yes, ma'am," he said politely.

"Didja come back to kick some butt?"

Nate met the spry old woman's mischievous grin and felt himself relax for the first time all day. Millie was one of the few people in his hometown who had ever bothered to give him the time of day.

"No, ma'am," Nate replied. "I gave up on kicking butt and taking names years ago. It just never seemed to do much good."

She appraised his appearance carefully, then said, "Pretty fancy duds for a kid from the poor side of town. Didja steal 'em?"

"No, ma'am. Paid in cash," he assured her, smiling in response to her gruff, no-nonsense interrogation.

"Turned out all right then, did you?" She pushed herself upright and gripped the handle of her grocery cart. "Glad to see it. Figured you would, though. What he did to you wasn't fair, not fair at all." When she shook her frizzy gray head, the plastic birds wobbled on the brim of her hat. "Tried to tell him so, I did. But the old fool wouldn't listen to me. Nobody ever listens to me."

Befuddled, Nate watched Millie shove off to the mom-and-pop grocery store. She was still mumbling to herself when she crossed the street.

Nate had no idea what Millie meant by her parting remarks, and he didn't have time to stand around woolgathering. The heartbreaking sight of Katy Bates compelled him down the street. Nate damn well intended to confront Katy again, away from the prying eyes of his local hate club—of which Brown and Jessup had elected themselves president and vice president.

Nate made a beeline for the library. Katy Bates was one of the three reasons he had returned to Coyote Flats. After encountering her at the café, she had been elevated to the top of Nate's priority list. If Katy thought she could duck and run away from him, she thought wrong. Their brief reunion had prompted a hundred questions, and Nate wanted answers—now.

Coyote Library sat a block north of Main Street. As Nate recalled, the small hole-in-the-wall structure had once housed a sleazy bar. The establishment was crying out for a coat of paint, and Nate suspected the town hadn't allocated much in the way of funds to keep the library up-to-date.

The instant Nate stepped inside the building, his speculations were confirmed. Unstained plywood shelves lined the main room. The floor was covered with vintage, gray-speckled linoleum left over from the days when tavern-goers boot-scooted to the strains of country music. Stains on the ceiling tile indicated there were a half-dozen leaks in the roof. The scarred wooden bar now served as the library counter. An outdated copy machine sat in the corner, and picnic tables and benches lined the walls.

Although the public library was neat and clean, the atmosphere was gloomy. Faulty fluorescent lights—that would drive Nate nuts if he had to spend the day working beneath them—flickered down on him.

This was Katy's world, Nate realized with a sense of shock and dismay. He took another assessing appraisal of the place and found it sorely lacking. This library was nothing compared to his ultramodern office in Odessa.

"May I help you?"

Nate glanced at the teenage girl who had her blond hair pulled back in a ponytail. She smiled at him, displaying the braces on her teeth. Something about her reminded him of the visual image of Katy that he had carried around in his head. There was a noticeable family resemblance....

My God...was this Katy's daughter? Could this girl have been Nate's daughter...?

The startling possibility made his knees wobble.

"Were you looking for a particular kind of book, sir?" Tammy Bates asked helpfully.

Nate flashed his best smile. "No, I would like to speak with Katy, please."

The girl hitched her thumb over her shoulder. "Katy is in her office. You can go on back if you like."

Nate zigzagged around the picnic tables—for God's sake!— that accommodated patrons who wanted to sit down and thumb through the limited supply of books on the shelves.

Nate was granted the opportunity to observe Katy unaware while she sat in profound concentration at her outdated computer, which looked exactly like the one Nate had pitched from his office eight years earlier so he could upgrade his equipment. Katy's shoulders were hunched the same way they had been when he encountered her at the café.

What the sweet loving hell had happened to that bubbly teenager he had fallen head over heels in love with all those years ago? Katy had been spirited and enthusiastic. A vivacious cheerleader. A snappy dresser with a dazzling smile. Katy had been the heartthrob of every male in town—Nate included.

Pity and disappointment slammed through Nate as he stared at this new and dramatically different Katy. While he had scratched and clawed to make something of himself, desperate and determined to rise above his miserable raising, hell-bent on making a triumphant return to this crummy little spot-on-the-road town, Katy had been backsliding.

What life-altering incident had broken her spirit, made her coil in on herself, as if she had all but given up on life?

God, seeing the hunch-shouldered woman with her downcast head and unsmiling face was agonizing for Nate. He had wanted to return to find Katy exactly as she had been—full of life, the picture of innocence and hope.

Ah, how many times had she delivered pep talks to him, assuring him that he could become anything he wanted, that he shouldn't let the stigma attached to his name get him down? She had believed in him when no one else saw the slightest potential. She had encouraged him when everyone else wrote him off as No-Account Nate who was destined for welfare checks and stints in prison.

"Katy?" he murmured, trying not to startle her as badly as he had at the restaurant.

She instantly flinched, then swiveled her head around to stare at him. Her huge blue eyes—eyes that he'd drowned in a thousand times as a kid—widened in surprise. She sat rigidly at the computer, her fingers frozen on the keyboard. Two lines of *K*s bleeped across the monitor.

Nate tossed her a grin. "You might want to ease your finger off the letter *K,* unless you plan to print out an entire page of them."

"Oh." She snatched her hand off the keyboard, as if she'd been snake-bitten, then stared at her lap, not him.

The fact that she refused to make eye contact for more than a split second annoyed and confused Nate. Sixteen years of separation and all she could think to say to him was *oh?* Nate's expectations of their reunion had been exceedingly high, he was the first to admit. But as far as reunions went, this one was the absolute pits.

The truth was that Nate had visions of Katy bounding from her vinyl chair—which was wrapped in duct tape to prevent the padding from sticking out—and launching herself into his arms to shower him with welcoming kisses.

So much for fantasy. This encounter was as huge a disappointment as the one in the restaurant.

Katy silently cursed the fact that Nate had tracked her down. She was thoroughly embarrassed and humiliated to have him see her at her worst. She looked like a blob of lime gelatin quivering on her chair, while he appeared dashing and vital and alive.

Why wouldn't he go away and leave her to her misery? It

was killing her to know she had made nothing of her life and that he had taken the world by the tail and given it a whirl. She was delighted for him, of course, had always known that he was teeming with potential, if only someone would give him a chance to make a fresh start.

She, on the other hand, had spiraled downhill, landed hard and never recovered. For two young kids who had made an emotional connection sixteen years ago, they had certainly ended up on opposite ends of the spectrum.

"Talk to me," he urged as he strode forward. "What happened to you, Kat?"

He filled her cubicle office with a strength and vitality that had become a distant memory to Katy. Heavens, she couldn't remember what *spirit* and *enthusiasm* meant these days, without looking them up in the dictionary.

"What do you want to talk about?" she asked with cool reserve. "If you need reference books, Tammy can help you at the front desk. I'm very busy, Nate. I'm typing a letter to the city council to request funds so I can afford to order more books and retain Tammy as my part-time employee."

"We haven't seen each other in sixteen years and all you can say is, 'I'm busy'?" Nate asked. His gaze bore into her with such intensity that she looked the other way. "No one else in this town is thrilled to see me. I didn't expect anything from them, but I guess I expected something more from you."

His voice rumbled with anger and Katy reflexively shrank away. When he abruptly jerked up his hand to rake it through that shiny crop of coal-black hair, Katy embarrassed herself by ducking and flinching. Oh, God, now he would know for sure that she was a sniveling little coward who was afraid of her own shadow.

Nate froze to the spot when he witnessed Katy's instantaneous reaction to his exasperated tone and sudden movement. It didn't take a genius to realize she had suffered from physical abuse. She reminded him so much of Taz, the mutt that he had taken into his home. The poor animal had been starved and kicked around by its previous owners. Taz tucked his tail between its legs and slunk from the room when Nate raised his voice. The mutt had seemed the perfect pet for a man who shared the same lowly breeding, and Nate had developed a natural affinity to underdogs in this world, because he'd been one for more than half his life.

Katy, he suspected, had been struck and browbeaten until she had all but given up on hope and happiness. It was there in the desolate expression in those beautiful blue eyes, the lines of grim acceptance that bracketed her mouth, in her braced posture.

My God, she behaved as if she expected him to storm over to her desk and backhand her! She should remember that he had *never* laid a hand on her, should know that he would never lay a hand on her.

Dear God in heaven, who had done this to her? Who had reduced her to an insecure, fearful, shrinking violet of a female?

Tears welled up in Katy's eyes when she saw that look of sympathy cross Nate's ruggedly handsome face. It was killing her, inch by anguishing inch, for him to see what she had become. For every positive step Nate had taken toward his future, she had taken two crawdad shuffles backward.

"Please leave, Nate," she whispered brokenly. "We have nothing in common anymore, except that we grew up in the same hometown. But know this…" Katy inhaled a deep breath and forced herself to meet his sympathetic gaze—at least she did for a few seconds before glancing at the air over his head. "I'm very proud of you. I admire you for turning your life around. I wish all the best for you. Never doubt that."

She spun around in her chair to delete the two lines of *K*s, then continued typing her letter, praying he would take the cue and beat a hasty retreat from her office before she broke down and blubbered.

He didn't budge from the spot.

"Do you have any idea how long I've carried your memory around with me, heard the words of encouragement you offered me when times were so bad I could barely tolerate them? You inspired me to make something of myself.

"Sheriff Havern gave me the chance that no one else in this town was willing to give me. I have you and Havern to thank for turning my life around. I'm not going to turn my back on you, Katy Marie Bates, you can count on it. And you know damned good and well that I never broke a promise to you. I'm sure as hell not about to start now!"

His parting remarks were heaven and hell in one. She wanted him to stay, to teach her how to mend her broken dreams. Yet she wanted him to walk away and never come back, because she had given up hope so long ago that it was difficult to remember what hope was.

When Nate finally turned around and walked away, Katy slumped over the keyboard. Nate had no idea how hard these past sixteen years had been on her. He refused to admit that the girl he remembered no longer existed. But Katy knew that enthusiastic teenager had not survived. That vibrant young woman was nothing more than a distant memory who lived in the past.

Overwhelmed by emotion, Katy did the very thing she promised herself she wouldn't do. She broke down and bawled her head off, just like the weak coward she was.

Chapter Two

Nate shot through the library and stormed down the street. If Katy didn't have the courage to tell him what—or who— had broken her spirit and made her give up so completely on herself, the former sheriff of Coyote County would. Fuzz Havern was another reason Nate was back in town, and Fuzz was going to help Nate understand what had turned his sweet, adorable Katy into a pitiful, drab-looking librarian who holed herself up in an office, surrounded by books.

He suspected that she had become content to live through the pages of all those books, watching the dreams of fictitious characters come true because her own dreams had fallen short. Those damn books had become her world, her only reality.

Well, Katy Marie Bates had another thing coming if she thought Nate was going to let her continue on the pathetic course she was on! He owed her more than he could possibly repay, but that wasn't going to stop him from doing whatever was necessary to help Katy.

Nate pounded the pavement to reach his car, totally ignoring Lester Brown and John Jessup, who had moseyed from the café to monitor his activities like a couple of tails staking out a known criminal.

"Been to the library, I see," Lester taunted. "Bet it's the first time you've set foot inside one, isn't it?" He flicked his thick wrist as Nate walked by without breaking stride or acknowledging his presence. "Atta boy, Nate. Climb back in that fancy-schmancy car and hightail it out of Coyote Flats. You're the reason my boy turned sour, and I don't need any reminders of that. Sonny was a good kid until you poisoned him with your bad blood. Get the hell out of here and don't come back!" he all but shouted at Nate's departing back.

"Yeah, what he said," John Jessup quickly seconded.

Nate plunked into the bucket seat and turned the key in the ignition. He revved the engine to drown out the scornful words. His knee-jerk reaction was to lay rubber and prove to those snippy old coots that he didn't give a flying fig what they thought of him. Luckily, Nate recovered his cool before he reverted to his teenage antics and behaved exactly as Brown and Jessup anticipated.

Like a conscientious, law-abiding citizen, Nate veered slowly from the curb and observed the speed limit as he drove toward his new home three miles from this dust-choked, outdated, economically challenged, one-horse town.

Don't let them get to you, he chanted to himself. *Don't let them whittle away at your pride and self-confidence. You're a self-made man who came up from rock bottom, and you've earned your success. If you start looking at yourself through their condemning eyes, your struggles and hard-won victories will count for nothing. You knew it would take time to prove yourself to the folks in this town. You knew you would have to earn a respectable reputation. Have patience, man. You knew damned good and well this wasn't going to be easy.*

Nate sucked in a cleansing breath and reminded himself that

he wasn't the same bitter, resentful kid who had been spirited out of town in a patrol car.

And Katy Bates sure as hell wasn't the same lively, optimistic teenage beauty queen he had left behind in a flash of lights and the scream of sirens.

That tormenting thought served to distract Nate from Brown and Jessup's taunts. Suddenly, his return to his hometown wasn't about proving something to himself and to the citizens of Coyote Flats. It was about bolstering the spirits of a woman who had all but given up on life. It was time to return the favor Katy had granted him sixteen years ago.

Nate made a pact with himself one mile later. Somehow, some way, he was going to put a smile back on Katy's lips and return the sparkle to those hypnotic blue eyes that dominated Katy's pale, thin face. She may have forgotten how to fight back, but Nate sure hadn't. And by damned, he was going to teach her how it was done!

"My gosh, Aunt Katy, who was that hunk?" Tammy Bates questioned as she propped herself against the office door.

Katy smiled ruefully at her niece, then handed over the letter she had prepared for the city council. "He's an old friend from high school," she replied as casually as she knew how.

"Man, and here I thought Brad Pitt, Leonardo DiCaprio and Matt Damon were incredible to look at! Wow! Talk about tall, dark and handsome!"

Tammy's love-struck expression was the spitting image of the dreamy smiles Katy had worn a lifetime ago while mooning over Nate Channing. Of course, Katy had had the good sense not to bring up Nate's name in front of her father, only in front of her friends. Judge Dave Bates had gone ballistic the few times he had caught Katy and Nate together. She had paid dearly for those secret rendezvous, too. Dave had decreed that Nate was off-limits, and her father had dreamed up ways to keep them separated.

Later, when Kate discovered to what drastic extremes her father had abused his power and used his influence to ensure Nate was out of her life for good, she had never forgiven him, had lost all respect for him.

Although Nate seemed determined to strike up a friendship with Katy, she knew it was utterly impossible to mend the broken bridges. She knew that, ultimately, she was the reason Nate had been forced out of town and never permitted to return.

She had also seen Nate's look of pity when he stared at her. She had nothing to offer the prominent, successful man Nate Channing had become. She was damaged merchandise. Her physical and emotional scars had left her with feelings of inadequacy and unattractiveness that she couldn't overcome.

Nate deserved better than a mousy female who had been in an emotional coma for years and couldn't remember how to laugh and smile. He needed someone exciting and attractive, someone who could stand up for herself, someone who could walk without a limp, someone who could look a man squarely in the eye and feel that she was his equal.

Nate had reinvented himself while she had shriveled up inside. She had nothing to offer him now or ever again.

"So, what's his name, Aunt Katy?" Tammy grilled her.

"Nate Channing."

Tammy frowned pensively. "I don't recognize the name. Is his family still around here?"

"No."

"So he just stopped by to visit you on his way through town?"

Katy shrugged her thin-bladed shoulders. "Please hand-deliver this letter to the city hall. I want the secretary to put my request on the agenda before the council's meeting."

"Sure." Tammy spun around, her ponytail bobbing as she walked away. "But I still think Nate Channing is incredibly good-looking. Maybe you should find out if he's staying overnight in town and invite him over for supper."

"Maybe you should stop playing matchmaker and mind your own business," Katy called after her.

Tammy pirouetted, then grinned unrepentantly at her aunt. "I'll mind my own business if you will admit that Nate is one great-looking guy."

"Okay, he's a knockout," Katy admitted honestly. "Happy now?"

"I would be if you would chase him down and invite him to supper," Tammy said before she whipped around and sauntered away.

Katy scrunched into her chair and stared at the blank wall where Nate's handsome face had superimposed itself. "Too vital, too good-looking. Far too deserving of someone like me," she said sensibly to herself.

There had been a time when Katy had dreamed of her darkly handsome knight riding back into her life to rescue her from a disastrous marriage and whisk her away from a domineering father who offered no moral support, who constantly sided with her husband. But no one had come to her rescue, and her own attempts to fight for her freedom earned painful blows.

It was too late for her to start fresh, too late to mend all her shattered dreams. This was as good as her life would get, she assured herself fatalistically.

Resolved not to let Nate make the mistake of trying to reestablish their friendship, Katy forced herself to concentrate on her work. For Nate's sake she had to discourage him from future contact. Katy had nothing to offer him now. Too much water had flooded under the bridge of her life. She had learned to accept what she hadn't been able to change, and she had learned to center her life around the books that lined the library shelves. The characters on the pages of those books were her friends and acquaintances. They were safe, and she was secure inside the walls of this building.

Eventually, Nate would realize that the happiness and confidences they shared a lifetime ago were like closed chapters in a book. He would look elsewhere for a fulfilling friendship and leave her to the life she had grown comfortable with. It was too late to change, Katy told herself. She wasn't even going to try.

Nate strode into his new ranch-style home to see Fuzz Havern, the retired sheriff of Coyote County, sprawled on the leather recliner. Fuzz had traded his police-issued pistol for the remote control to the big-screen TV.

Fuzz was all smiles when he glanced up to see Nate stride into the spacious living room. Nate wished he felt half of Fuzz's obvious pleasure and satisfaction. Unfortunately, seeing what had become of Katy Bates had turned Nate wrong-side-out. He still couldn't believe Katy had changed so dramatically.

"Pinch me, Nate," Fuzz insisted. "I swear I must be dreaming all this. How can I possibly be sitting in this luxurious house, living like a king?" Fuzz swiped a meaty hand over his military-style gray hair and beamed in pleasure again. "After all the tense situations in the line of duty, here I am, kicked back, surfing channels and loving every minute of it." He glanced around the expensively furnished room. "This place is really something else, Nate."

"I'm glad you agreed to our arrangements," Nate said as he plopped down on the matching leather sofa. "I told you sixteen years ago that I would repay you for what you did for me."

Fuzz nodded, remembering. "Yeah, well, all I did was give you the break nobody around here was willing to give you. You took the opportunity I arranged for you, and you ran with it." He tossed Nate a knowing glance. "I don't imagine you thought I was doing you any favors those first few months after I left you in Bud Thurston's charge."

Nate returned the grin. "No, I didn't," he recalled. "That ex-marine sergeant knew how to put a wayward youth through the drills, didn't he?"

"Amen to that," Fuzz agreed. "But Bud taught you discipline, the value of a hard day's work, just as I asked him to do."

Nate remembered the big, burly, gruff-mannered man who stood six feet six inches tall and weighed in at two-eighty— every pound solid, unyielding muscle. Bud Thurston had clamped a beefy fist around the ribbing on Nate's T-shirt, jerked him off the ground and told Nate what was what. Bud had also taught Nate to be courteous, considerate, respectful and cooperative—or else.

Way out in the middle of nowhere, on Thurston Ranch, Bud was a law unto himself, and he was man enough to back up any command or threat he spouted. Nobody in his right mind messed with Bud, not if you planned to walk away from a confrontation in one piece.

Then, of course, there was Fuzz Havern, who checked on Nate once a month like a parole officer. Between the two men who had served together in the military, Nate had been nudged down the straight-and-narrow path and gotten his miserable life on course. It had taken a year for a bitter, mule-headed kid to change his ways, but it had been worth the effort. Nate was eternally grateful somebody was willing to help him make the needed changes in his behavior and attitude.

"You'll notice that I didn't extend the same generosity to Sonny Brown that night I hauled your sorry butt out of town," Fuzz remarked, then channel-surfed to his heart's content. "That boy never could overcome his raising, not with Lester there to defend him every time he made a bonehead mistake. The only way to save Sonny would have been to shoot his father. I couldn't stretch the law that far."

"Where is Sonny these days?" Nate asked.

"Doing time up in Big Spring," Fuzz reported. "Every

time he does another hitch in jail he learns another trick and tries it out when he walks back into society. And every time Sonny is taken into custody, Lester claims his kid is innocent.''

"He is still blaming me for driving Sonny to ruin," Nate commented.

"Of course he is. Lester isn't the kind of man who's big enough to admit to his own failings and mistakes. It has always been someone else's fault that his boy was worthless. It was the fault of bad weather conditions and plummeting cattle-market prices that caused him to lose his shirt in the ranching business."

Fuzz shook his head. "Nope, you couldn't convince Lester Brown that his laziness, his lack of ambition and lack of discipline for himself, and Sonny, caused his misfortune, not even if you dedicated an entire month of your life to explaining it to him... Why the sudden interest in Lester? Did you run into him already?"

Nate squelched his frustration and ignored the taunts still buzzing around his head. "Yeah, Lester and John Jessup headed up the unwelcoming committee when I drove into town to open a bank account and fill out the forms to have mail delivered to this address."

Fuzz stared grimly at Nate. "Don't let Lester get to you. I warned you that he would be on your case, along with his comical sidekick, Jessup. That was the first test you had to pass. You'll have to turn the other cheek when those two lay into you."

"They already did, twice today," Nate confided.

Fuzz stared at Nate for a long, pensive moment. "Why don't you just tell them flat-out why you came back? Maybe they would cut you a little slack."

This wasn't the first time Fuzz had questioned Nate's strategy. Personally, Nate didn't think the reasons for his return to

Coyote Flats would change the low public opinion of him. No, Nate had to do things his own way, in his own good time.

The first phase of Nate's crusade was already in place. He had constructed this spacious house on the site of his birthplace. He had convinced Fuzz Havern to share his home, rather than puttering around in that tiny garage apartment the retired sheriff rented after his wife died eight years earlier. Nate knew Sally Havern's long bout with cancer had drained Fuzz's savings account and plunged him into debt. Fuzz's retirement pension barely covered expenses. Convincing Fuzz to move in with him was Nate's way of repaying this man who had seen to it that a troubled kid had a chance to turn his life around.

Nate had specifically designed this house so Fuzz would have a private living area, bedroom, bath and kitchenette in the west wing. Of course, Fuzz could make use of the rest of the house any time he felt like socializing with Nate. That was the deal—no rent, no utility bills. Fuzz could stock his kitchenette with his favorite foods, buy personal supplies and maintain his pickup truck. Nate took care of everything else.

Although Fuzz had insisted on sharing a larger portion of the living expenses, Nate wouldn't hear of it. This was his way of repaying a tremendous favor, and Fuzz just had to accept that.

The patter of canine feet on the kitchen ceramic tile prompted Fuzz to glance over his shoulder. He rolled his eyes as Taz trotted into the living room to shove his snout under Nate's hand, demanding a pat on the head.

"I gotta tell ya, Nate. That is the ugliest mutt I've ever laid eyes on." He regarded Nate shrewdly. "Is Taz the same kind of charity case I am?"

Nate stroked the affection-starved mongrel that was a cross between a blue heeler, border collie and German shepherd, but his full attention was riveted on Fuzz. "Let's get one thing straight here," he said firmly, directly. "You are not a charity case. You are, and always were, the only man in this Podunk town who gave a damn about me. When I was a kid, you saved me from a few beatings at my old man's hands."

"But there were times when I wasn't around to stop them," Fuzz murmured regretfully.

Nate didn't particularly want to revisit those hellish memories. Living the nightmare was bad enough. Being knocked around, stepped on and locked out of the house for punishment was behind him now. His daddy hadn't been anyone's idea of a role-model parent, that was for sure. Gary Channing had done his stint in Vietnam, and the hell he'd endured screwed up his life royally. Nate wasn't about to make excuses for his old man, who took his torment out on his kid, but the more he read about the trauma suffered by war veterans, the more he understood that Gary Channing was too busy battling his own demons to offer guidance to his son.

All Nate received from his father was a hefty life insurance policy that had been bought and paid for by his father's parents. When Gary died in prison seven years earlier, Nate had acquired a financial base to invest in the oil industry, where he had been working for the previous three years.

It was Bud Thurston and Fuzz Havern, ex-marine sergeants, who had vouched for Nate when he applied for the job working endless hours on the oil rigs. Nate had been praised by his new employer for his hard work, respectfulness and cooperation.

Bud and Fuzz's behavior modification program had worked like a charm. It was Bud who first employed Nate on the ranch west of Odessa and taught him to work and to be responsible for equipment and machinery. Fourteen-hour days, seven days a week on Bud's ranch and on oil rigs was no picnic, but it left Nate no time to revert to his old ways. Nate had been too exhausted to do anything except plop his aching body into bed and sleep.

During those years on Thurston Ranch Nate had strung

miles of barbed wire fences, had been launched off the backs of more ornery horses than he cared to count. He had been run down, kicked and stepped on by jittery cattle during roundup. But he had always managed to hoist himself to his feet to face another exhausting day.

Oh, yeah, Bud was one hell of a taskmaster, but Bud had been fair, honest and straightforward. He hadn't put up with any crap from Nate or the other boys delivered to his care, and Nate had every intention of repaying "Sarge." The first-born calves from Nate's cattle herd, which was presently grazing in the surrounding pastures of the property he had purchased the previous year would become a gift to Bud Thurston.

Nate Channing fully intended to repay every kindness extended to him. Furthermore, he was going to find a way to turn Katy Bates's life around. He couldn't abide by what she had done to herself—or rather, what some maniacal beast had done to her.

Nate continued to stroke the mongrel's broad head. "I ran into Katy Bates in town this morning."

Fuzz winced. "Did you?"

Nate's gaze narrowed on the retired sheriff. What caused that reaction? he wondered.

Fuzz stared out the bay window, which provided a panoramic view of cattle grazing in the pasture. "You, I managed to rescue in time. She, I couldn't," he said regretfully.

A knot of apprehension coiled in the pit of Nate's belly. He really didn't like the sound of that. "Tell me about Katy."

Fuzz arched a thick brow and smiled knowingly. Nate figured he must have given himself away by the way he murmured her name.

"She's another reason you came back to town, isn't she?" Fuzz nodded thoughtfully. "I figured as much, but you didn't mention her name when you gave me that sales pitch about how you wanted me to move into this palace with you and help you out by checking on your cattle herd while you were tied up with overseeing the construction of your local branch office for your Sunrise Oil Company.''

Fuzz flicked off the television and settled himself more comfortably in the easy chair. ''You really had it bad for that girl when you were a kid, didn't you? Not that I blame you. Katy was really a vision in those days. Cute as a button when she was in kindergarten, then blossomed into an eye-catching young woman.''

When Nate didn't respond, Fuzz snickered. ''Aw, come on, son. You think I didn't know how you mooned over that girl? You think the judge didn't trot into my office and demand that I slap a restraining order on you after he found out the two of you were meeting on the sly?''

Nate's eyes widened in surprise. He'd had a few confrontations with old man Bates, none of them pleasant. Dave Bates had warned Nate to stay away from his precious daughter, threatened to blow him to smithereens if Nate so much as set foot on the front porch. According to old man Bates, Nate was the worst kind of white trash that ever drew breath and he wasn't fit to breathe the same air as Katy. But Nate hadn't known the influential Judge Bates had tried to twist Fuzz's arm into taking legal action, in attempt to halt the blossoming romance.

''Oh, yeah,'' Fuzz said, then chuckled. ''Dave bent my ears all the damn time. He claimed you were stalking his daughter, insisted that she was terrified of you. But I knew better. While I was cruising around the school grounds, I saw the way Katy looked at you when the two of you were speaking privately.''

''But you didn't knuckle under to the judge's pressure,'' Nate presumed.

''No, I told Dave there was no evidence of wrongdoing. I also told him that I had talked to Katy, and she confirmed that you had done nothing whatsoever to deserve a restraining order.'' Fuzz grinned wryly. ''But I did cruise through that residential section of town enough times to notice that rattletrap car you used to drive was often parked a few doors down the street from Katy's house.''

Nate squirmed uncomfortably. He'd had it bad in those days. He couldn't begin to count the nights he had driven to Katy's neighborhood and sat there in his car, staring at that house, wishing he were welcome. He would sit there puffing on a cigarette, wishing he wasn't a social pariah, wishing Katy wasn't off-limits, wishing he had the right to escort her around town and let all the other boys know she belonged to him. Oh, yeah, and he'd also wished he could win the lottery so he could afford to take her out to fancy restaurants, like the kids of Coyote Flats' high society did when they dated.

In those days Nate barely had enough pocket change to fuel his gas-guzzling, bucket-of-rust car and put food in his mouth. His ill-fitting clothes were hand-me-downs that the United Methodist Women's Society donated to his family once a year, along with a Thanksgiving basket of food.

It had been humiliating to be dirt poor and to be head over boot heels in love with a girl whose weekly allowance was higher than the salary he made as part-time attendant at the service station.

Embarrassment and humiliation didn't keep Nate from caring deeply for that warm, sweet young woman who treated him as if he were special, though the other members of her social clique flung up their noses and pretended he didn't exist. Nate honestly didn't know what Katy had seen in him back in those days, but she had bolstered his confidence, defended him to her snooty friends, treated him with the kind of respect he had never encountered in Coyote Flats.

Nope, Nate reminded himself. There had been no one like Katy Bates. Every woman he'd been with since then had never measured up to her. She had been kind, caring, supportive and generous of heart. Nowadays, women were easily accessible because of his financial success in the oil industry. But Nate hadn't had time for lengthy relationships, not when he was obsessively driven to succeed in business, to keep the promise he had made to himself when Sheriff Fuzz Havern had loaded his sorry butt into the squad car and driven straight to Bud Thurston's ranch. During that late-night drive, Fuzz had told Nate that he was going to get one chance to make something out of his life. If he blew it, he would be on his own.

That long-winded lecture from Fuzz was something Nate had never forgotten. He'd been scared and desperate enough to listen that fateful night.

"Katy has changed drastically over the years, hasn't she?" Fuzz said, jostling Nate from his pensive musings.

"I almost didn't recognize her," Nate admitted. "What happened?"

Fuzz rose to his feet. "I'm going to rob your fridge of a Coke to wet my whistle. Want one?"

Nate nodded as he rose to let the mongrel outside. When he returned, Fuzz handed him an iced-down cola, then sprawled in his chair. "The only reason I can tell you about what happened to Katy is that the two detrimental influences in her life are dead and gone, so you can't revert to your old ways and beat the hell out of them."

Nate winced. God, how grim was this tale? he wondered. It must be bad if Fuzz predicted Nate would be tempted to tear off on a mission of revenge.

Fuzz sipped his cola, then focused solemnly on Nate. "I chose to transport you out of town that night, despite the fact that Judge Bates wanted you incarcerated so he could have you delivered to a detention center. From that day forward, the judge took Katy firmly and relentlessly in hand. You already know about Dave's crusade to pick her friends for her."

Nate nodded. He remembered that Katy often confided her frustration with her old man. Dave saw his daughter as a reflection on his prominent position in the county. He was convinced that he and his children had a lofty image to uphold.

The family was wealthy and high-class, and they were not supposed to associate with white trash, not even in this small community with its cross section of socioeconomic classes. Katy resented her father's snobbish airs, but Dave ruled his roost with a stern hand, and when he pounded his gavel, he considered his decrees forevermore written in stone.

"Judge Bates decided the Butlers, who owned the big ranch south of town, would make an ideal connection. The Butlers had money coming out their ears," Fuzz explained. "They also had a son and daughter who were close enough in age to Katy and her brother, James, to make a double match."

Nate swore under his breath. He had never had a smidgen of respect for the high-and-mighty Judge Bates, who looked down his nose at the less fortunate. But Dave's patriarchal matchmaking filled Nate with disgust.

Fuzz took another sip of his drink, then continued. "Dave pushed his son at Butler's daughter, shelling out money so James could escort Shelly to the fanciest restaurants, the best movies and musical concerts held in Odessa." He glanced pointedly at Nate. "Of course, if James wanted to date someone else, there was no pocket change handed out."

"In other words, the judge used money to bribe his son into turning his attention to Shelly Butler," Nate muttered.

"You got it," Fuzz confirmed. "As for Katy, she was only allowed to date Brad Butler. If anyone else asked her out during high school she wasn't allowed to go."

"Brad Butler," Nate murmured thoughtfully. "Wasn't he the hotshot football star who went to play at West Texas State for a couple of years after graduation?"

"Right," Fuzz replied. "Bradley's dad made generous contributions to the college athletic program to get his kid on the roster. Brad was big and mean and loved full-body contact sports, on and off the playing field."

The bitter sound of Fuzz's voice caused alarm signals to

clang in Nate's brain. Sure as hell, he was going to hate hearing what came next.

"With Dave Bates pushing and prodding both his kids, they married into the Butler family. James was married a month after he graduated high school and had a child within the year."

"A girl who works at the library with Katy?" Nate asked.

"That'd be Tammy," Fuzz confirmed. "Her mama ran off with another man when Tammy was six, causing the Butlers and the judge all sorts of embarrassment. James only comes around a couple of weekends a month. He is married to his profession as a legal consultant for one of those highfalutin corporations in Dallas. Tammy lives with Katy most of the time."

"And Katy's husband?" Nate questioned. The first thing he had noticed when he recognized Katy at the café was that she wasn't wearing a wedding ring. According to what Fuzz had said earlier, Nate knew that Brad Butler had died. "What happened to the football star?"

"Six feet under," Fuzz said without an ounce of regret. "Same as Judge Bates, who had a heart attack and keeled over on the courthouse steps. Dave and Brad are probably rotting in hell together as we speak."

No love lost there, Nate noted. It was easy to tell that Fuzz wasn't a member of Dave or Brad's fan clubs.

Fuzz squirmed in his chair, clearly unenthused about continuing this briefing. "You got any chips and dip in that fully automated refrigerator of yours?"

Nate smiled faintly as he came to his feet. He remembered how Fuzz had carried on about the ice-and-water dispenser in the door of the freezing unit. The man loved to watch crushed ice plunk into his glass.

"Sure, Fuzz, dip and chips coming right up."

Chapter Three

Nate grabbed the sack of Doritos and spicy salsa, then strode back to the living room to set the snacks on the end table beside Fuzz. "I've been thinking about hiring a cook and housekeeper," Nate commented. "Do you think Mary Jane Calloway might be interested?"

Fuzz grinned devilishly. "You sly young scamp. You haven't outgrown your ornery streak entirely, have you. If you hire Mary Jane away from Coyote Café, the whole town will be up in arms. It's the only decent place in town to eat, the place where Lester Brown hangs out, shooting off his big mouth."

Nate returned the wry grin. "As I see it, I would be doing Mary Jane a favor. She's a widow who has a hard time making ends meet. If she comes to work for me, she'll have shorter work hours and better pay. You think she might be interested?"

"You want me to ask her?"

Nate bobbed his head.

"Done." Fuzz rubbed his lean belly. "I can almost taste her mouthwatering homemade pies from here. She can make chicken-fried steak and gravy that is to die for. Mmm…and her pot roast—"

"You're stalling," Nate broke in. "You were going to tell me about Katy's marriage."

Fuzz crammed a chip in his mouth, chewed, then swallowed. "You're right, son. But I'm not one of those people who gets his kicks from reporting disasters. That was exactly what Katy's marriage was—pure dee-saster."

Nate sipped his drink, wishing he could have been there to rescue Katy. But that had been impossible. The night Nate was driven to Bud Thurston's ranch, Fuzz made him promise not to make contact with anyone in Coyote Flats. Nate suspected Judge Bates would have been waiting for him, looking for any excuse to shove No-Account Nate into the Texas penal system—and keep him there indefinitely. The judge had the power and connections to get it done.

Until today, Nate hadn't realized the full extent of Fuzz's intervention. The judge had wanted a quick conviction and jail time. Fuzz had bucked the judge and insisted on an alternative plan. No doubt, Fuzz had promised that Nate would have no future contact with Katy.

Fuzz champed on a few more chips, then sighed audibly. "Well, hell, there is no delicate way to describe Katy's marriage, so I may as well be blunt. Katy gave up fighting the judge's domineering decrees after you left town. Her daddy sang high praises to Brad Butler and put on a spectacular wedding that boasted all the bells and whistles. I didn't have much contact with Katy after her daddy packed her belongings and moved her off to college with Brad. I do know the judge saved Brad's bacon several times when he was picked up for drunk and disorderly conduct on campus and DWI."

Nate had a sick feeling in his gut about this prearranged

marriage. He suspected the judge had been embarrassed that his son's marriage had ended in divorce. Therefore, Dave vowed to prevent his daughter's marriage from reaching scandalous proportions.

"The judge wouldn't let Katy walk away from her drunken husband, I don't suppose," Nate muttered bitterly.

"Of course not," Fuzz said, then snorted. "Wouldn't look good for the judge, you know. Katy wanted out, but the judge refused to let her come home, refused to pay her college tuition and living expenses if she divorced Brad. Katy tried to run away and make it on her own, but the judge hired a private detective to track her down in Colorado and bring her back."

Nate's opinion of Judge Bates went right down the toilet. Dave's attempt to prevent Katy's actions from being seen as a bad reflection on himself was deplorable. He had no concern for his daughter's well-being or happiness, only for his reputation.

"When Brad got booted off the football team, because of the incident involving rape—"

"Good Lord!" Nate erupted in outrage.

"What can I say?" Fuzz grunted in disgust. "The Butler kid was a creep. I didn't know all the details until Katy and Brad moved back to Coyote Flats to work on Butler Ranch for his father. I saw Katy every once in a while, sporting a few bruises, but Brad would never let me close enough to question her, always had some excuse about how clumsy she was."

Nate's hands curled into tight fists. He had been granted a second chance in life, but Katy had had no chance at all. Her situation had gone from bad to worse after her wedding. Nate's imagination ran wild, visualizing Brad getting snockered and knocking his wife around for kicks. Apparently the son of a bitch delighted in exerting his strength over a woman.

"No wonder Katy stopped standing up for herself," Nate muttered. "Her own father manipulated her, then handed her over to an abusive beast. God, I wish I would have been there to go a few rounds with that Neanderthal bully Katy was forced to marry.''

Nate stared at Fuzz, noting the former sheriff's bleak expression, realizing that, as bad as this tale was, it was going to get worse. Fuzz's mouth was set in a grim line, and frustrated anger glittered in his eyes.

"Six years ago, Brad and Katy were on their way out to Butler Ranch for Christmas dinner. They had a wreck because Brad was legally intoxicated. He went through the windshield and Katy was trapped in the car, which was wrapped around an electric pole.''

Nate grimaced, realizing what had caused Katy's limp. "She was hurt badly,'' he presumed.

Fuzz nodded. "She was three months pregnant at the time. We cut her from the twisted metal with the jaws of life, and the judge had her airlifted to Dallas for surgery on her broken hip. He paid for the year of physical therapy needed for Katy to walk without crutches or a cane.''

Nate blew out his breath, wishing he could spout the F word a few times. Unfortunately, he had given up saying the queen mother word at the same time he quit smoking. But right now, he would sure feel better if he could chain-smoke and curse a blue streak.

The picture Fuzz painted was so depressing that Nate could understand why Katy's will to live had been stripped away. His youth had been a nightmare, but her young adult years had been hell. She'd had no one to provide moral support, no one to rescue her from pain and anguish. And so she had drawn into herself, hiding behind a shell, going through the motions of living, existing only in books that lined the shelves in the library. Nate guessed that Katy only read books that guaranteed happy endings. It was her only escape from tormenting reality.

"These days Katy keeps to herself, raises her niece and

quietly goes about the business of helping the unfortunate in the community," Fuzz continued. "If a family is dealing with death or illness, you can count on Katy to arrive at the bereaved family's home, laden down with food, supplies and flowers.

"Katy moved into her father's home after his fatal heart attack. She sold the house where she and Brad lived after he was suspended from college. She uses the money she made from the sale to fund the library and aid needy families."

Nate suspected Katy hadn't wanted to live in the house where she was knocked around and treated like Brad's convenient whore. Not that living in the judge's house was much better. But then, the Bates home was a monstrous structure and a woman who had turned into a recluse had plenty of space to move around.

"Katy took some of the money from her inheritance and set up two college scholarships for high school students who want to make a better place for themselves in society," Fuzz reported.

Nate smiled ruefully. He couldn't help but wonder if Katy was providing for the other Nate Channings in Coyote Flats— the down-on-their-luck kids who faced grim futures. That sounded like something Katy would do. Those qualities of kindness, caring and generosity were still there, he realized. Though Katy had cut herself off from the world, it was her nature to help the less fortunate.

Nate felt so damned sorry for her that he wanted to weep.

"Wipe that look off your face right this very minute," Fuzz scolded abruptly.

Nate jerked up his head to see Fuzz wagging an index finger in his face. "What look?"

"That pitying look, that's what," Fuzz grumbled. "That is the one thing Katy can't tolerate from folks. I oughta know, because I made the mistake of feeling sorry for her and telling her so."

Nate winced when he recalled how he had welled up with sympathy at the library. He remembered how Katy had spun around in her chair and promptly dismissed him. She was sensitive about being looked upon with pity, and he had hurt her feelings unintentionally. Well, damn.

"Knowing how you operate," Fuzz continued, frowning darkly, "You will probably decide to storm over to Katy's house and tell her how sorry you are that she suffered through a hellish marriage and lost her unborn child, then endured injuries that left her with a noticeable limp."

Fuzz pushed forward in his chair to stare Nate squarely in the eye. "Hear me and hear me well, Nate. That is not the proper approach to take with Katy. Am I coming through loud and clear?"

"Crystal clear," Nate confirmed.

"If you have visions of drawing Katy from her shell, you can't march over there and tell her that you want to take up where the two of you left off all those years ago. I'm no psychologist, but I've dealt with enough traumatized and abused victims to know they bottle their emotions inside, just like Katy does. She will never be able to get on with her life until she lets go of her past, until she feels a strong, compelling reason to let go of her pain. My experience tells me that you will have to earn Katy's trust and confidence, slowly but surely. The men in her life have abused and betrayed her. Any changes she makes in her attitude toward men will be gradual."

Nate's shoulders slumped and he sighed audibly. "Hell, here I was, hoping for instant, miraculous results."

"Then expect to be disappointed," Fuzz said as he reached for another chip to dip into the salsa. "It took sixteen years of browbeating, manipulation, physical and mental abuse to turn Katy into a hermit. It may take sixteen years to teach her to trust men, to live and laugh again." He shot Nate a stern glance. "Don't start some noble crusade that you might not have the patience and dedication to finish, because you will only make matters worse for Katy if you do.''

Nate flopped back in his chair and scrubbed his hands over his face. Fuzz had read him well. Nate had learned to attack business problems with swift, relentless efficiency. The skills he had perfected on the road to financial success were worthless when it came to dealing with Katy.

"So where do I start?" Nate asked helplessly.

Fuzz grinned broadly. "Right here." When Nate frowned, bemused, Fuzz made a sweeping gesture with his arm. "Bring her out to your ranch, tell her how you burned those bad memories from your past to the ground and constructed this palace, with its panoramic view of the rugged gullies and rocky ravines of West Texas. Maybe if she realizes that you wanted to make a fresh start, she'll want to do the same thing."

"Hell of an idea, Fuzz," Nate complimented him.

"Hey, son, I wasn't born yesterday, you know. I've got a gray hair for every damn one of life's experiences." His smile faded from his wrinkled features. "I encountered a similar problem when my wife was diagnosed with cancer. Sally was ready to give up the fight, and she tried to push me away, make me angry enough to quit on her, the same way she quit on herself. But I refused to back off. I was determined to eke out every moment of happiness during that last year. We traveled when she felt up to it. We attended every community activity, and we made the most of every day we had left together.

"Maybe if Katy realizes you have no intention of giving up on her she'll come around," Fuzz added before he switched on the big-screen TV.

"I'm going for a walk," Nate announced, rising to his feet.

"Take that mutt with you," Fuzz requested. "Taz has been cooped up in the house most of the day, trying to coax me into petting him constantly. He needs to chase a few rabbits and burn off some energy."

When Nate had changed into a T-shirt and jeans, he called to Taz and took a long, meditative stroll across the rolling pasture. Checking on his cattle herd was the least of his concerns at the moment. His thoughts were centered on his campaign of reaching that vibrant young woman who had been his inspiration, his unattainable dream way back when. Nate knew he needed a game plan—the best.

"Got any bright ideas about how to handle this situation, Taz?" Nate asked his four-legged companion.

When a jackrabbit bounded up in front of them, Taz took off at a dead run, yipping at the top of his lungs.

Nate realized, and not for the first time in his life, that he was on his own when it came to solving his problems. Turning Katy's life around would have to be a one-man crusade, and it would take him a few days to work out his plan of action.

Katy was in the process of pulling a bubbling chicken casserole from the oven when the doorbell rang. It had become her habit to let Tammy answer the door in the evening, but Tammy had gone back to school to design posters for the basketball king-and-queen coronation and dance that was scheduled for the upcoming weekend.

Setting aside the casserole, Katy limped to the front door. Her breath gushed from her lungs when a vision from the past returned to haunt her. Nate Channing, dressed in faded blue jeans and a T-shirt that had seen better days, was standing on the porch—the exact place her father had refused to let him set foot all those years ago.

His dark hair, ruffled by the evening breeze, drooped on his forehead, giving him a devil-may-care appearance. He was leaning against the supporting beam of the porch in a negligent stance that had been his trademark as a teenager. A knock-'em-dead smile pursed his lips, and Katy reacted instinctively to it.

He held a bouquet of roses in one suntanned hand and a

box of candy in the other. It was difficult for Katy to maintain the distant, remote attitude she practiced in the presence of men. This was one devastatingly attractive man, and despite the fact that Katy knew it would be better for her and Nate not to renew their friendship, there was a lot of history between them—and no closure whatsoever. Nate had been whisked from her life, never to be seen or heard from in sixteen years.

"I always wanted to do this, Katy Marie," Nate said in that sexy Texas drawl that turned her knees to the consistency of tapioca. "But sixteen years ago I didn't have enough cash to shower you with gifts." He glanced at the wrought-iron railing surrounding the porch. "Never thought I'd even get this close to your front door, either."

Katy inhaled a steadying breath, only to be assailed by the alluring scent of expensive cologne—a vivid contradiction to his bad-boy appearance. Nate looked tough, invincible and adorably appealing to her, just as he had in the old days. His appearance resurrected memories and sensations that Katy hadn't allowed herself to revisit for fear of driving herself crazy.

But here stood Nate Channing, looking larger than her lifesize memories, smelling absolutely wonderful, filling up all her senses to overflowing. God, how she had missed him those first few years, lived on the hope that he would contact her, save her from the life her father had mapped out for her.

Nate extended the box to her. "Chocolate-and-pecan Turtles," he said in that husky baritone voice that sent gooseflesh flying across her skin. "Your favorite, if memory serves."

Katy accepted the candy, unable to meet Nate's gaze. "Thank you."

"And roses," he murmured softly, taking a whiff of their fragrant scent. "I wanted to ask you to the prom my senior year and present you with a bouquet of roses and a box of candy, but I never got the chance."

The reminder caused Katy to flinch as she accepted the flowers. Because of her father, Nate hadn't been allowed to attend the prom or graduate with his class. God, how would Nate react if he knew the truth about that night he was spirited out of town? Katy wasn't sure she could find the nerve to tell him.

"May I come in, Kat? I always wondered what the inside of this house looked like. Heaven knows I spent countless evenings staring at it from the street, wishing I was welcome here."

The admission startled her, and it must have shown in her expression, because Nate's obsidian eyes twinkled down at her. "I confided a lot of things to you in the old days, Kat, but I guess I was too embarrassed to tell you how I sat by the curb in my bucket-of-bolts car. I used to stare at your house, wishing…"

He shrugged impossibly broad shoulders in that lackadaisical way that once upon a time concealed his feelings of inferiority and frustration. Yet, this handsome hunk—as Tammy had referred to him—had nothing to be ashamed of now. He had obviously made something of himself. Not with laundered drug money, as Lester Brown had everybody thinking.

Despite the fact that Nate had been caught for possession of marijuana and cocaine that night he was arrested, Katy knew he never touched those illegal substances. Because of Gary Channing's addiction to booze, Nate had developed a fierce aversion to liquor and drugs.

It outraged Katy no end to hear the cruel gossip Brown and Jessup were spreading around town, in an attempt to turn everybody against Nate. If Katy could have found the nerve to confront those two blowhards she would have rushed to Nate's defense at lunch at the café today. But she had learned the hard way that to contradict a man could incite violence.

Instead of bounding up to refute Brown's nasty gossip, she

just sat there in her corner booth, staring at her plate, listening to that old cuss plant seeds of mistrust and contempt for Nate.

"May I come in?" Nate prompted, jolting Katy from her musings.

She stepped back to allow him inside. How could she refuse him? Nate deserved the opportunity to tour the house that Dave Bates had decreed off-limits to him.

"Wow," Nate said as he surveyed the spacious living area that was furnished with expensive, refinished antiques. "No wonder the judge didn't want me in here. He was probably afraid I'd break an irreplaceable heirloom."

Katy smiled remorsefully. "This room was off-limits to me and my older brother, too," she confided. "It was nothing but a showroom for Dad's influential guests. James and I were confined to the playroom until we graduated from high school. I doubt that anyone sat on the flowered fainting couch or hand-carved gliding chair, except our forefathers who originally owned them."

Nate breathed an inward sigh of relief. He finally had Katy talking. That was the most she had said to him since his arrival in town. He had made it a point to be on the sidewalk outside the library when she went to work the past three days, but she had merely nodded, ducked her head and limped into the library.

Maybe he was being sneaky by dressing as the dirt-poor kid she remembered and preying on her sympathy. But hell, this was the best strategy he'd come up with, even after three nights of profound deliberation. Fortunately, the strategy had worked. He was in the house, and Katy was talking to him, though she still refused to make eye contact for more than a nanosecond at a time.

"I don't want to impose, but do you have time to give me the grand tour?"

"If you like," Katy murmured, then ducked her head. "Let me get a vase for the roses."

Nate followed at a respectable distance behind Katy as she limped through the formal dining room to the spacious kitchen—which had been remodeled and boasted every high-tech convenience. Nate expected that from Dave Bates. Nothing but the best for his children and himself. The sorry son of a bitch.

"Damn, maybe I'm glad I didn't know what I was missing in the old days," Nate commented, admiring the shiny oak cabinets, antique Hoosier cabinet and jelly cupboard. I would have been feeling even more sorry for myself when I went home to that pile of rubble that served as my house."

When Katy failed to comment, just reached into the cabinet to retrieve a vase, Nate gestured toward the casserole dish that was steaming on the stove. "Am I interrupting? Are you expecting guests for supper?"

"No. Alice Rother's son fell off the slipper slide during recess this morning and broke his arm. I fixed supper so the family would have something to eat when they return from the doctor's office."

"Skinny Alice has a kid?" Nate asked. "When I left town, she'd never even had a date, not to my knowledge."

The comment provoked Katy's smile. Nate felt as if he had worked a small miracle. There and then, he promised himself to find ways to make Katy smile more often.

"Alice married Cody Phelps after he divorced Mandy Slater. You probably wouldn't recognize Alice if you saw her. She was a late bloomer who turned out to be quite attractive."

"Yeah? Well, I'd have to see it to believe it," Nate said, and chuckled.

Before Katy could take Nate on a tour of the house, a sharp rap resounded on the back door. "Excuse me a moment."

She scuttled off, quickly closing the door behind her. Curious, Nate tiptoed over to peek through the kitchen window. To his amazement, he saw a teenage boy standing at the bottom of the steps. The kid had his hands crammed in the front pockets of his baggy jeans. He wore his dingy baseball cap backward, pulled down low over his mop of unruly hair.

"Need lunch money, Chad?" Katy asked her visitor.

Nate watched the teenager nod, then shuffle his oversize feet. Nate's heart twisted in his chest, knowing that he was staring at a younger version of himself. Chad's clothes and self-cut hair indicated a shortage of funds.

"You know the deal, Chad," Katy said. "No drugs, only food. Don't let yourself be sucked into the pressure put on by the kids you hang around with. I know they are razzing you, but don't give in to them. Promise me?"

Chad bobbed his shaggy head. "Yes, ma'am."

Katy pulled a twenty dollar bill from the pocket of her jeans and handed it to the teenager. "I've requested funds from the city council to hire a janitor. If the funds are approved, the job is yours. It will give you an excuse not to get involved with those troublemakers who have befriended you."

"It's not easy to break loose from them when nobody else will accept me," Chad grumbled sourly, then swiped a hand across his faded shirt. "I can't dress well enough to be accepted by the 'in' crowd in town."

"You can spiff up your wardrobe when you get the job," Katy encouraged him.

"I can't afford to buy duds fancy enough to make Tammy sit up and take notice," Chad challenged.

Nate watched Katy bless the kid with a tender smile. "She notices now, Chad, but she is old-fashioned enough not to chase after boys, and she is just as self-conscious and unsure of how to approach you."

"Yeah?" Chad asked hopefully.

"Uh-huh, so you'll have to do the asking when it comes to dating."

"Right, like I have pocket change for that," Chad said, then scowled. "What am I supposed to do? Borrow the neighbor kid's bicycle and ask Tammy out? Like, that would really impress her, wouldn't it? Like, she'd leap at the chance to go out with a guy from the poor side of town to have a Coke date, because that's all the cash I could scrape together to spend on her."

Nate stepped away from the window and resumed his position by the door, so he wouldn't get caught eavesdropping. Katy returned a couple of minutes later.

"Sorry for the interruption," she said.

"No problem."

When Katy limped upstairs, Nate followed in her wake. He appraised the grand old home, finding it as neat and tidy as he expected. It was a far cry from the disheveled, filthy shack where he'd grown up. His mother had never been around much. When she was, it was only to sleep off the most recent hangover. Nate had been responsible for all the handyman jobs he could manage and for tidying up the place. There was only so much you could do with a drafty old shanty that should have been condemned during the Dust Bowl days.

Nate wondered if the kid named Chad who came calling at the back door hailed from a similar background. Probably.

Nate halted abruptly at the door that was filled with Katy's soft scent, then studied her bedroom. Vivid images leaped to mind; he wondered how the two of them would look cozied up in that priceless antique four-poster bed, improving on those intimate secrets they had shared in the back seat of his car.

Those stolen moments had been indelibly etched in Nate's memory. Despite his bad reputation, his first experience with sex had been Katy's first experience. He hadn't known what the hell he was doing, only that his feelings for her demanded to be communicated physically, emotionally.

To this day Nate could still remember how sweetly and trustingly she had responded to him. And he wished with all his heart that he and Katy could have spent the past decade learning all the intimate ways of pleasuring each other. Instead, Katy had been used, abused and treated so abominably that she had lost faith in men, in herself.

The thought caused Nate to grind his teeth until he practically wore off the enamel. He clenched his fist, wishing he could retaliate against the men who had brought Katy such pain. Judge Bates and Brad Butler should consider themselves extremely fortunate they were dead, because Nate would have gladly reverted to his old habits and beat the living hell out of them.

Chapter Four

"Something wrong?" Katy guessed when Nate stared silently at her bedroom.

Nate flashed a smile he didn't feel. "I was just thinking how I used to sit in my car and stare up at the lights in your bedroom window. You must have spent most of your time up here. Either that or you didn't need to worry about conserving on the electric bills the way I did."

"This was my haven," she admitted quietly. "I only went downstairs when it was time for one of Dad's many lectures."

Katy was amazed how easily she had slipped back into confiding in Nate. For years she had kept her own counsel. But when Nate arrived to stroll down memory lane it seemed only natural to tell him about those difficult years with her tyrannical father. She always wondered, if her mother hadn't died shortly after childbirth, if Victoria Bates would have served as a buffer and go-between for Katy and James, if things had turned out differently... As it was, the judge had handed down his decrees and sentences to his children the same way he delivered legal rulings from the bench. The man had never been able to separate his personal and professional lives.

"Come on, Kat. I've seen your place, now I would like to show you mine."

When Nate reached for her hand, Katy reflexively withdrew. And felt like a fool. Although she expected to see a look of confusion or sympathy on Nate's face, he merely smiled and patiently held out his hand a second time.

"Still the best of friends?" he asked softly. "I would like to have two allies in this town. Sheriff Havern is one. I would very much like for you to be the other, Katy."

Katy stared at his long, lean fingers. She hadn't liked to be touched, had avoided contact every chance she got. The remembered pain and humiliation had taught her to keep her distance from men. In years past a touch had become an insulting grope, a slapping reprimand for disobedience, then blessed oblivion from the pain.

Suddenly, Katy remembered what Nate had told her the first day he returned to Coyote Flats. He had reminded her that he had never hurt her, that he would never hurt her. Could she trust him to keep his word when the other men in her life hadn't?

Hesitantly, she slipped her hand into his, though she couldn't quite meet his gaze. Her heart bled when he brought her hand to his lips and grazed her knuckles with a kiss. The old Katy would have pressed up on tiptoe, flung her arms around his neck and kissed him full on the mouth. The new Katy didn't dare take initiative, because old habits died hard.

"Thanks, Katy, you'll never know how badly I needed to do that. Just touch you, I mean."

Gently, Nate squeezed her clammy hand. He could tell she was self-conscious, wary and nervous as hell. Already, he was moving so slowly and cautiously with her that it nearly killed him. But if slow and cautious were the only ways of drawing

Katy from her self-imposed shell, then he would damned well inch along like a snail.

Never in his life had he expected to count his progress in inches. But hey, even a snail got somewhere—eventually—Nate reminded himself.

Hand in hand, Nate and Katy strode down the hall. Nate was careful not to pull her behind him, because he suspected that bastard she'd married had pulled and dragged her around constantly. Nate made damned sure he and Katy remained on equal footing.

"I'm anxious for you to see my house," Nate continued on the way down the steps. "I built it on the same spot where the shack used to sit. It seemed symbolic and necessary to erect my future on the ashes of the past."

She slipped her hand from his, then limped toward the kitchen. "Maybe I can come out some other time, Nate. I have to deliver the casserole and pick up Tammy from school."

"I'd be glad to drive you." Nate flashed what he hoped was his most engaging grin. "Surely you aren't going to deprive me of the chance of seeing Skinny Alice again, are you? A real knockout these days, you say?"

It came again. A smile—one shade brighter than the first. Still, though, it didn't reach Katy's eyes and make them sparkle with the inner spirit he remembered from the old days. But when a man was counting his progress in quarter-inch increments, he took what he got and was glad of it.

Katy knew it was a mistake to allow herself to associate with Nate, even for a few hours. They were too different these days, and she had nothing to offer except limited friendship. But darn, it was hard to say no to that charming grin, to the incredibly handsome man who appealed to her on so many levels. The fact that she was still impossibly attracted to Nate assured Katy that not all her emotions were frozen solid. She simply couldn't resist that compelling field around him that offered strength, comfort and pleasure.

"You and Tammy can stay for supper," Nate invited. "Fuzz would love the company. He spent so many years cruising around all by his lonesome in the patrol car that he's practically talked my ears off since he moved in with me."

"So the rumor circulating around town is true? Fuzz does live with you?"

Nate nodded. "Yep, I designed the house to accommodate him. It is my way of repaying him for giving me a second chance, though I had to promise not to make contact with you or anyone else after I left. Otherwise, I would face punishment at the judge's hands."

Katy flinched. Her father had gone to extremes to ensure that she had no future contact with the young man she had fallen hopelessly in love with at the tender age of sixteen. Dave Bates had known how to break her spirit and bend her to his will. He had taken away the only person who meant something to Katy. Her father had made Nate disappear and left her with no hope of his return.

Katy shoved aside the bitter thoughts to inform Nate of what he was up against in town. "According to Lester Brown, you moved the former sheriff in with you so you would have good connections, in case you ran into trouble with the law during your drug dealings."

Nate blinked in surprise. "That's the scuttlebutt in town? Well hell, Lester doesn't miss a trick, does he?"

"I wanted to pop him in the mouth when he blurted out that lie at the café today," Katy muttered.

The comment, spoken with more emotion than Nate had seen, or heard, Katy display, gave him hope. Katy had obviously become a master at maintaining a neutral tone for fear of igniting her husband's volatile temper. But she was obviously offended by Lester Brown's attempt to turn the town against Nate.

"Thanks, Katy, I'm glad to hear you're in my corner, even

if you didn't wallop Lester upside the head. So...will you come with me tonight?''

Nate could tell by the way she sidestepped that she was still reluctant to break her habit of avoiding men. Nate reached out slowly, so as not to startle her, then took her hand in his.

''I doubt that anyone else in town would accept the invitation, me being a no-account drug lord who has surrounded himself with hoodlums and headquartered at my house where I keep a former law official under my roof. But I really would like to show off the place to someone. I really would like for that someone to be *you,* Kat.''

''Okay,'' she said finally. ''But just for a little while. I'm sure Tammy has homework, so I don't want to keep her out late.''

Another small victory, Nate thought as he strode over to grab a hot pad so he could scoop up the casserole. Although he had developed the Midas touch when it came to financial investments, his profits seemed insignificant in comparison to coaxing Katy from her house, to spend time with him.

How far do you plan to take this crusade of yours, Nate? he asked himself on the way to his car. *Given the rumors circulating around Coyote Flats, Katy might catch flack because of her association with you. For God's sake, don't hurt her more than she's already been hurt!*

Nate wondered if maybe he had jumped the gun by trying to draw Katy from her hermitage so soon after his return. Maybe he should have waited until he had earned the trust and acceptance of the citizens first—if ever. Maybe Fuzz was right in criticizing his methods and strategy of constructing a branch office of Sunrise Oil Company in town without announcing ownership. Maybe he had screwed up after only a week in his hometown.

Yet, one look at Katy slumped on the bucket seat renewed his determined resolve. Teaching Katy to live again had become his number one priority. If he had to take on the lynch mob, commandeered by Lester Brown and his sidekick, then he would. Nate owed Katy for building up his ego all those years ago, for believing in him, for offering her innocence to him with such extraordinary trust and affection.

Somehow, he was going to make this work, he told himself. Even if Lester had the citizens of Coyote Flats believing the devil incarnate had returned to town, hurling pitchforks and breathing fire, he was going to give this economically strained town the boost it needed.

Of course, there was a strong possibility that he would have to drag the residents—kicking and screaming—every damn step of the f—

Nate came to a mental halt. He was not going to start slinging around derivatives of the F word, just because he had returned to his old stomping ground. He had reinvented himself and he was not—repeat *not* with great emphasis!—going to backpedal.

"Every blessed step of the way," he corrected himself aloud.

Katy stared curiously at him. "Pardon?"

"Nothing." Nate flashed a grin. "I was just talking to myself. Now, give me directions to Skinny Alice's place. I can't wait to take a gander at the male magnet you claim she has become."

Katy watched Alice Rother Phelps recoil in the doorway of her expensive brick home when she realized who was standing behind Katy. "N-Nate Channing?" she stuttered, wide-eyed.

Katy felt the fierce need to protect Nate from Alice's stunned reaction. Nate had been hurt enough by the citizens of this town. Knowing she was the reason Nate had been sent away left Katy feeling personally responsible for ensuring that he was granted a new start in Coyote Flats.

Smiling, Katy extended the casserole to her longtime friend. "Hi, Ali. I'm glad to see that you recognized Nate. He looks

wonderful, doesn't he? He has become exceptionally successful since he left town.''

When Ali frowned dubiously, Katy realized her friend had
been treated to a heavy dose of negative gossip about Nate.

''Don't pay the slightest attention to the lies Lester Brown
has been spreading.'' Katy practically shoved the casserole at
Alice, who was still frozen to the tiled floor of her entryway,
still gaping at Nate. ''I brought chicken cacciatore so you
wouldn't have to scramble around to fix supper tonight. What
did Dr. Wilson have to say about Tony's arm?''

Alice shook herself from her daze and accepted the baking
dish. ''Tony is going to be fine.'' Her gaze bounced back to
Nate, then she refocused on Katy. ''It was a clean break that
didn't require surgery, just a plaster cast.''

''We're all very thankful for that,'' Katy replied.

''Breaking an arm is tough on a youngster,'' Nate added.
''Is your son active in sports?''

Alice bobbed her head jerkily. ''Yes, Tony loves to play
baseball and football. Hopefully, the cast will come off before
we get into the thick of baseball season.''

''Glad to hear it,'' Nate replied. ''I'll have to stop by the
park this summer and catch a game. What position does Tony
play?''

''Um…''

When Ali hesitated, Katy's hackles went up. She predicted
that Ali had been led to believe that Nate wanted to contact
youngsters so he could get them addicted to drugs. Damn that
Lester Brown! He was poisoning everyone's opinion of Nate,
long before he had the chance to prove himself.

''Er…he plays first base,'' Ali said eventually. ''Uh…
thanks for the casserole, Katy. That was very thoughtful of
you.''

''I'm glad to be of help.''

With a decisive click, the door shut in Katy's and Nate's

faces. Annoyed by Ali's leery attitude, Katy wheeled around and stamped off the porch.

"Katy?"

She half turned to meet Nate's smile. "What?"

"Thank you for standing up for me. No one else around here would have done that. It means a lot to me."

"This is so unfair. I'd like to strangle Lester Brown and John Jessup for what they are trying to do to you."

Nate caught up with her in two long strides. Reflexively, Katy outdistanced him, then slowed her pace. She reminded herself that she was no longer dealing with Brad. It was Nate who was on her heels, and he had no intention of roughing her up. That had never been Nate's style. Katy *had* to stop reacting to Nate the way she had reacted to Brad in order to protect herself. But damn it, years of terror and torment were difficult to forget.

Although Katy was irritated with Ali's cool reception, Nate didn't let it bother him. He was too elated that Katy had emerged from her shell long enough to come to his defense. Quick as a wink, she had done exactly as she had done in the old days. It gave Nate a warm, fuzzy feeling to know that a smidgen of the past history between them was still alive and breathing. Deep down, buried beneath Katy's heartache and anguish, she still cared about his feelings. That was a start. If he could get her to care about him, he prayed he could get her to care about *herself* again, too.

"You were right about Alice," Nate said as he caught up with Katy. "She did blossom. Pretty face and attractive figure. Did Cody Phelps leave his wife for Alice?"

Katy resettled her ruffled feathers as she limped to the car. "No. Mandy suffered from the same affliction of roving eye that ruined my brother's marriage. Cody was hesitant to get involved with another woman. He was humiliated when his ex-wife married his best friend the day the divorce was final.

But Alice caught Cody's eye and they hit it off from the beginning."

Although Katy had seemed ill at ease each time he was alone with her, Nate noticed she was beginning to warm up to him. Conversation was coming more easily for her since he had tried his best to reassure her that he would never be the slightest threat to her. However, he reminded himself, Katy was probably still irritated and distracted by Alice's wary attitude toward him. But whatever the reason, Katy didn't freeze up the second they were enclosed in his car.

"I should have tossed that blasted casserole in Ali's face when she reacted to you like that," Katy huffed. "I've never seen her act like that before, and I prefer not to again!"

For a moment, Nate could only stare at her in amazement. Signs of misplaced spirit erupted from nowhere. Katy Marie Bates, champion for lost causes and underdogs, might have stopped living for herself, but nothing could smother her innate need to come to someone else's rescue and defense.

She could cope adequately when she confronted another *woman*, Nate amended. Katy was still noticeably unsure of herself when dealing with those of the male persuasion.

"What are you grinning about?" Katy demanded suddenly. "There was nothing amusing about the way Ali treated you."

Chuckling at Katy's forceful tone, he turned the key in the ignition. "You remind me of how you used to stand up for me back in high school, when your cliquish friends insisted that you should tell me to get lost, because I wasn't good enough to hang around you."

She stared straight ahead, hands folded in her lap. "They were wrong then, and folks in town are wrong now. And I do have my moments occasionally, when I can't help but speak up," she explained. "Injustice still rubs me the wrong way."

"Good. I'm not too crazy about rejection and injustice, either."

"Speaking of injustice..." Katy's voice trailed off and her

shoulders slumped. Although she had gotten fired up by Ali's attitude toward Nate, she still couldn't bring herself to tell him what her father had done to him. He had the right to know, and she needed to tell him.

Later, she promised herself. But not now. She wasn't going to spoil the evening for Nate. He was anxious to show off his new home. Nate had encountered one negative reaction tonight already. If she told him about her father's devious betrayal, it would ruin his cheerful mood.

"You were saying?" Nate prompted when she lapsed into silence.

"Nothing important," she mumbled. "If you will stop at the gymnasium I'll round up Tammy."

While Nate drove like the responsible, law-abiding citizen he had become, Katy studied his handsome profile. Broken dreams swirled through her mind. She caught herself wondering if she and Nate could make a new beginning. Yet, as quickly as the whimsical thought gelled, Katy quashed it. She wanted the very best for Nate, wanted him to find someone who was whole and complete and eager to offer him the intimate pleasures of a healthy, meaningful relationship.

Katy knew she was no longer that woman. She would only torment herself if she tried to welcome a man's sexual advances after the hell Brad had put her through.

Just friends, Katy convinced herself. That was all she and Nate could be now.

"Wow! Awesome!" Tammy exclaimed as she bounded into the back seat of Nate's Lincoln. "Man, this is sweet."

"In case you're out of touch with teenage jargon, that means Tammy really likes your car," Katy translated.

"Geez, this is even fancier than Dad's car," Tammy rattled on.

"Say hello, Tammy," Katy prompted her impolite niece.

"Oh, sorry. Nice to see you again, Nate," Tammy said, smiling sheepishly.

"How are the decorations for the basketball coronation coming along?" Nate asked.

"It's going just as I expected. The girls are doing all the work, and the jocks are lounging around, trying to out-cool one another." Tammy pulled a face. "The guys think making posters and stringing banners is girls' work."

"Being male, I suspect the guys are simply strutting their stuff to gain your notice," Nate replied. "It comes with their hormones."

"Well, I wish they would quit crowing and help out. Chad Parker was the only one willing to lend a hand. Of course, everybody ragged him for being there at all, because he doesn't play basketball and isn't allowed to mix with the guys who do."

Nate cast Katy a discreet glance, certain the Chad whom Tammy had mentioned was the one who had come knocking at the back door earlier this evening. Katy, however, didn't change expression.

"Did Chad back off after the other boys ridiculed him?" Katy asked.

"Naw, he climbed up the ladder to tape the banners on the wall, then helped me set up the archway for the coronation."

The kid must have it bad for Tammy, Nate decided. Chad Parker had withstood the taunts and teasing just to be near Tammy. Nate could relate to that. He had been there and done that in the old days, grabbing for any excuse to spend time with Katy.

"Do you have much homework tonight?" Nate asked as he cruised past the city limits.

"Naw, just a few algebra problems that I didn't have time to finish in class. Aunt Katy said we get to take a tour of your new house. Cool!"

"And stay for supper if that doesn't cut into your homework time," Nate added.

"Really?" Tammy grinned at him in the rearview mirror, then darted a glance at the back of Katy's head. "That's fine by me."

Nate had the unmistakable feeling that Tammy had in mind to do a little matchmaking. That was fine by him, too. But he doubted Katy was going to be cooperative. He felt her withdrawing from him as the minutes ticked by. It was as if she had suddenly remembered that it was important to keep an emotional distance from those around her, to discourage Nate from expecting more than a platonic friendship.

Ah, if only Nate could have been satisfied with that. He wasn't sure he could. Every moment spent with Katy left him yearning to recapture the closeness they had once shared. Yet, considering the damaging gossip that was swirling around him, he couldn't tolerate the thought of Katy being caught up in the backdraft. He had to find a way to make this work, to rejuvenate her spirit, he told himself. But Lester Brown, that cantankerous old hound, wasn't going to make it easy on anyone who paid Nate the slightest attention.

"Whoa! That house is *so* huge!" Tammy erupted when she caught sight of Nate's home. "Looks like something a movie star might live in."

"I'm glad you approve." Nate tossed Tammy a grin. "Since I don't claim to be any authority on class and style, I consulted architects, landscape experts and interior designers for guidance...."

Nate barely had time to punctuate his comment before Tammy vaulted from the car and stared across the pasture to note the sparkling pond at the base of a rugged ravine. Smiling in satisfaction, he watched Tammy admire the spectacular view, then he glanced back to gauge Katy's reaction.

She didn't disappoint him.

She never could.

"Oh, Nate, this is absolutely spectacular," Katy complimented him. She inhaled a deep breath of country air. "This must be what freedom feels like, the view of wide-open spaces, the whisper of wind." She wrapped her arms around herself and smiled. "I can almost picture this setting in a book."

Forget the books, thought Nate. *Picture you and me in reality.*

"You like?" he said instead.

"I love," Katy said sincerely. "You're right. There is something very symbolic and gratifying about building on this site. Very appropriate."

When she glanced at him momentarily, he saw renewed sparkle in those sky-blue eyes. His breath caught, and sweet memories bombarded him. It wouldn't take too many more glimpses of Katy's blossoming spirit for him to fall in love with her all over again. Could she deal with that? Would she be afraid to try, after the hell she had endured in her marriage? Would she ever trust him enough to try?

One step at a time, Nate cautioned himself. *Don't rush her. She can't transform herself into the old Katy overnight.*

"Come inside and I'll show you around," he invited Katy and her niece.

The moment Nate opened his front door, Taz was there to greet him—practically beating Nate to death with that wagging tail. The mongrel whined pitifully for a pat on the head. Nate reached down to comply.

Tammy giggled as she watched the love-starved mongrel lean heavily against Nate's leg. "This mutt lives in your fancy house?"

"Tammy Marie!" Katy chastised her niece immediately.

"It's okay," Nate insisted, scratching the dog behind the ear. "Taz isn't much to look at, but he's loyal and lovable. If he gets carried away trying to make your acquaintance and begging for pats, just tell him to sit. That's about the only command I've had time to teach him.''

Sure enough, Taz slobbered all over Katy and Tammy in his effort to be petted. Ugly or not, Taz had a unique method of winning friends. It was those sad eyes, the way he tipped his head sideways in silent pleading. Nate wondered if he should take lessons from his dog. Both women cooed and fussed over the mutt, as if he were as special as a purebred that sported an impressive pedigree.

Katy stopped short when she saw Fuzz Havern sprawled in a recliner, watching an Andy Griffith rerun on the oversize TV. She felt uncomfortable in his presence, knowing full well that he had seen her several times after Brad had knocked her around, then threatened worse if she told the sheriff the truth about her bruises.

She wondered if Fuzz had filled Nate in on her not-so-blissful marriage. The thought made her stiffen, recoil. Was Nate being especially nice to her because he pitied her? She glanced sideways to see Nate smiling at her, giving none of his thoughts or emotions away.

''You remember Fuzz Havern, don't you?'' he asked Katy. ''Tammy, this is the former sheriff of Coyote County. He is now my personal consultant and ranch foreman.''

Fuzz brought his lounge chair to an upright position, then waved away the glorified titles Nate bestowed on him. ''Don't pay any attention to all that baloney, Tammy,'' he said as he came to his feet. ''I'm retired, and all I do is gaze out the window at irregular intervals to see if the herd of cattle has broken through the fences.'' He hitched his thumb toward Nate. ''He does all the work around here.''

''Nice to meet you, Fuzz,'' Tammy said respectfully.

Fuzz frowned when Taz walked circles around Tammy's legs, just in case she felt inclined to reach down to pet him. ''That mutt bothering you, girl?''

''No, sir.'' Tammy patted the mutt's broad head. ''I always

wanted a dog, but Dad isn't home much, and he said I shouldn't impose on Aunt Katy by making her keep up with my pet.''

"You should have said something, honey," Katy murmured. "I wouldn't have minded you having a dog."

"Excuse me a minute," Nate said as he turned on his heels. "I'll tell the cook to set a couple of extra plates for supper."

"The cook?" Katy glanced curiously at Fuzz.

He nodded and grinned broadly. "Mary Jane Calloway is now on staff here."

Katy blinked in disbelief. "Nate hired her away from the Coyote Café? No wonder Lester Brown was more out of sorts than usual at lunch today. I wondered why my meal was below par."

"Yesterday was Mary's first day here," Fuzz explained, still grinning. "She loves it here, by the way. She's doing half the work for more pay. As far as Lester-the-Mouth is concerned, he deserves to go home and eat his own cooking. That is, if he can get off his lazy patoot and cook for himself."

Fuzz walked over to take Katy's hand and patted it fondly. "So how are you doing these days, Katy? I haven't seen much of you lately."

"I'm fine," she said neutrally.

"Still dealing with those tightfisted old coots on the city council, in hopes of increasing the library funds?"

She nodded, withdrew her hand, then glanced at the original oil paintings that graced the walls. "Nate really has a lovely home, doesn't he? I'm so pleased that he has made a good life for himself."

"Amen to that. The boy deserved a chance to break loose from the mold cast for him. I did what I could, and he has repaid me a hundred times over for the good deed." Fuzz waved his arms in expansive gestures. "I still can't believe I'm living in this palace, after years of being cramped up in that cracker-box garage apartment."

''Dinner will be served in thirty minutes,'' Nate announced as he ambled through the hall. ''Wanna take the tour now?''

''I'm ready!'' Tammy enthused as she strode forward, tugging Katy alongside her.

Chapter Five

Katy oohed and aahed at the doorway of every room, while Tammy put in a "Wow, cool!" The place was indeed impressive, Katy noted. Each room had a cozy country atmosphere that spelled *home*. She could have curled up in any room and been content to stare at the marvelous artwork.

Picture windows provided plenty of sunlight and breathtaking views of the wild tumble of arroyos that slashed through the plains. The carpet was so thick Katy was sure she could have camped out on it for the night and awakened well-rested. The leather furniture looked soft enough to mold itself around her body—it would be like floating on air. And the bathroom! Katy sighed appreciatively at the Jacuzzi bath, oversize shower stall, spacious counters and marble sink. She could almost visualize herself lounging in that monstrous tub, letting the pulsating jets massage her aching leg, while she sipped wine by candlelight....

She brought her thoughts to a screeching halt, telling herself that she would never enjoy the luxuries that were found in Nate's home. *Just friends* didn't bathe at each other's houses or sleep over....

The runaway thought made Katy flinch. No, she definitely wouldn't find herself romantically involved with Nate. She would only disappoint him, repulse him. Heaven knew Brad had told her countless times that she was a cold fish swimming in arctic waters, that she didn't know how to please or satisfy a man. Katy couldn't bear the thought of disappointing Nate, and she was sure she had been a disappointment to him that first time they made love in the back seat of his car. Of course, he had been too polite to say so.

Brad didn't have that problem. He ridiculed Katy constantly.

"And this is my room," Nate said as he led the way down the hall.

Hesitantly, Katy approached the doorway. She wasn't sure she wanted to picture Nate in his bed. The vision would be too tormenting. Yet, it would have been difficult to explain why she preferred to bypass this particular room, so she edged into the doorway.

Katy noted the oversize, floor-to-ceiling picture windows and king-size bed that was covered with a luxurious comforter of soft gold-and-brown earth tones. Her breath sighed out in appreciation. The room suited Nate perfectly.

The private bath with its solar-tube lighting, whirlpool and shower was every bit as impressive as the main bath, Katy also noted.

"Gosh!" Tammy chirped. "I could sleep in that tub. It is humongous!"

Nate chuckled. "You'll have to fight Taz for it. I've caught him in here once or twice. He seems to prefer sleeping where the sun shines down on him."

Nate glanced at Katy for approval. The look reminded Katy of days gone by—when he was a teenager fighting to make a place for himself in a town that refused to accept him. Her heart melted and dripped like butter down the ladder of her ribs when she stared up at him. She was assailed with the fierce need to assure him that he had made perfect choices while designing his home.

"If *Better Homes and Gardens* hasn't contacted you yet, they will soon," she insisted. "This house is a fairy-tale dream come true. You have a walk-in closet, too, I suppose?"

While Katy and Tammy marveled at the oversize closet, Nate glanced at his watch. "We better take a quick look at the indoor pool, then let Fuzz give you the guided tour of his quarters. I don't want him to feel slighted."

"You have an indoor pool?" Tammy questioned, amazed. "Fuzz has his own private quarters?"

"Yes and yes," Nate responded to the rapid-fire questions. "Swimming helps me unwind after a hectic day. As for Fuzz, I wanted him to have enough private space that he wouldn't feel hemmed in."

"Lead the way," Katy requested. "We don't want to miss a single detail of this marvelous house."

Nate strode off, feeling immensely satisfied. Katy had given her wholehearted approval. He wondered if she had any idea what that meant to him. Truth be told, he had found himself wondering if Katy would appreciate the house plan and decor each time he made a decision about the blueprints and the furnishings. He hadn't realized that she had colored his thoughts to such extremes...until now.

He hadn't realized he had never gotten over needing her approval and acceptance until now, either. Had he simply fixated on that one bright, shining memory from his youth? Or was there still something simmering beneath the surface, waiting to be tested, nurtured, rekindled?

Would Katy be willing to retest the affection they once shared? Had the bastard she was forced to marry killed her desire for future relationships?

Nate knew Katy had lived with so much fear and tension that she had learned to be afraid of men. She had lived with so much ridicule that she had lost her self-confidence. Would he ever have the old Katy back? Would he ever see that sweet, loving, generous young woman who could smile that dimpled smile and make his world seem twice as bright?

Nate raked his fingers through his hair and called himself nine kinds of crazy when visions of Katy lying in his arms practically jumped up and bit him. This was his first official outing with Katy in sixteen years, and there were two chaperones underfoot. Three, if you counted Mary Jane Calloway, who had a habit of buzzing in and out of rooms like a house afire. Yet, here he was fantasizing about close encounters of the most intimate nature. But damnation, he was inexorably drawn to Katy, though she downplayed her femininity these days and she didn't offer a man the least bit of encouragement.

But the chemistry was still there for Nate, at least. Even when Katy was hesitant to let him stand too close or hold on to her too long, he could feel the fires of desire smoldering beneath his nonchalant façade.

Lord, he'd like to come right out and ask her if she felt something, too, because the chances of burning himself into a pile of frustrated ashes were increasing with every moment he spent with her.

On the way down the hall Nate glanced longingly at his private bath. He wished he could spare time for a cold shower before supper. These forbidden longings that kept creeping under his skin when he let his guard down needed an icy dousing.

"We really should get back to town," Katy said uneasily as Nate led her away from his house.

Although Katy had felt relaxed and at ease during the past hour, while savoring Mary Jane Calloway's fried chicken, mashed potatoes and cream gravy, wariness assailed her when Nate insisted they take a stroll down to the pond.

"This will only take a few minutes," Nate told her, leading the way down the rocky ravine. "I want to show you the place where I hid out when my dad went on one of his binges when I was a kid."

The comment prompted Katy to quicken her pace. Despite her awkwardness with spending a few minutes alone with Nate, she did want to see the spectacular view so she could visualize him as that lost, lonely kid he had once been.

It was because of Nate, for Nate, that she agreed to this hike at sunset.

Nate halted on the pond bank, then gestured toward a wild tumble of rocks below the cliff. "I used to sit there in the dark as a kid, tucked between those rocks. I preferred to take my chances with scorpions and snakes rather than confront my old man when he was in one of his crazed moods," he confided. "I'd sit down here while he bellowed my name and threatened more bodily harm, then I'd sneak into the hayloft in the barn to sleep for the night."

He stared across the rugged landscape, watching the sun cast its colorful rays and slash long shadows across the winding arroyos. "I guess the peace and comfort I found sitting out here as a kid is what lured me back to this site to build a home."

"While my bedroom was my haven, you had the view of the whole outdoors to comfort you," Katy murmured. "I'm so sorry your childhood was hell, Nate."

As reluctant as Katy was to be drawn back to Nate, she felt another set of emotions stir inside her. Nate had endured so much misery in his youth. It was impossible to remain distant and remote from him when she could so easily picture Nate as a kid, huddled against the jagged rocks, hiding from the madman he called father.

Nate smiled faintly as he gazed across the rugged terrain.

"Yeah, well, according to Fuzz, it is important for me to confront my unpleasant memories, accept that part of my past, and thank the Lord that all those heartaches are behind me."

Hint, hint, Nate thought to himself. A psychiatrist he wasn't, but he was doing all he could do to convince Katy that she also needed to face her past and conquer her demons.

"You've come a long way, Nate," she whispered, tears in her eyes. "I'm so proud of you."

"Thanks, but it feels more like I've come full circle," he murmured. Very slowly, carefully, Nate stepped up behind Katy—not close enough to touch or frighten her away. "You'll probably think I'm crazy, but something about this wild, untamed country has always called to me on a level that I can't logically explain."

"Like you've been here before? At another time?" she asked.

"Yeah. Some weird kind of déjà vu, as if I were here when some of my Comanche ancestors roamed this area. Nuts, huh? You wanna start backing away from me now?" he asked.

Katy shook her head and continued to stare at the spectacular scenery of winding gullies that flattened into wide-open plains. "Not so nutty," she assured him. "I've read dozens of accounts about baffling, unexplainable occurrences that resemble flashbacks."

Nate moved a step closer—drawn to Katy like metal to a magnet. He slid his arms around her waist, then rested his chin on the top of her head. He felt her tense, as if prepared to bolt and run at the first sign of threat. But Nate didn't move a muscle, refused to make her wary of him. He just held her carefully, loosely in his arms and continued talking.

"I used to sit here and wonder what it would be like to wander like a nomad along the caprock that slashes through the high plains. This part of Texas hasn't changed much the past two hundred years. You either adapt to it, accept it for what it is, or you move on. I think I became a part of this land when I was a kid, became too connected to it to be satisfied living in another location. I guess you'd have to say this land is in my blood.''

Katy ignored the uneasy sensation sliding through her, battled the forbidden pleasure of having Nate's muscled arms encircling her. She couldn't let herself think about what they once shared. She focused her concentration on picturing Nate as a renegade Comanche warrior thundering across this wild terrain on horseback. He would make the perfect hero for some of the Indian romances she'd read.

Katy smiled at the thought and instinctively relaxed in his arms. She didn't realize she had laid her arms over his until she glanced down to note the contrast between her pale skin and his bronzed flesh. Sharp contrasts, vast differences, she thought to herself. Yet the attraction was still there, she realized with a sense of panic.

No, don't go there, Katy. Don't do that to yourself. Back away from Nate. What was between you is over, and you swore you didn't want another man near you after the hell Brad put you through.

Reflexively, Katy stepped sideways, out of Nate's reach. He didn't jerk her back against him, just let her go without objection. Katy breathed an inward sigh of relief, reminding herself that Nate wasn't Brad. She didn't have to expect the same hurtful reactions she had grown accustomed to during her marriage.

''I guess I've detained you and Tammy long enough,'' Nate said as he pivoted on his heels. ''We'll rescue Tammy before Fuzz talks her ear off. Give me your hand and I'll help you up to the top of the ridge. Believe me, it's easier coming down than it is going back up.''

Hesitantly, Katy lifted her hand up and felt the strength in his fingertips. She had touched Nate too many times already, and each moment gave rise to forbidden memories that she couldn't allow herself to revisit. She didn't want to feel, was afraid to feel. But Nate was right. With her gimpy leg, this staircase of stone and loose dirt made a difficult path to follow. Twice, Nate steadied her when she stumbled. The feel of his arms closing around her sent her into instant panic, and she struggled with herself to prevent pulling away from him.

During the uphill hike to the house, Katy recalled what Nate had said about confronting the tormenting past and getting on with life. Good advice, to be sure. But for Katy, it was easier said than done.

"Gosh, I wonder what's burning?" Tammy clamped her hands on the edge of Katy's bucket seat as Nate drove them back to town.

Katy came to immediate attention as they neared town. "Oh, no! It's the grocery store!" she wailed in dismay.

Nate watched the cloud of thick, black smoke mushroom into the air, then roll north. He saw the crowd of bystanders closing in around the volunteer firemen, who were battling the blaze. Nate found the nearest parking space and maneuvered the car to the curb.

Katy was out of the car in a flash, limping hurriedly toward the mayor, who was standing on the sidewalk. "What happened?" she asked anxiously.

"Nobody knows for sure. The fire marshal is on his way to check things out," Eugene Wilks replied, staring at the leaping flames with fanatical fascination. "Could have been anything from faulty electrical wiring to premeditated arson."

While Katy was speaking to Eugene, Tammy hurried off to join her friends, who were clustered on the curb across the street, and Nate made a slow, deliberate sweep of the crowd. When he saw Millie Kendrick leaning heavily on her shopping cart, Nate made a beeline toward her. If anyone had a clue what had happened it would be Millie. She was an observer of life who was always on the sidelines, watching, contemplating situations.

Nate edged up beside Millie, who stood apart from the crowd. She tipped her head back to peer up at him. The plastic birds on her straw hat wobbled on their wire legs.

"You know what happened." It wasn't a question, merely a statement of fact. Although no one paid Millie much heed, Nate knew she had always been the eyes of this town.

"Yup, I do," she confirmed, then turned her attention to the fire that consumed the building, despite the valiant efforts of the firefighters. "But I ain't telling the sheriff, so don't expect me to."

"Wouldn't expect you to," Nate replied, following her gaze to the roaring blaze. "The way I see it, you and I are a lot alike, Millie. We always were. We were pretty much overlooked and written off by this town."

"Yup." She nodded her frizzy gray head. "More alike 'n ya think, boy."

Nate glanced down to see a wry smile purse the old woman's lips. That was Millie through and through—always talking in riddles, then smiling as if she were enjoying a private joke. Nate reckoned that habit was the reason most folks didn't pay much attention to Millie. But there was something about the way Millie was staring up at him, the way her dark eyes gleamed, that prompted him to do what most people never did. Nate asked her to explain what she meant.

"How so, Millie?"

She snickered, leaving him dangling on the hook, as if checking to see if he had the patience to outwait her. Most folks didn't. They just turned and walked off, mumbling that she was loony.

Nate never wanted to be like "most folks." It must have been that rebel streak in him that he'd never quite been able to cure. "You gonna tell me, woman? Or just stand there grinning like a baked possum? Either fish or cut bait."

"We're blood kin, boy," she cut in, delighting in shocking him. "That's why we're a lot alike."

Nate's jaw scraped his chest. "We are?" he tweeted like a sick sparrow.

She bobbed her Brillo-pad head. The plastic birds fluttered on her hat. "Yup. I'm your aunt, your ma's sister. Who'd ya think left those little stashes of money in your kitchen cabinet when there was nothing between you and starvation? Wasn't your mama. My baby sister never had her head on straight, from the time she was in training bras. Had a chip on her shoulder, too. Didn't want anybody, least of all me, telling her what to do and how to do it. She wanted all the credit for what she did, and she gets it, too. She ruined her life, and darn near ruined yours, all by herself."

Nate opened and closed his mouth, but words refused to come out. All these years he'd thought his mother had cared just enough to set aside a little money for groceries. All these years he'd given his mother more credit than she deserved. She had cared more about herself than about him.

As if she knew what thoughts were running through Nate's mind, Millie smiled at him. "Couldn't tell ya way back then. You were having a rough time of it, and Lil needed somebody to look after her. She didn't want a thing to do with me, so that just left you to watch out for her, boy."

Oddly enough, Nate understood Millie's reasoning. "I take it the two of you never got along well."

Millie snorted. "Nope. After you were bustled off in the patrol car, she packed up and left town. To this day, I don't know what became of her. She always steered clear of me, resented me for giving advice, for having a decent marriage, short though it turned out to be. Your uncle died in a farming accident." Her lip quivered, and her eyes misted over. "I never got over it, sort of like you with that Bates girl." Her gaze swung to Katy, who stood beneath the streetlight, talking to the mayor.

The information Millie imparted left Nate in an emotional tailspin. He recalled all the times he'd swaggered down Main

Street, trying to look confident so folks would think he felt good about himself. Nothing could have been further from the truth. His demeanor had been an act. No one but Millie acknowledged him, paid him the slightest attention. Now Nate knew why. Millie had been the silent financial benefactor who made his misguided youth barely tolerable.

Millie was his aunt? He had one relative left in this world? The thought gave him a sense of belonging that he couldn't remember feeling in decades.

"Pack of boys did it," Millie said out of the blue. "Saw 'em bustling around the corner to that open lot behind the store. Smoking cigarettes and acting cool.

"Purely accidental is my guess. Must've neglected to snuff out the cigarette completely. Then the wind came up and blew the grass fire toward the building," she added. "Not intentional arson, though that's probably what the fire marshal will decide." She gestured her head toward the five teenage boys who stood at a distance. "Every one of them reminds me of you, back in the old days. Lost, confused, and trying to find their way. They don't need a charge of arson dumped on their heads. Got a rough time of it as it is."

Nate's heart dropped to the soles of his boots. He recognized Chad Parker immediately by his stance, by his downcast head. The kid's hands were crammed in the pockets of his baggy jeans, and he shifted uneasily from one oversize tennis shoe to the other. Nate knew Katy was trying to reach Chad before he got into serious trouble. It would break her heart if one of her lost sheep went too far astray. Worse, Tammy and Chad had a mutual crush—just like he and Katy in the old days.

"Do you see yourself standing over there, boy?" Millie asked in a gravelly voice. "Whatcha gonna do about it? Tattle what you know to the new sheriff? Peterson is a good man, but he is too by-the-book to handle the problems these boys have. Somebody who understands them needs to intervene."

Nate had made his decision long before Millie gave him the verbal nudge. He strode off—and got as far as the next streetlight before Lester Brown and his sidekick stepped up to block his path.

"Figured you'd return to the scene of your crime, No-Account Nate," Lester jeered in a voice loud enough to catch the onlookers' attention. "What did you do? Pay some of those thugs to set the fire? Trying to prove to the rest of us that you returned to take over this town, and you'll burn it down around us if we don't accept you?"

"Yeah," John Jessup chimed in, his barrel-size chest thrust out, his pointed chin tipped upward. "Since we tried to run you outta town, you decided to destroy the grocery store, didn't you?"

Nate's hand balled into a tight fist. Brown and Jessup didn't have a clue how close they'd come to receiving one-two knockout punches. Willfully, Nate restrained his irritation, then glanced around to gauge the crowd's reaction. Looks of suspicion and condemnation focused on him.

"We know you're dealing drugs," Lester spouted. "You're probably hanging around, waiting for that oil company to get itself in operation, so you can get yourself what looks to be a respectable job. But we know it'll only be a front for transporting and distributing drugs."

"Now wait just a blessed minute, Lester!"

Nate didn't know whether to curse or applaud when Katy's voice rang out. He didn't turn around when he heard her storm forward—her limp gave her pelting footsteps a distinct staccato sound. Nate was pleased to see that Katy had regained some of her lost gumption, but he didn't want her standing up for him and alienating herself from the citizens of Coyote Flats. She would be condemned by association.

Nate felt the need to protect Katy, even though he was the one who was being verbally crucified in front of the whole cursed town. He wasn't sure how to handle this situation. He didn't want to become involved in a shouting match with these two troublemakers. Yet he didn't want Katy to get into an argument with them in front of a captive audience. Well, hell!

"Lester," Katy huffed as she approached. "I have tolerated all your snide, unfounded, slanderous remarks about as long as—"

"Come on, Katy, let me drive you and Tammy home," Nate cut in as he steered her away from the confrontation.

"No, I—"

"It's okay," he whispered for her ears only.

"No, it's not okay," she muttered angrily. "For once I've worked up the nerve to say what I should have said to that spiteful windbag a week ago. Now you won't let me at him!"

Nate grinned at her spunky display. Wow! Katy had really girded herself up for battle, hadn't she? Now he could compute his progress of transforming Katy into her old self in whole *inches.* Maybe suffering through Lester's damning insults and becoming his whipping boy was worth it. If the incident provided Katy with the incentive to revive her spirit, Nate would gladly make the personal sacrifice. However, Katy might damage her reputation in Coyote Flats if she stood up for him. Nate couldn't let that happen.

"Tammy!" Nate flapped his arms to gain the girl's attention. "Let's go."

Reluctantly, Tammy joined Katy and Nate on the street. Nate was quick to note the girl's gaze darted toward the group of boys standing apart from the crowd—to Chad Parker in particular. Chad's gaze swung momentarily to Tammy, then he dropped his head.

Well hell, thought Nate. If that kid was involved in the destructive fire, his future was sealed. Chad would be as condemned as Nate had been at the same age. Damn it, Nate felt as if history was repeating itself, and he *had* to do something to stop it!

* * *

Katy was bewildered by the flood of emotion coursing through her. One moment she had been speaking calmly to the mayor, discussing the fire and the possibility of receiving allocated funds for the library. And then, whammo! She had heard Lester and John verbally attacking Nate, and she had exploded into action, as if that was a natural reflex. Fact was, she hadn't reacted so impulsively in years!

Katy had been truly amazed at herself when she stormed toward Brown and Jessup. Eight hours earlier she had hunched in her booth at the café and listened to Lester's slanderous remarks without acting. This evening, she had come to Nate's defense when Alice Phelps had behaved rudely, then she'd launched herself at Lester and John on a street filled with bystanders. She had just gotten wound up, prepared to let loose with two loaded barrels when Nate detoured her into the street and whisked her into his car to drive her home.

Without a word, Nate had left Katy and Tammy standing in the driveway and sped off into the darkness.

Hands still shaking with suppressed frustration, Katy poured herself a cup of tea, then attacked the box of chocolate pecan Turtles like a shark in a feeding frenzy.

"Are you okay, Aunt Katy?" Tammy questioned worriedly.

"No," she grumbled between bites of chewy caramel. "Sometimes the folks around here make me ashamed to call this my hometown! What Lester and John said about Nate was untrue and totally uncalled for. You and I know perfectly well that Nate has been with us all evening. How could anyone possibly think he ignited that fire or coerced a bunch of kids into doing it as an act of spiteful retaliation!"

Tammy's eyes popped. "Man, you're really ticked off, aren't you? I've never seen you get worked up like this before." Tammy grinned in approval. "Really cool!"

Katy sucked in her breath, striving for hard-won control, then asked herself why she should crawl back behind her wall of self-reserve now. Or ever again. It suddenly dawned on her that if she didn't stand her ground and show some gumption, she was essentially allowing Brad and her father to dictate to her from beyond the grave.

Withdrawing into herself had been her only means of survival against Dave Bates and Brad Butler. But they were gone, Katy reminded herself. If she continued on the same self-destructive course she had followed the past six years, then she would be allowing those two men to defeat her. By damned, she wasn't going to give them the satisfaction!

Tonight, for one glorious moment, adrenaline had pumped through her and she'd felt like fighting back, *needed* to fight back, because Nate had simply stood there while Lester hammered him with insults. Since Nate hadn't defended his honor and integrity, she had felt the compulsive need to do it for him.

Only he hadn't let her.

Why the hell not?

"Boy, Nate sure bustled us off in a hurry, didn't he," Tammy commented as she helped herself to the candy.

Katy frowned pensively. "I think he was trying to protect us from an ugly scene. When a disaster strikes, people have a bad habit of trying to lay the blame at someone's feet, whether it belongs there or not."

When Tammy squirmed uneasily, then stared at the refrigerator, as if it suddenly demanded all her attention, Katy frowned warily. "What's wrong? You know something, don't you, Tammy? What is it?"

Tammy shrugged noncommittally and chewed vigorously on the candy.

"Do you know who might have started that fire?" Kate grilled her.

"Not for sure. I just heard talk."

Clearly, Tammy didn't want to be drawn into a discussion on the subject. Well, tough. Katy was not going to allow Nate to be persecuted for something he didn't do. Heaven knew he

had been blamed for just about everything that went wrong in
this town while he was a kid. Katy had always hated the way
her influential father cast aspersions and made Nate the convenient scapegoat.

All because Katy showed an interest in him.

"Tammy…" Katy said softly. "Tell me what you heard."

Tammy flopped back against the counter. Her breath gushed
out sharply. "Please don't make me tell you, Aunt Katy. I
don't want to rat on anybody, especially not him!"

A knot of apprehension coiled in Katy's stomach. She had
the unshakable feeling she knew who "him" referred to. Chad
Parker, Tammy's secret admirer, the object of her growing
affection. Well damn, Katy had tried so hard to reach Chad
before the gang who tried to include him in their circle poisoned his thinking and ruined what little reputation the kid
had. Chad wanted something better, but he was battling the
social prejudices that excluded him from the cliques that operated at the high school.

Katy knew all about those social dynamics, had stood firm
against them as a teenager—for all the good it did her then.
But now, the obstacle in her path was gone. Dave Bates wasn't
here to label teenagers he considered undesirable and prevent
her from defending them. Katy knew as sure as the sun rose
that Dave Bates would have refused to allow his one and only
granddaughter to associate with the likes of Chad Parker. In
Judge Bates's eyes, the kid wouldn't be good enough for
Tammy. She deserved better, she was entitled to the best, because of her good breeding. That's what the judge would say
if he were here.

How many times had Katy heard that monotonous lecture
while she was infatuated with Nate Channing? Too darn many
to count, that was for sure.

"So you think Chad might have been involved," Katy said
belatedly.

Tammy ducked her head and gave the very slightest of

nods. Tears clouded her eyes. "That's what the other kids said tonight, but I refused to believe it. He's not like the other guys who hang around him. I swear he isn't. He's nice and polite and friendly to me. He certainly treats me better than those cocky jocks who think they're such ladies' men!"

"I think Chad has great potential, too, Tammy," Katy assured her.

When Tammy jerked up her head, her blond ponytail bobbed against her neck. "You do?"

"Yes, but Chad may have gotten involved unintentionally. Those other boys had been trying to draw him in, because there is safety in numbers. The more the better, according to their logic. Those boys lack security and they are trying to find it in one another. They are rebellious and eager for attention, even if it's the negative variety. When kids aren't noticed at home or school, when they don't feel accepted, they crave notice of one kind or another."

"Yeah," Tammy said pensively. "Those other guys get into trouble at school and seem kind of proud of it. You must be right. They just want to be noticed by somebody. But Chad doesn't call attention to himself in that way. He makes decent grades, and he doesn't blow off homework assignments, even if his friends razz him and call him a bookworm."

Here was yet another indication that Chad Parker was trying to break free of the stigma and make something of himself. But if he was arrested, even under *suspicion* of setting the fire, his chance of making a new start and getting the job as library janitor would be impossible. The city council would not approve of having a known arsonist working in the public library.

"You better finish your homework," Katy insisted. "Besides, I need to be alone with my thoughts if I'm going to figure out how to help Chad through this crisis."

Tammy peered intently at her aunt. "You'll try to help him? Really?"

Katy nodded, refusing to confide that she had already helped Chad financially for six months. That was between Katy and Chad.

When Tammy ambled to her room, Katy plunked down at the kitchen table to devour a few more Turtles, then she stared appreciatively at the bouquet of roses Nate had given her. She faced a frustrating conundrum here. If she tried to prove Nate wasn't involved in setting the fire, she would likely get Chad into hot water with Sheriff Peterson. If she didn't offer her speculations, then Nate would remain the convenient scapegoat. Lester and John would continue to sway public opinion about Nate.

To save one, she might have to sacrifice the other. Talk about getting caught between the proverbial rock and hard place.

"Damn," Katy mumbled around a mouthful of candy. How was she, who had practically turned into a recluse and let her appearance go to hell the past few years, going to have enough credibility and influence on the folks in this community? She was just poor Katy who'd had a rough time of it and kept to herself. Folks around here had offered sympathy but hadn't followed up the emotion with charitable acts. They let her wallow in her misery and never tried to draw her out, include her in activities.

But now Nate Channing had come back to town, and he cared enough to make a difference in her life. His insistence in getting her out of the house this evening lent testimony to that.

Katy frowned thoughtfully. In less than a week, Nate had managed to stir up emotions Katy thought she had buried. He, alone, had befriended her, included her by giving her a tour of his house, inviting her to dinner and renewing her acquaintance with Fuzz Havern.

In an effort to protect her from Lester and John's vicious tongues, Nate had spirited her away tonight. He had to know that Lester and John would view the incident as another victory in their ongoing feud against Nate. He hadn't defended himself by announcing that he had spent the evening with Katy and Tammy.

He had been willing to sacrifice his attempt to gain respect in his hometown in order to protect Katy and Tammy. The noble gesture could cost his already questionable reputation dearly in this suspicious town.

Tears welled up in Katy's eyes. Life had been so unfair to Nate…and Katy had been the reason he was forced out of town sixteen years ago. She could never let herself forget that she owed him for the loss of respect he suffered the night he was spirited away.

Katy sat up a little straighter in her chair and raised her chin a notch. Perhaps she would never regain enough self-confidence and self-esteem to share an intimate relationship with Nate because Brad had taught her to fear sexual advances, had pounded it into her head—literally—that she was a pathetic sexual partner. But she felt the compelling need to stand up for *Nate,* even if she had forgotten how to stand up for *herself.* Maybe she was only a partial coward, she decided. Maybe if she projected a new image in town, she could earn enough credibility to become Nate's champion.…

If she didn't chicken out the way she usually did during heated confrontations and revert to the old habit of running for cover.

No more negative thoughts, Katy Marie, she told herself firmly. Nate Channing deserved a second chance in this dusty, dried-up, opinionated town. And Katy was going to find a way to ensure Nate got a chance. If the first step in phase one was to improve *her* image and appearance, to hold up her head and assert herself, then that's what she was going to do.

Yes, she decided, she was going to ignore the barrage of second thoughts that ricocheted around her head. She could do this, for Nate Channing's sake. She was going to recapture a little of that fire and spirit her father and husband had smothered. She had told Nate countless times in the past that he was worthy and honorable and capable. All she had to do was tell herself the same thing.

Given time, she might even begin to believe it.

Chapter Six

Chad Parker nearly jumped out of his skin when an ominous figure loomed within the shadows on the front porch of his house. "What the hell are you doing here? Who are you?"

"Your worst nightmare, kid...if you refuse to cooperate with me." Nate took an intimidating step forward, then another, until he had forced Chad to back down the sidewalk.

"You better beat it, mister, or I'll holler to my parents," Chad threatened nervously. "My dad'll blow you away."

Nate scoffed at the bluffed power play. He knew this routine, had used it himself in the past. But the fact was that he had used his cell phone to check with Fuzz Havern, and he had the lowdown on Chad and the gang of boys who had most likely caused the fire at the grocery store.

"Your mother isn't home. Rarely is," Nate told the fidgety kid. "I know you don't have a father."

Chad elevated his chin and tried out his tough look, but Nate wasn't impressed. He looked at Chad and saw himself

ten times over. Behind all that bluff and bluster was a scared
kid who had very little guidance, direction or encouragement.

"What the hell do you want?" Chad snapped hatefully.

Nate broke into a devilish smile. "Your soul for starters,
kid."

A wary expression crossed Chad's face as he shifted uneasily from one well-worn sneaker to the other. "*Who* the hell
are you?" he demanded again.

Nate leaned forward to get right in the kid's face. "The
name is Nate Channing. I know you and your buddies started
the fire. Are you the one who tossed aside the cigarette that
caused the dry grass to set off like a lit fuse and ignite the
grocery store?"

Chad's face turned the color of vanilla pudding. "How'd
you know about—"

"Because I'm right in your head with you, pal. Been there,
hated my lot in life, resented being looked down on, as if I
wasn't as good as everybody else. Even believed it myself for
a while. And you know what, kid?"

Chad gulped. "What?"

"I made it out of the gutter where everybody thought I
belonged. I left behind a ramshackle shanty that looked worse
than the one you're living in. Somebody in this snobbish town
saw potential in me, and she never let me give up on myself.
Her name is Katy Bates, and no—" he hurried on before Chad
assumed Katy had confided Chad's identity "—she doesn't
know that I know who you are. She doesn't know that I saw
her slip you a crisp Jackson when you skulked into her back-
yard."

Chad's face turned a lighter shade of pale, but Nate didn't
let up, because he had gotten the kid's undivided attention and
he intended to press his advantage.

"You know what else, kid? You aren't going to get by with
the excuses you've been relying on anymore because they
won't cut it with me. You want a better life, a new image, a

chance? Well, guess what, I'm your lottery ticket, and you win.

"Starting tonight, I'm going to make a winner out of you. If I hear any excuses about the lousy start you've had, about your lack of parental guidance, then you'll leave me no choice but to cram them back down your throat. Don't force me to do that, kid, because I gave up the F word, smoking, drinking and fistfighting years ago. But not so long ago that I don't remember how to deliver a brain-scrambling punch that causes temporary amnesia. You got that, kid?"

"Yeah," Chad chirped nervously.

"That is 'yes, sir,' to you," he corrected him sharply, amazed that the instant he approached this kid and lit into the boy, he sounded exactly like Bud Thurston and Fuzz Havern all rolled into one intimidating authority figure.

"You've got just one chance," Nate continued gruffly. "You blow it and you'll rot away in this dump of a house, in this town. You won't have the chance to walk away from the bad example your parents set for you. You won't learn something positive and become a better man, worthy to be seen in public with someone of Tammy Bates's caliber."

Chad's eyes rounded. He stared up at Nate as if he were telepathic or psychopathic—the kid couldn't figure out which.

"My dad was an alcoholic who turned mean and nasty when he was drunk. So did my mother, so don't whine to me about a deadbeat dad and the uncaring mother you got stuck with. Don't whine to me about not having the funds to date the prettiest girl in town. When I was your age, I couldn't even set foot on my girlfriend's doorstep because her snobbish daddy didn't think I was good enough to get within a hundred yards of his high-class daughter.

"And you want to talk modes of transportation?" Nate added with a snort. "My bucket-of-rust car was broken down more than it ran. I couldn't even afford a car until I was a senior in high school. If I didn't learn to fix that junk heap, then it didn't get fixed, because I couldn't afford a professional mechanic. Right now you don't have wheels, but you're going to earn the money to buy one.''

''Doing what?'' Chad mumbled. ''Picking up aluminum cans beside the road? There's not much work for kids in this town.''

Clearly, having wheels was a high priority on Chad's list. His ego was smarting because he was afoot. Nate understood the embarrassment, but Fuzz and Bud had taught Nate that sarcastic back talk was a no-no. Chad had to learn that straight away.

''You say something to me, kid?'' Nate snarled for effect.

Chad reflexively jerked to attention. ''No…sir.''

''I didn't think so. If you had, you would have used a polite, nonhostile tone.'' Nate cuffed Chad by the rib knitting on his T-shirt and hauled him down the street.

''Where are you taking me?'' Chad shrieked in alarm.

''For a ride in my shiny black Lincoln, just so you'll know you could have one just like it someday if you wanted one, provided you don't give up on yourself, provided you refuse to live down to people's low opinion of you.''

Nate jerked open the door and shoved Chad roughly into the car, the very same way Fuzz had manhandled him sixteen years ago. It had made a lasting impression on Nate. He was pretty sure it would have a similar effect on Chad. The kid was going to realize immediately that, no matter how tough he thought he was, Nate was bigger, stronger and tougher.

''Wow!'' Chad breathed in awe as Nate plunked down behind the wheel. ''This car is really loaded.''

''Darn right. Bought and paid for with hard-earned money, not illegal funds, no matter what you are likely to hear to the contrary from some folks in this town who refuse to accept me because of the frustrated kid I was when I left, not the man I am now. You, kid, are going to leave this place with a better reputation than you have now so you don't have to deal with this kind of suspicion and mistrust if you ever decide to come back.''

"So where are we going?" Chad asked as Nate pulled through the alley and veered to the street.

"To pick up your so-called friends. You're going to tell me where to find them. You're also going to tell me who tossed aside the cigarette, because I think you have more sense than to pull an irresponsible stunt like that.''

Nate glanced sideways, noting that Chad had clamped his mouth shut. "I'm not going to beat the crap out of your friends, at least not if they cooperate the same way you are going to. You want them to have the same break you're going to get? Or do you care if they make it out of the gutter?''

Thus far, Nate had followed Bud and Fuzz's policy of informing a juvenile of exactly how he was expected to behave. He wasn't going to tell Chad and the other boys what *not* to do, but what *to* do, how to respond in certain situations. Nate was going to prepare them to become responsible, law-abiding citizens. This would be the payback Nate owed society. He was going to set up his own behavioral-modification program and attitude-adjustment classes. Chad Parker might not know it yet, but he was going to become Nate's star pupil—like it or not!

"So where do I find those soon-to-be-converted thugs?" Nate demanded sharply.

Chad kept silent for a long moment. Nate didn't push and prod. He let the kid mull over the rapid-fire comments and make the right decision. And Chad would make the right decision or Nate would move directly to plan B. Fear, Nate knew for a fact, was a strong motivational technique. He hoped he wouldn't have to resort to strong-arm tactics with Chad.

The other boys, Nate wasn't so sure about.

According to the background information Fuzz Havern had provided, the other four hoodlums weren't hard-core but they were borderline. Nate prayed he could reach them before they followed in Sonny Brown's footsteps, before they gave up completely on themselves and turned to lives of crime.

"The guys are probably at the hamburger joint," Chad said finally.

An unseen smile quirked Nate's lips as he hung a right and cruised down the side street. His new charges were hanging out at the Coyote Grill, were they?

This Podunk town lacked creativity, Nate thought to himself. There was no Sundown Café, no Fluff-and-Dry Laundromat, just plain old Coyote Café, Coyote Grill, Coyote Service Station and Coyote Grocery, which had recently gone up in smoke. No wonder kids just sat around howling at the moon. No wonder the hidebound snobs in town dragged their feet and resisted change. The whole lot of the folks in town were stuck in a rut. Nate hadn't realized that until he shook the dust of Coyote Flats off his boot heels, then returned to view the town from a new perspective.

His thoughts trailed off when he saw four boys sipping drinks from foam cups while they leaned negligently against a light pole. All four juveniles had their ball caps turned backward and were trying to act like the coolest of the cool in Coyote County. It was just an act, Nate knew from experience. These kids were suffering from attention deprivation and severe cases of inferiority complex.

"Go round 'em up," Nate ordered brusquely. "We're going for a ride."

Chad did as he was told. Nate watched Chad deliver the summons, saw the thugs glance at the Lincoln with its tinted-glass windows. They held a short powwow, then finally the foursome swaggered behind Chad when he returned to the car.

Nate made a long, pensive study of the foursome who approached and he immediately picked out the ringleader. The kid was a stout bully type with a chip the size of the Rock of Gibraltar on his shoulder. Of course, the kid was the first one to shoot off his smart mouth when he plopped carelessly on the back seat of the car.

"Whatddya want with us—"

Nate twisted around, snaked out a steely arm, grabbed the kid by the front of his T-shirt and hauled him forward before he knew what hit him. When dealing with troubled kids, like Nate used to be, he knew attention-grabbing was important. He employed yet another technique Fuzz and Bud had used on him, noting that it worked as well now as it had way back when.

"You set your last fire around here and smarted off for the last time, son." Nate breathed harshly on the kid's reddened face. "I'm the only thing standing between you and a stint in a juvenile detention center. I promise you that you don't want to tangle with the badasses locked up in there. This is your lucky day, pal. You get to deal with me instead.

"When I ask you a question you will respond truthfully and politely. The name is Nate Channing," he told the cocky ringleader. "When you reply you can use my name or sir, whichever you prefer. That goes for the rest of you. Any deviation from Rule Number One will land you in deep trouble with me. Is that understood?"

He released his hold on the ringleader. "Is everybody clear on how to behave respectfully?"

"Yes, sir," Chad said, setting a good example for the boys in the back seat.

Nate smiled discreetly at his star pupil when the fearless foursome tucked their tails and mumbled, "Yes…sir."

During the four-mile drive to the construction site, Nate silently thanked Bud and Fuzz for teaching him how to deal with wayward youths and make them respond. These half-pint thugs would come around because Nate refused to let them give up on themselves. Katy's crusade to help underprivileged, neglected and troubled kids had become his crusade.

When Nate cut the engine, he was the first one out of the

car. He waited for the boys to pile out, then directed their attention to the monstrous steel building that would soon house a branch office, research and development center, and supply warehouse for Sunrise Oil Company.

"I'm hiring all five of you to clean up the premises," he announced. "I want every packaging paper from insulation, every scrap of steel, every discarded bolt and hex-head screw picked up off the ground and placed in the trash bins. When the shrubbery arrives to landscape the grounds, we will shovel, rake and plant the garden sites according to my specifications. The interior of the building will be swept clean nightly so the electrical and framing crews don't have to work around clutter and risk injury. When the time comes to build the fence around the property, I will be your foreman.

"You will report to me exactly one hour after school is dismissed each day and at nine o'clock on Saturdays. You will be paid two dollars an hour above minimum wage, and you will be docked five dollars for tardiness. There will be no smoking or drinking on the premises.

"Since my parents were both alcoholics, I have zero tolerance for what booze can do to people, to families. I know exactly what you have endured in life because I endured it myself as a teenager, so don't think flimsy cop-outs will work with me. They won't. I will also be checking in with the teaching staff to ensure your job doesn't cut into your grade-point average. If you aren't making the kind of grades to brag about, then it's time to start. The Nate Channing School of Etiquette and Work Ethics doesn't tolerate sloppy appearance, rotten attitudes and self-imposed ignorance. Any questions?"

"Yeah," Jake Randolph said, smirking. "You and what army is gonna make us follow your stupid rules?"

Nate got right in Jake's face, forcing the kid to look up at him, establishing his role of authority.

"You want to rephrase that question, kid?" Nate growled venomously. "I don't think I heard you correctly, did I?" Nate practically stood on top of him, his gaze boring down like laser beams.

"No…s-sir," Jake squeaked when a painful twist was applied to his hair.

"Now, what was it that you wanted to ask me?" Nate prompted through gritted teeth.

"Nothing…sir…I…understand the rules," Jake said grudgingly.

Still, standing toe to toe with Jake, he glanced sideways to see Tyler, Will, Richie and Chad staring uneasily at Jake. "Anybody else need me to repeat the rules one more time?"

Four moppy heads shook in response.

"Pardon? I didn't hear you," Nate snapped harshly.

"No, sir," the boys chorused.

"Good, get back in the car so I can drive you home. I'll be at the library tomorrow to give you a ride to the construction site. You can use your hour to study at the library. The first thing you're going to learn is effective time management by doing your homework promptly."

When the four boys filed back to the car, Nate stared the kid squarely in the eye. "I wasn't as smart as you are going to be, Jake. The chip on my shoulder was a size larger than the one on yours, I'm sorry to say. I learned to respect authority—the hard way. At the time I was too bitter, stubborn and immature to realize they were doing me the kind of favor no one ever bothered with before. They *cared* what happened to me, *cared* about me.

"Know something else, kid? I care about you, even though we don't know each other very well yet. I care, because there aren't enough people in this town who do care about those of us who have to scratch and claw to get ahead in life.

"I'm not helping you because I'm getting paid for it, not because I've been asked to do it. I'm trying to help, because I want more for you than I had when I was your age. I want to show you the way out of the trenches, Jake. You can hate my guts for forcing you to make an attitude adjustment, but you are going to change because the path you're on leads to a dead end. I'm offering you a detour. Take it and you'll have a chance to be somebody. I guaran-damn-tee you'll like it better than being a nobody. The penal system is overloaded with losers.''

Nate turned Jake around and directed the kid toward the car. If Nate could reach the ringleader and Chad, who was a step ahead because of Katy's encouragement, the other boys were sure to follow.

''You're a genuine son of a bitch…sir,'' Jake muttered as Nate walked him to the car.

Nate threw back his head and laughed good-naturedly. ''You're right, Jake. I am…now. But when you earn my re-spect, and you will earn it the right way, you and the rest of the guys will get a deserved raise for your hard work. And you're going to like having money in your pocket instead of lint. And Jake?''

The kid stumbled to a halt, then glanced sideways. ''What?''

''No matter what anybody else tells you. *Anybody* else,'' he emphasized. ''You *are* worth it. You're worth your effort and my effort.''

Nate slid beneath the wheel and drove off. There was dead silence in the car until he dropped off Chad.

''Thanks for the ride, sir,'' Chad murmured as he climbed out.

''Glad to do it, Chad. See you tomorrow at the library.''

More silence as Nate drove away.

''Just drop us off at Coyote Grill…sir,'' Jake requested, a hint of hostility in his voice.

''Nope,'' Nate refused. ''I'm taking you home. Nothing could be worse than the dump where I grew up, so don't go getting self-conscious on me. Doesn't matter where or how you live now. It's where you're going that counts. Oh, yeah, and one more thing. I know you were involved in the incident at the grocery store. I also know I'm obstructing justice by keeping silent. I'm not blackmailing you with my knowledge, because I don't believe what you did was intentional, just a careless, thoughtless, regrettable mistake.''

Nate glanced in the rearview mirror to see the boys slumped guiltily on the seat. ''Folks in this town will be unconvinced until the grocery store is rebuilt and the accident is behind them. I'll probably end up being the one who takes the heat for the incident because people have a tendency to remember me as I was, not what I've become. I have to prove myself to them, just as you have to. In some ways you're more fortunate, because you don't have to wait sixteen years for folks to see the positive changes in your behavior.''

Nate glanced in the rearview mirror again to see four pensive gazes zeroed in on him. These kids would understand what he was talking about when Lester Brown and John Jessup spread a few more malicious rumors with his name attached to them. When these misguided kids realized the blame would lie at his feet, rather than theirs, Nate wondered how they would react. Would they feel guilty? Would they see the injustice directed toward Nate and know that he had taken the pressure off them?

Time would tell, Nate mused as he dropped off the last of his young charges and drove home to give Taz a long-awaited pet and listen to Fuzz talk his ear off.

''Aunt Katy?'' Tammy stopped short and stared, wide-eyed, at her aunt. ''Gosh, you look terrific!''

Self-consciously, Katy ran her hand through her recently cut and styled hair. ''Do you really think so?''

Tammy bounded forward, beaming with encouragement. ''Your haircut is really cool. You're wearing makeup, too,'' she observed. ''I don't remember seeing that business suit before. Is it new?''

Katy smoothed the wrinkles from the skirt that was several inches shorter than her usual garments. She had stayed up late last night to raise the hem and take a few tucks in the oversize blouse. "No, I simply did some alterations on the mix-and-match outfits in my closet."

Tammy gave her another thorough glance. "Well, whatever you did looks great. You really look fabulous, Aunt Katy."

Katy felt pride in her appearance for the first time in years. If she was going to exert influence in town she had to muster her pride and belief in herself. With every stitch she'd sewn, she had given herself a pep talk. It must have worked, because she had marshaled the nerve to march herself over to Mayor Eugene Wilks's office and inform him that she had been making personal contributions to support the library for years and that it was time for the city council to step up to the needs of the community.

She also told Eugene that students were making use of research material for term papers and they were being deprived of opportunities found in more progressive communities. She informed Eugene that she had applied for several federal grants and was doing all she could to improve the library, and she didn't want to be the only one around here doing it.

When Eugene hemmed and hawed, Katy had planted her hands on his desk and told him that an increase in funds was crucial, and she expected *him* to lead the crusade at the city council meeting. He, after all, had a grandson who was making use of the library, and the boy wasn't getting everything he needed for his term paper because the research material was outdated.

Eugene had gaped at her, as if she had antlers sprouting from the sides of her head. Finally, he had nodded agreeably.

Katy had maintained her assertive image until she exited city hall. Then she half collapsed against the side of the building to haul in a deep breath. She told herself that she was acting on behalf of every student in this backward town, on behalf of every citizen who appreciated the knowledge and pleasure that books and interesting magazines provided. For heaven's sake, the encyclopedias in the library didn't even cover Desert Storm. It was shameful!

Katy's thoughts trailed off when Chad Parker, accompanied by four boys, trooped into the library and plunked down at a picnic table. Without a word, they opened their textbooks, retrieved paper and pencil, and began doing homework.

Katy glanced curiously at Tammy, who shrugged, bemused. To Katy's surprise, the teenagers didn't make a peep for forty-five minutes. They pored over their books in profound concentration.

Five minutes later, Nate Channing walked in. Katy felt herself tense the moment his onyx-colored gaze flooded over her. She realized she was holding her breath, hoping for his approval—something she had learned not to expect or count on this past decade.

Then it came, the lift of his thick brow, that sexy quirk of a smile, the nod of male appreciation. Katy felt a grin of satisfaction spread across her lips. She felt as if this was the first day of the rest of her life, a new start, felt as if she had passed her first test.

Okay, so it was clichéd and sappy, but that's how she felt. Her father and Brad weren't here to batter her self-confidence and ridicule her the way they had in years past. She was allowed the pleasure of feeling good about herself.

Nate was afraid to speak for fear his voice would sound like the croak of a waterlogged bullfrog. Katy's startling change in appearance caught him completely off guard. Her blond hair was a tumble of curls that gave her a bouncy, carefree appearance. Eyeliner and mascara enhanced her vivid blue eyes. Blush added color to her cheeks, and lipstick accentuated the cupid's bow curve of her mouth—a mouth that looked so tempting that Nate had the wildest urge to march right up to her, bend her over his arm and kiss her until they were both gasping for air.

This was the Katy he had expected to see when he returned to Coyote Flats. The Katy who had pride and confidence in herself, not the shadow of a woman, oppressed by domineering men, who had used her without appreciating her special qualities and endearing personality.

When Katy raised her eyes and smiled at him in return, Nate's heart smacked against his ribs—and stuck there. Direct eye contact and a hundred-fifty-watt smile that lasted more than a millisecond? Hot damn, now they were getting somewhere!

"You look..." Nate's husky voice trailed off. He didn't want to focus so much attention on her transformed appearance that she thought that was all that mattered to him. But Nate didn't want to downplay the effect she had on him, either. How was Nate supposed to respond, except to be totally honest with her?

"You take my breath away, Katy," he said, because that was exactly the way he felt.

She blushed, and he grinned rakishly. He couldn't remember the last time he had been in the presence of a woman who knew how to blush. Most females of his acquaintance preened in response to a compliment. Not Katy. She had learned the hard way not to call too much attention to herself for fear of being pounced on.

"I feel shamelessly sloppy in comparison," Nate admitted, plucking at his faded T-shirt and paint-splattered jeans. "I'm scheduled to do physical labor this afternoon."

"You look fine," Katy assured him hurriedly.

She glanced at the cluster of boys, then back at Nate. "I was wondering if you wanted to come by for supper this evening. I put a roast in the oven when I went home for lunch."

Nate didn't want to refuse the invitation, but he had to ride herd over his young charges during their first day of labor. He couldn't swagger off and set a lousy example if he wanted to teach positive, responsible responses, now, could he? Neither did he have the heart to disappoint Katy when she was projecting this improved image—whether it was for his benefit, he didn't know.

A man could only hope.

Nate must have hesitated too long in thought because Katy's gaze plunged to the gray linoleum floor, and she clamped her hands in front of her the way she did when she withdrew into her protective shell.

Well, hell, thought Nate.

"I'd love to join you for supper," he said quickly. "I just have a scheduling problem. I have to work tonight. Would you mind stopping by Coyote Grill to pick up burgers and fries and bring them to the construction site? It will be my treat for the inconvenience I'm causing, of course. Hot beef sandwiches for tomorrow night, maybe?"

He must have looked pretty desperate and pleading because Katy nodded and smiled. Spring-loaded curls bounced around her makeup-enhanced face. "Okay, it was short notice on my part. I left a message with your cook, but she didn't know where to reach you."

Nate decided, right there and then, that Mary Jane Calloway needed to have his cell phone number. No way was Nate going to screw up future invitations from Katy.

Nate pulled several bills from his wallet and handed them to Katy. "Bring along several extra burgers and drinks." He gestured his head toward the boys. "My crew won't be able to concentrate on their jobs while the aroma of food is floating around them. I'll reward their work with a meal."

Katy blinked in surprise when Nate called to Chad, and the boy came immediately to his feet. Amazingly, the rest of the boys closed their books, grabbed their papers and filed from the library. "You hired all these boys to work for you?"

He nodded. "I'm offering to pay them a day's wages for a hard day's work."

Katy beamed in pleasure, and Nate's knees turned to cooked noodles.

"Oh, Nate, I'm so pleased to hear that. They need guidance so badly."

"I know." Nate couldn't help himself. Katy looked so grateful, so enthused by his effort, that he was leaning forward to press a kiss to her forehead before he could stop himself. To his everlasting relief she didn't recoil.

Yup, she looked awkward and ill at ease. But she didn't retreat from him. More progress, he thought, pleased.

"Bring Tammy along if you want to," he said as he wheeled toward the door. "We'll have a picnic supper."

And then he was gone, and Katy stood there, absorbing his tantalizing scent, the gentleness in the touch of his lips, the tingling awareness she thought had died so many years ago.

Those emotions had lain dormant. Definitely not dead, she realized.

"Get back to work, you ninny," she scolded herself. Mechanically, she turned herself around and limped to her office to plunk in her chair.

Was there a chance that she and Nate could become more than friends? More than former schoolmates? More than pals?

Even as the thought circled around her mind, doubts rolled in like thunderclouds. There was a vast difference between a kiss on the noggin and heated physical intimacy. What if she and Nate got up close and personal and she gave into the sensations of desire he aroused in her…and then she froze up? She would humiliate herself and repel Nate.

Maybe he wasn't interested in her in that way, she reminded herself sensibly. He had only offered her a friendly kiss on the forehead. He probably meant nothing by it. She shouldn't make too much of it. Besides, she had learned to be satisfied with the romantic relationships of the characters in the books she read. That was safe. The endings to the stories were happy because she refused to read any other kind.

Katy would die if she disappointed Nate. The very thought terrified her.

Nothing ventured, nothing lost, Katy told herself sensibly. She was too self-conscious and embarrassed about her scars. Furthermore, she couldn't tolerate Nate's pity. It was better if she didn't expect too much from her relationship with him.

"Just friends," she chanted while she worked. "The very best of friends. Kindred spirits. Deal with it, Katy Marie." Having given herself that good advice, she concentrated on completing her work.

Chapter Seven

Surrounded by his teenage charges, Nate drove his extended-cab pickup to the construction site. As far as he knew, Katy, Fuzz and the boys were the only ones in town who were aware that the offices and warehouse belonged to him. Nate planned to keep it that way. He had deliberately purchased the land for the complex that sat outside the city limits under the company's name, so that no one could nose into his business until he was prepared to announce plans to hire additional staff.

He had spent most of the day at the site, approving work orders and dictating messages to his secretary at the main office.

"Rats," Nate muttered. He had forgotten to make the requests that had come to him in the middle of the previous night, while he was tossing and turning when he should have been sleeping.

Hurriedly, he picked up his cell phone and dialed.

"Cindi? Nate. Grab a notepad, will you? I have some last-minute requests to fill before the staff shoves off for the weekend.''

Nate glanced in the rearview mirror, noting that the teenagers were listening attentively. It figured. When you wanted kids to turn a deaf ear their mental antennae were operating at full power. When you wanted their attention, they were space cadets.

"First off, Cindi, contact Jim in promotion and public relations. Ask him to donate six of our older computers to Coyote Flats school system and four to the local library here in town. It's time for us to upgrade in our offices. We will replace our conference tables and donate our discarded furniture to the library.''

"My goodness, boss. What's going on up there in that one-horse town?'' Cindi teased. "Why this sudden burst of generosity?''

Nate ignored her playful tone. He had business to conduct the instant he arrived at the site, and he was working on a short clock. "I'm getting together a city beautification crew here.'' He glanced back at his young charges. "We're going to add a little spit and polish to this run-down community. When the transportation department hauls in the furniture and computers Monday morning—''

"Monday morning!'' Cindi hooted. "Who lit a fire under you, boss?''

Nate would just as soon not discuss fires. He knew he was going to catch hell for the most recent one in Coyote Flats. "Have all the extra cans of paint sent on the delivery truck,'' he said, rushing on. "I know we have spare cans in the warehouse that might as well be used up.''

"Anything else, boss? Want any other mountains moved by Monday?'' Cindi asked with a chuckle.

"No, that should cover it.''

When Nate replaced the phone and turned into the driveway, Jake Randolph stared at him, bemused.

"Why are you doing all that stuff...sir? Nobody in this sorry-ass town has gone out of his way to do anything for you. You were right. Word is that you were responsible for that fire. I heard two old coots flapping their gums about it outside the café while I was walking to school this morning."

Nate refused to answer that question. He preferred that his charges mull it over awhile and see if they could come up with an explanation for his generosity. "Not one word about my plans to anyone," he ordered firmly. "You wouldn't have been privy to that conversation with my secretary if I hadn't been pressed for time. If I hadn't put those work orders through an hour before closing time, the less-ambitious staff members would have tabled it until Monday and then delivered by Wednesday at the earliest. You want something done, you get right on it, pronto. Those of us with drive and ambition have to keep a mental step ahead of the complacent masses."

"What's *complacent* mean...sir?" Richie Baker asked.

"Unconcerned, showing a lack of industriousness or interest," Nate defined. "Hard work always pays off. Maybe not immediately, but eventually. Some folks don't have the patience to wait for their rewards. If it doesn't come easily they quit and look for illegal ways to make fast money."

Lord, how many times had Bud and Fuzz drilled that into Nate's head while he was working his butt off, sweating like a racehorse? Again, Nate had opened his mouth and poof! The gospel according to Bud and Fuzz came pouring out.

Nate bounded from his truck and started spouting instructions. When he had directed his crew to the jobs, he flung up his hand to halt them in their tracks. "I'm buying supper tonight. Until it arrives, we're going to get this lawn cleared of trash. If you loaf, you get to work while the rest of us are gobbling up burgers and fries. Go!"

Nate watched in satisfaction as his charges jogged to the work site to clean up after the crews who had loaded up their trucks and left for the day. It annoyed the hell out of him that so many of the construction crews tossed around their trash, expecting someone else to pick up after them. Candy wrappers, paper cups, wall insulation wrappers and plastic soda bottles were scattered like casualties of war.

Nate expected his oil field crews to leave a site clean, rather than living down to that nonsense about being oil-field-worker trash and proud of it. Apparently, corporate officials in other industries didn't share his beautification fetish. Nate supposed he insisted on tidiness because he had lived in a trashy dump of a house half his life. Nowadays, he couldn't tolerate messiness and disorganization.

All the while that Nate was sacking garbage and carrying it to the bins, he kept an eye on his charges. He could hear them yammering while they worked, but they didn't break stride so he didn't object. He wondered if this was the first honest day's work they had put in. Probably. If he taught these teenagers anything else it would be the self-discipline to stick with a job—no matter how crummy it was—until it was completed.

The boys were probably cursing him, but at least they were working. A man had to start somewhere, he figured.

At seven o'clock, Katy and Tammy arrived with supper. Nate was pleased that he didn't have to exclude anyone from eating. The crew had fulfilled their end of the bargain satisfactorily. They had worked as hard and fast as Nate had. In fact, he caught all five boys watching him from time to time, as if trying to emulate his efficiency of movement, attempting to keep the pace he set.

However, the boys' hormones kicked in when Tammy Bates showed her pretty face at the site. Amused, Nate noted every juvenile had developed a strut in his walk when answering the summons to supper.

Nate wondered if he had, too, back in the old days when he caught sight of Katy.

After the boys gobbled down supper and took a few minutes to kick back and take a breather, Nate put them back to work.

There wasn't time for a single juvenile to grouse or complain, because Tammy, bless her heart, bounded to her feet and offered to pitch in with the cleanup. She reminded Nate so much of the younger version of Katy that he was lost to tender, bittersweet memories.

Of course, it was little wonder that Tammy was a kind, caring, good-hearted young lady, Nate reminded himself as he gathered his trash from supper. Katy had practically raised her niece, instilling good work habits and strong moral ethics.

"I can't believe the startling changes in those boys," Katy marveled as she limped alongside Nate. "Sir? They call you sir? And they say it with respect? What kind of magic wand did you wave over their heads?"

"The same kind that included tough love and a no-nonsense approach that Bud Thurston and Fuzz Havern used on me," Nate replied. "I—"

His voice dried up when he pivoted to face Katy and saw her silhouetted against the burning orange sunset. She reminded him of an earthbound angel, what with the bright light glinting off her curly hair, molding itself to her shapely contours.

God! He wanted to scoop her up in his arms and kiss away all the demoralizing hurt and pain she had suffered during his absence. He wanted to protect her from being the brunt of gossip because of her association with him.

"Nate? Is something wrong?" Katy watched his admiring smile evaporate, and she felt the immediate loss of self-confidence when he stared at her with a hint of sadness in his dark eyes.

He raked his fingers through his wind-blown hair, then sighed audibly. "Every time we're seen together, I suspect Lester's wagging tongue is working overtime. It's the only part of him that is, to be sure. I don't want to see you hurt, Kat, especially not because of me. It could happen, you know. Lester will stop at nothing in his attempt to drive me out of town, up to and including making something sordid of our friendship.''

The aching tenderness in his voice, the intensity in his eyes, compelled Katy toward him. Never once in her hellish marriage had she instinctively moved toward Brad. Only away from him, always desperate to avoid him. But Nate was completely different. Even her learned reactions seemed to recognize the difference and respond to the feeling of trust and security Nate generated inside her.

At that moment Katy thought Nate was the one who desperately needed a hug and words of reassurance. She knew Lester's poisonous gossip had to be getting to Nate. He tried not to let it show, but it did occasionally.

Katy slipped her arms around his lean waist and pushed up on tiptoe. He cocked a thick brow and waited for her to make the next move. She wondered if he had any idea what that meant to her. Probably—Nate Channing seemed to know exactly how to handle her, just as he knew how to relate to the juveniles he'd taken under his wing.

''Katy Marie,'' he said in a low, husky drawl, ''I swear you have every intention of kissing me, right out here in front of your niece and my owl-eyed work crew.''

She returned his contagious grin, felt warm self-assurance gliding through her. ''It's just part of their training program,'' she insisted as she reached up to trace the sensuous curve of his lips. ''If the kids are looking, they'll see gentleness and respect.''

He nipped playfully at her fingertips. ''I gotta tell ya, Kat, their male antennae are probably picking up on my difficulty to show self-restraint. Truth is, I want your mouth on mine so badly I can taste it.''

''You do?'' Katy glanced down momentarily, gathering the courage to continue. ''I thought maybe you were satisfied just being friends.''

A low rumble of laughter bubbled in his chest. Katy felt the vibrations echoing through her, stirring her, leaving her wanting in ways she had forgotten existed. She had only experienced desire with Nate—in another lifetime.

"I'm trying to be the perfect gentleman with you," he admitted as his arm glided around her waist to draw her full-length against him. "But don't be fooled, Katy Marie. There's still a lot of the bad boy of Coyote Flats left in me, though I'm trying to control it. I want you. That probably scares you half to death, but I want all you are willing to give, any way you want to give it." He gazed down at her with glittering intensity. "And if you don't kiss me in about one second I swear I'm gonna go into nuclear meltdown and disintegrate."

"Yeah?" Katy beamed in pleasure and newfound confidence.

"Uh-huh," he confided on a tormented groan. "The burger and fries were just swell, but I've got a powerful craving for dessert. I think you better kiss me now."

He had the knack, Katy realized as she melted against him, to send all her wariness and learned inhibitions into orbit. He allowed her to set her own pace—unthreatened and unafraid that he would push too hard, too fast. He left her wanting and eager for a taste of him, for a touch—all those things that Brad made so repulsive and hurtful. Nate gave those actions new, pleasurable meaning.

When her lips touched his, an interim of torment vanished, replaced by a gentleness so overwhelming that Katy felt her knees wobble, felt the ground shift beneath her feet. She could feel the evidence of his desire pressing against her hip, but he didn't spoil the moment by crushing her painfully against him, tearing at her clothes, groping at her with brutal impatience. Nate cherished her, cradled her, left her with her self-respect. He made her feel an equal participant in a kiss that she wished could go on forever and ever.

Gradually she became aware of the sound of giggling in the near distance. She broke the kiss and turned in Nate's encircling arms to see six adolescent faces beaming mischievously at her. She should have been embarrassed, but Nate made it feel so natural, so right, to be with him.

"What are you clowns snickering about?" Nate asked, his voice slightly unsteady.

"Nothing, sir." Chad tried to keep a straight face—and failed.

"How about you, Jake?" Nate asked.

"Nothin'...sir." Jake didn't make the slightest attempt to conceal his devilish grin.

"Richie? Tyler? Will? Tammy?"

"Nothing, sir," they said in unison, then ruined the effect by bursting out in giggles.

Nate nodded in mock sobriety. "I get it. You're wondering if I'm going to kiss you guys for a job well done, is that it?"

The boys howled in laughter. Tammy giggled again.

"Sorry, fellas," Nate said. "All you're going to get from me is a pat on the back and a heartfelt thank-you. Now, get back to work. You're wasting your time and my money."

The crew, still grinning, went back to work. Nate couldn't bring himself to release Katy. He felt as if they had passed another monumental milestone, and he didn't want to let go of the moment. When a woman as emotionally and physically inhibited as Katy finally offered an invitation, Nate hungered to savor every last drop of pleasure.

Truth be told, his male body was roiling with so much sexual frustration that he wanted to drop down on all fours and howl at the moon. He wanted the uninterrupted privacy to finish what they started, to strip Katy down to her silky skin and see to it that every fantasy that was keeping him up nights became reality....

Don't go there, Nate, he cautioned himself. *Don't expect more than Katy can give. Take things slow and easy, pal. You're making progress in yards, not inches, now. Don't blow it by scaring her away.*

"Thanks for delivering supper," Nate murmured as he bent to graze his lips across the side of her neck. His voice dropped an octave as she turned in his arms to face him, her body brushing against the hard ridge behind the zipper of his jeans. "And most especially, thank you for dessert. I really needed that. You're the only one in town who gives any positive feedback."

"No," she contradicted him as she reached up to comb her fingers through the tuft of raven hair that drooped on his forehead. "Thank you, for giving these boys a chance, for—" she grinned impishly "—that spectacular kiss."

He chuckled. "Why, 'tweren't nothin', ma'am," he said in his best Texas drawl. "Mighty happy to oblige. Just call me any ole time you'd be needin' a good kissin'."

"Tomorrow night? Hot beef sandwiches?" she asked.

"I'll be there," he promised.

Katy stepped away, then called to Tammy. For the first time in years she felt alive, content. It was as if she had been reborn, injected with some of that long-forgotten spirit.

Yet, there were still these lingering self-doubts that kept creeping up on her. She wondered how she would react if things between Nate and her became hot and heavy. Would she spoil the moment? Would he back away when he saw her ugly scars? Would he care that she wasn't as physically perfect as he was? Would he become angry if she froze up, reacting instinctively to unpleasant memories from the past that might suddenly assail her? Just how much patient understanding did she expect Nate to provide when it came to intimacy?

A sinking feeling riveted Katy when she remembered that she was keeping a secret from Nate that he needed to know. She had to tell him of her father's involvement in the incident that forced him out of town sixteen years ago. She had to tell him sometime. When was the right moment?

Katy glanced over her shoulder at Nate as she limped toward her car. Maybe she should get it over with before things got more complicated....

"Aunt Katy?" Tammy held out her hand for the car keys, jostling Katy from her troubled thoughts. "Can I drive us home?"

"Sure."

As Tammy pulled from the parking lot, she glanced back at the work crew. "Chad and the other guys seemed different tonight."

"Did they?"

"Yeah, lots," Tammy confirmed.

"They must have gotten a dose of Nate Channing magic," Katy replied.

Tammy flashed Katy an elfish grin. "You obviously got a dose, too. I'm glad. Really, really glad about that."

Katy gestured toward the highway. "Just drive, Cupid. I have a few sewing projects to attend to this evening, plus I have to whip up a couple of pies for tomorrow's senior citizens' luncheon at church."

"More hemlines going up in your wardrobe?" Tammy teased, then giggled when Katy pulled a face at her.

"Good thing your father is coming home in the morning," Katy said, turning her gaze to the highway. "You need some instruction in respect for your elders, rather than razzing them unmercifully."

"Um...Chad asked me out for a Coke date tonight. It is Friday, you know."

"Yes, I'm very good at days of the week, dear," Katy assured her, grinning. "And what did you tell Chad?"

"I said yes. He doesn't have a car, and he asked if I minded just walking to Coyote Grill. Nate overheard the conversation and told Chad he could borrow the pickup."

Katy smiled to herself. Nate's generosity and willingness to make a difference in the lives of those misguided boys filled her with such satisfaction that she wanted to tell Tammy to turn the car around so she could squeeze the stuffing out of Nate.

Although he was the subject of insulting gossip, he was determined to make a difference in this town, to give more than he had received. You had to love him for that.

Katy was afraid she already did, afraid she had never really stopped loving him...but she wasn't sure she was woman enough these days to communicate all the wondrous feelings he inspired in her.

It was hell wanting Nate this badly and battling feelings of inadequacy. She didn't want to disappoint him and she didn't want to walk away ashamed and humiliated, either. Darn it, her mind told her to remain just friends, but her feminine body was rejecting the good advice sent down by her brain.

Nate stood in front of the small wood-frame house, with its chipped paint, lopsided shutters and overgrown flower bed. Willfully, he squelched the frustration that was eating away at him.

He had stopped by the hardware store to buy paint, nails, lumber and screws for his Saturday project. The moment he strolled into the store, silence descended on the other customers. Everyone stopped and stared at him. Nate figured Lester Brown had been hard at work, sabotaging him again, because folks turned away as if they feared they were about to contract the plague.

Sometimes—like this morning—Nate found himself asking why he was putting so much time, effort and money into a town that rejected his presence. Lester continually filled folks' ears with tales of Nate's checkered past, then twisted Nate's motivations to make him sound manipulative and devious.

Well hell, there were times when Nate wanted to throw up his hands and tell everybody around here where they could go and what they could do with themselves when they got there.

The cold, remote attitudes toward him were breaking down

the self-confidence he'd spent years constructing. Okay, so maybe he hadn't come from great breeding, same as his mutt, Taz. But damn it, he was trying to make a new start! Didn't that count for anything in Coyote Flats?

Apparently not.

His depressing thoughts trailed off when he heard the rumble of his extended cab pickup as it pulled into the driveway. Nate had told Chad to keep the truck overnight after his date with Tammy, then pick up the other boys for work this morning. The fivesome piled from the truck and glanced curiously at him.

"Isn't this Crazy Millie's house?" Jake asked. "What are we gonna do here?"

Nate gestured his head toward the house. "It needs a facelift. Millie isn't physically or financially able to do the work herself."

"She asked you to do this?" Richie questioned, bemused.

"Nope."

"Then why?" Tyler asked.

Nate merely smiled at his befuddled crew. "Figure it out while you're grabbing the scrapers, rollers and paint."

Dressed in a threadbare T-shirt and tattered jeans, Nate went to work removing the dangling shutters on the windows while the boys scraped wood and rolled on paint.

Millie appeared on her porch, her straw hat tipped down on her wrinkled forehead like a gunfighter prepared to square off for a showdown. "What the blazes do you think you're doing, Nate?" she demanded gruffly.

"Fixing up the place."

"Didn't ask you to."

"I know."

Millie glared at the boys, who were spreading a glossy coat of white paint everywhere. "You there." She indicated Chad Parker. "Tell your boss man that you aren't doing this job!"

Chad paused with a roller in his hand. "Sorry, ma'am, but I can't do that. I'm here to work."

Millie harrumphed at him. "Are you, now?" She focused her steely gaze on Jake. "What about you, boy? How come you signed up with this paint brigade?"

"Because..." Jake's voice trailed off, and he frowned pensively.

"Well?" Millie prodded him.

"Because...I want...to help."

Nate nearly dropped the shutter. The kid was finally starting to get it. Glory be! Saints be praised! Hallelujah!

"And what about the rest of you young rascals?" Millie demanded.

"We're helping, too," Tyler, Richie and Will said in unison.

"And what if I said I don't want your help?" she challenged.

"You don't always get what you want, Millie," Nate replied as he unscrewed another shutter. "Deal with it."

Millie toddled around, hands planted on hips. "You think I don't know that you're the one who sneaked into my house yesterday afternoon while I was taking a walk and left that stash of money on my table?" She huffed and puffed. "I don't need charity, you whippersnapper!"

"Wasn't charity," Nate said calmly while he worked. "I was only paying you back for the loans you gave me when I was a kid who was short on pocket change. One good turn deserves another."

"I didn't give you that money when you were a scrawny brat, expecting you to pay me back," she snapped.

"I know you didn't."

"Then why are you doing this? Spiffying up my place and all?"

Nate turned to face her, knowing his charges were watching intently and awaiting his reply. "Because I feel like it, you sweet, lovable old woman. Because you deserve it. Any more questions? I'd like to get to work.''

Millie stared him down, then focused on every boy in the paint brigade. A wry smile pursed her lips as she pivoted in front of Nate, then waddled into her house.

"You think she appreciates this?" Chad asked. "She darn sure doesn't act like it."

"We'll see. Maybe she's one of those people who is a little long on pride and has to adjust to the idea of someone helping her out, just because we feel like it."

Nate watched the boys chew on his food for thought while they worked. Slowly but surely, he realized he was getting through to these kids, that he had gotten hold of them before they became hopeless causes.

Of course, Millie, sly old biddy that she was, had helped Nate out by bringing up the fact that he was repaying her for a kindness done years ago, and by firing questions at the boys that made them think. If folks in this town would pay attention to Millie occasionally, they could learn a thing or three.

As Nate anticipated, Millie found a way to return the favor. She reappeared on the porch an hour later with fresh-baked cookies and lemonade. You'd have thought Nate's young charges had never been catered to—and they probably hadn't. With Katy, Millie and Nate providing positive examples, these boys were learning more than how to work. They were learning values to carry with them into adulthood. Nate never heard—hadn't expected to hear—so many "Thank you, ma'ams" tossed around by these boys.

Nate was so deeply involved in conversation with the boys and Millie during their midmorning break that he hadn't realized a crowd had gathered on the opposite side of the street. The enjoyable moment vanished when Lester Brown hiked up his sagging jeans and stepped front and center.

"Well, well, well. Isn't this a touching scene," he said, then smirked. "All the firebugs in town are trying to put on a show

for us law-abiding citizens, trying to make us think you're a
bunch of do-gooders, instead of a tribe of thugs following the
chief drug lord's orders."

Nate felt Jake tense beside him, saw the mutinous glare
leveled on Loudmouth Lester. When Jake tried to vault to his
feet, Nate clamped a hand on the kid's rigid shoulder and
forced him back down.

"Easy, Jake. Don't let Lester antagonize you. That's exactly
what he wants, for you to lose your cool and prove what he
is saying about us. He talks big when he has a crowd to protect
him. That's the way cowards operate. You can count on it."

"That's the same son of a bitch who was insulting you on
the street yesterday morning," Jake growled bitterly.

"There are a lot of Lester Browns in this world, kid," Nate
said. "Like it or not, you have to prove your worth to bitter
old hounds like him. He holds a grudge against me, and I'm
sorry that he's taking it out on you."

When Fuzz Havern picked the wrong time to pull up in his
battered pickup, Nate silently cursed. No doubt, Fuzz's arrival
would fire up Lester.

Sure enough, it did.

"Well, whaddya know. Here comes the former sheriff, the
one Nate has in his pocket," Lester taunted unmercifully.
"Running interference for the drug gang these days, are you,
Fuzzy? What's-a-matter? Your retirement pension not big
enough? Had to turn to corruption and crime?"

"Go soak your head in a washtub," Millie Kendrick trum-
peted, hands planted firmly on her broad hips. "Don't see you
getting off your lazy duff to do any good deeds around this
town. You couldn't raise your own no-account son up right,
so don't be poking fun at my boys!"

When Lester's sunken chest puffed up like an inflated bag-
pipe, Nate groaned. He appreciated Millie's attempt to leap to
his defense, but she was antagonizing Lester. The man was
primed and ready to spout off at the source of his grievances.

Lester's face turned the color of raw hamburger meat as he thrust out his arm to wag a stubby finger at Nate. "Here is the reason my good boy went to the bad!" he shouted. "Nate Channing taught Sonny the meaning of trouble and disrespect. Sonny was a fine boy until Nate sank in those devil's claws of his. That's exactly what's gonna happen to these here boys, too. He'll teach 'em to lie, cheat, steal and deceive. And Lord knows what else! Do us a favor, Nate. Pack up and get out of town. We don't want you here. Never did, never will!"

Five young faces turned to Nate, expecting him to fight back, to leave Lester in a bloody pile beside the curb. Oh, yeah, Nate would have delighted in accommodating the boys and himself. But that had been his answer to anger and insults sixteen years ago. It hadn't solved the problems then, and it wouldn't help redeem his reputation now.

"Break's over, guys," Nate announced, climbing to his feet. "Thanks for the cookies, Millie. They were delicious. We better get back to work."

"Why?" Lester jeered sarcastically. "Are you putting a little spit and polish on Millie's house so you can use it as a drop-off for your drugs?" He wheeled toward the silent crowd. "Don't let your kids hang around here. Old Millie will be doctoring cookies with dope. She's one of them now."

"Lester, you never did outgrow being a jackass," Millie spouted. "Now, skedaddle, you braying mule. Some folks around here got work to do. You don't know the meaning of the word!"

"You tell him, Millie," Chad muttered.

"You see that, boy?" Millie said, hissing between her clamped teeth. "That's an example of what *not* to be when you grow up." She flapped her arms at the crowd. "Now, all of you go on about your business. Take that lazy windbag with you!"

The crowd dispersed, and Lester had no choice but to galumph away. Without the protection of the crowd behind him, he had nothing more to say.

"What'd I tell ya, boys," Millie said, then snorted in disgust. "Lester is just a rooster crowing in the wind. You don't see him over here helping, now, do you?"

Fuzz darted Nate a glance when the boys picked up their rollers and paintbrushes and went to work. "How long has this been going on?"

Nate knew Fuzz was referring to Lester's harassment. "Every blessed day, regular as clockwork. I think he's found his true calling in life."

"Got that right," Fuzz grunted. "Gimme a brush. I have a hankering to do some painting."

Fuzz's presence allowed Nate to set aside his frustration. He knew he was going to have to do something about Lester soon. But what? Nate decided to worry about that later. He had a house to paint and an official dinner date with Katy. And by damned, nothing was going to spoil his anticipation of spending the evening with her. Not even that blowhard, Lester Brown, was going to ruin the moment. The man just wasn't worth the trouble. If the citizens of Coyote Flats weren't smart enough to figure out what Lester was doing, then Nate plain felt sorry for the whole bunch of them.

Chapter Eight

Katy stepped back to survey the candlelit table in the formal dining room. Maybe it was too formal an atmosphere for left-over hot beef sandwiches. Maybe she should serve supper in the kitchen where she and Tammy ate their meals. Maybe Nate would take one look at the dimly lit table and think she was setting him up for seduction.

Katy rolled her eyes and shook her head in dismay. Never once in her adult life had she invited a date to her home. She had been issued orders and demands from men for as long as she could remember. Offering invitations was out of her league.

How was a woman supposed to know what kind of signal she was sending out? How was a woman supposed to behave in order to send the message: I want to be with you, but I'm uncertain how far I can go before I freeze up solid and run screaming from the house.

"This is so ridiculous," Katy muttered as she limped to the

kitchen to ensure the brown gravy wasn't bubbling over the saucepan.

She checked her watch for the umpteenth time. Nate should arrive in a half hour. Should she change into one of the dresses she had hemmed last night? Or should she keep things casual by wearing jeans and a knit top?

And how, Katy wondered nervously, was she supposed to keep her blood pressure and heart rate within the normal range when hounded by these uneasy questions and feelings of inadequacy? Geez, maybe this supper invitation hadn't been a good idea, after all.

The phone jingled, jostling Katy from her musings. She jerked up the receiver after the first ring. If Nate was calling to cancel, maybe that was for the best.

"Aunt Katy? It's me."

Katy slumped against the kitchen counter. "Hi, Tam. How is your dad?"

"Just like he always is after a marathon business trip. He's vegetating on the couch in front of the TV. I guess he's exhausted after his nonstop, two-week work schedule. I asked him twice if I could go out on a date tonight, and he didn't hear me."

Katy sighed in disappointment. James was turning out to be a lousy father, a workaholic who rarely communicated with his daughter. Katy had mentioned that fact to him a few times, but he got defensive. She had the feeling Tammy's appearance reminded James too much of his two-timing wife. But at least James had a child, Katy thought to herself. She didn't. The prospect of having children of her own was looking bleak.

At thirty-two, Katy had convinced herself that raising Tammy completed her. It had, to some extent, yet…

"I just called to tell you that Chad was kind of upset about what happened at Millie Kendrick's house today."

Katy frowned. "What happened?"

"That Lester Brown person showed up with a crowd to

Play the
"LAS VEGAS" Game
and get
3 FREE GIFTS!

FREE GIFTS!

FREE GIFTS!

1. Pull back all 3 tabs on the card at right. Then check the claim chart to see what we have for you — 2 FREE BOOKS and a gift—ALL YOURS! ALL FREE!

2. Send back this card and you'll receive brand-new Silhouette Special Edition® novels. These books have a cover price of $4.50 each in the U.S. and $5.25 each in Canada, but they are yours to keep absolutely free.

3. There's no catch. You're under no obligation to buy anything. We charge nothing — ZERO — for your first shipment. And you don't have to make any minimum number of purchases — not even one!

4. The fact is thousands of readers enjoy receiving books by mail from the Silhouette Reader Service™. They like the convenience of home delivery... they like getting the best new novels BEFORE they're available in stores... and they love our discount prices!

5. We hope that after receiving your free books you'll want to remain a subscriber. But the choice is yours — to continue or cancel, any time at all! So why not take us up on our invitation, with no risk of any kind. You'll be glad you did!

Visit us online at
www.eHarlequin.com

FREE!
No Obligation to Buy!
No Purchase Necessary!

Play the
"LAS VEGAS"
Game

PEEL BACK HERE ▶
PEEL BACK HERE ▶
PEEL BACK HERE ▶

YES! I have pulled back the 3 tabs. Please send me all the free Silhouette Special Edition® books and the gift for which I qualify. I understand that I am under no obligation to purchase any books, as explained on the back and opposite page.

335 SDL C23Y   **235 SDL C23U**

NAME   (PLEASE PRINT CLEARLY)

ADDRESS

APT.#   CITY

STATE/PROV.   ZIP/POSTAL CODE

7 7 7   **GET 2 FREE BOOKS & A FREE MYSTERY GIFT!**

🍀 🍀 🍀   **GET 2 FREE BOOKS!**

🍒 🍒 🍒   **GET 1 FREE BOOK!**

🔔 🔔 🔔   **TRY AGAIN!**

Offer limited to one per household and not valid to current Silhouette Special Edition® subscribers. All orders subject to approval.

(S-SE-05/00)

◀ DETACH AND MAIL TODAY ▼

BUSINESS REPLY MAIL

FIRST-CLASS MAIL   PERMIT NO. 717   BUFFALO, NY

POSTAGE WILL BE PAID BY ADDRESSEE

SILHOUETTE READER SERVICE
3010 WALDEN AVE
PO BOX 1867
BUFFALO NY 14240-9952

NO POSTAGE
NECESSARY
IF MAILED
IN THE
UNITED STATES

poke fun at Nate and the guys who were painting Millie's house and doing repair work. Chad and the other guys were ready to take on Lester, because of the hateful things he said and for insisting that they were just putting up a front for their drug gang.''

"What!" Katy howled in outrage.

"Yeah," Tammy grumbled. "Chad and the guys really like Nate. I think he's worked wonders with all of them. You know, giving them some pride in themselves and their work, like you say is important. But Nate didn't stand up for himself in front of that loudmouth. Chad can't figure out why."

Tammy switched topics to inform Katy that she and Chad had another Coke date and Katy responded with her customary "Have fun. Be careful. Wear your seat belt."

Katy hung up the phone a few minutes later, silently smoldering. Lester's bad publicity infuriated her. She wanted to bust Lester in the chops. That stupid old goat! Why couldn't he leave Nate alone?

For one hour—just one!—Katy would have liked to revert to a sixteen-year-old's mentality and seek revenge. She would slit the man's tires, toilet-paper his ratty lawn, spray-paint graffiti on the exterior of his run-down house and…heave a blueberry pie in his face! Lester would never get the stains out of his dingy shirt.

Lester's crusade to destroy Nate's reputation and turn the whole town against him made Katy furious enough to retaliate!

When Katy simmered down she tried to view the situation from Nate's perspective. He was trying, she was certain, not to revert to bad habits, trying not to add fuel to the fire blazing off Lester's tongue. Nate wanted to project a new image. Cramming his fist down Lester's throat would only verify the point that old coot was itching to make—that Nate hadn't changed and never would.

Yes, Katy could understand Nate's reasoning, but damn it all, she didn't want Lester to destroy Nate's confidence and pride. Nate had worked hard to make something of himself. He could have established a branch office of Sunrise Oil anywhere in the county. Yet, he chose to do it here. He was trying to help this ungrateful town, but no one gave him the benefit of the doubt. No one gave him a chance to prove himself— hadn't given him a chance way back when, either.

The rap at the door put Katy in motion. She moved at an uneven pace and found Nate standing on the porch, smiling past the exhaustion that showed in the lines of his face. She knew he was knocking himself out, ramrodding his community projects, handling business dealings and overseeing the building construction. It showed. He definitely needed to kick back and relax.

"Come in, Nate. You're right on time."

When he walked in, the enticing scent of his cologne wrapped itself around Katy's senses. His brand-spanking-new blue jeans and bright yellow polo shirt accentuated his dark complexion, his broad shoulders and his lean hips. There was a splatter of white in his hair that looked suspiciously like dried paint.

Nate looked so adorably handsome that Katy wanted to hug him, hold him…and hope that if something intimate happened between them that her reflexive reaction didn't spoil the moment.

"Mmm, smells good," Nate murmured, his gaze drifting over her.

"It's the meat and gravy," she informed him.

"No," he said, looping his arms around her waist. "It's you. Got any kisses to spare? It's been one of those days."

Katy tipped back her head in invitation and was rewarded with the tenderest of kisses. She wanted it to go on forever, and she was disappointed when Nate raised his head. There was a sadness in his expression that tormented her. She knew immediately that Lester's negative propaganda was getting to him. There wasn't much confidence in his smile, very little sparkle in his eyes.

"You realize, of course, that I am going to have to murder Lester Brown if he doesn't straighten up pretty quick," Katy announced.

Nate laid his forehead against hers and chuckled softly. "You'll have to get in line. My work crew, headed by Millie Kendrick, wants a piece of him first."

"Maybe you should let them have a piece of him," Katy replied.

Nate shook his head. "That would prove what Lester is saying, that I'm the ringleader of a gang that does my dirty work for me. I've cautioned the boys about retaliating, and I've tried to make them understand why. But it's not easy when the boys are accustomed to fighting injustice with their fists. They have to learn that the violence they've grown up with is part of the attitude I want them to leave behind."

"You're so very good for them, with them," Katy assured him.

He looked terribly sad. "Am I? I wonder. I'm also wondering if the flak I caught this afternoon at the service station is going to bring trouble down on your head, too."

"Now, what?" Katy demanded irritably.

"Word around town is that I'm preying on you because you inherited a considerable amount of money from your dad and large life insurance payments from your husband. Rumor has it that I'm paying attention to you so I can get my hands on your money."

"Of all the ridiculous, insane…oh! That really does it!" Katy spluttered. "I'm going to have to shoot, poison and stab Lester Brown, then hang him high. Maybe even launch him off on the next NASA rocket!"

"That'd be just great," Nate groaned. "Then the whole damn town will claim I've manipulated your thinking and turned you into my hired assassin."

Katy grabbed his hand and tugged him along behind her. "Come sit down and we'll conspire over supper. Maybe I can come up with something a little more discreet. Say, accidentally running over Lester on the street. Considering all the mysteries I've read over the years, surely I can devise an untraceable, incredibly creative method of shutting him up permanently."

"Hey." Nate set his feet, then waited for Katy to turn back to him. He was getting giddy, just listening to the spirited tone of her voice, the bubble of energy radiating through her. Part of the woman she used to be was rising to the surface. Nate felt ten times better just being with her, pleased with the metamorphosis that was taking place. She could make him feel better about himself in nothing flat, just like in the old days.

"Hey what?" she asked when he just stood there, looking at her.

"Just thanks. I almost called for a rain check tonight, because I doubted I would be very good company. But..." He shrugged, leaving the word dangling between them.

"But planning a murder perked you up, right?" She patted his cheek playfully. Sliding into the role of comic cheerleader came easier than she expected. It was amazing what magic this man worked on her. For him, because of him, it seemed she was capable of anything.

Almost anything, at least.

"Now then, park your carcass in the dining room, and I'll bring supper," Katy insisted. "Maybe we'll start working on Lester with teenage pranks. You know, short-sheet his bed. Stick globs of petroleum jelly on his doorknobs. You can get petroleum products at a reduced rate, can't you? You being a hotshot oil tycoon and all."

Chuckling, Nate held up both hands in defeat. "Enough. You're starting to sound like Millie. She voted for tar and feathers.... And guess what? I found out a few days ago that Millie is actually my mother's older sister."

Katy pulled up short and spun around. "Really? No kidding?"

He nodded. "Actually, Millie was the one who planted cash in the house to feed me. My mother drank up her welfare checks."

"So that's why you decided to paint and repair her house," Katy presumed.

He bobbed his raven head. "Tried to talk her into moving in with me and selling her house, too."

"And she said?" Katy prompted.

Nate followed Katy into the kitchen to help her dish up the meal. No way was he going to let Katy wait on him hand and foot. He suspected she had done that at Brad's demand.

"Millie said it would spoil her image as the crazy old broad who wandered around town with her shopping basket and silly hat. She couldn't keep surveillance in town if she was stuck out in the boondocks with me."

"I suspect she doesn't want to impose." Katy poured bubbling gravy into a bowl, then retrieved the reheated roast from the oven.

"Yes, I suspect so," Nate agreed. "But I think she was tempted. I told her she was all the family I had and that we should stick together." Nate picked up the bowls of tossed salad and buttered corn. "I could build another wing near the indoor pool. Aquatics would be good for Millie's arthritis.... Hey, what did you do that for?" he asked when Katy up and planted a smacking kiss on his lips.

"Just because you're you," she replied. "I happen to think you're a pretty swell person, Nathan Daniel Channing."

"You do?"

"The swellest," she confirmed, all smiles. "Let's eat. I plan murders better on a full stomach."

Nate followed in Katy's wake, marveling at the steady transformation that had taken place the past week, delighted by the return of her invigorating spirit. If he was partially responsible for Katy's new lease on life, he could withstand Lester's cruel taunts.

Even if leaving town was the only way to prevent Katy from getting hurt, he would do it. He didn't want to leave her behind a second time, but he could do it, he convinced himself. He could walk away from her, if it was in her best interest, knowing that she had regained her fighting spirit and her will to live.

Nate sincerely hoped it wouldn't take leaving town to resolve the situation. But he could not, would not, allow Katy to be hurt again. She had endured too much pain and heartache already.

Katy had cleared off the table and was ready to wash dishes when the phone rang. She tucked the portable receiver under her chin and continued her cleanup chores. "Hello?"

"Are you out of your ever-loving mind?"

Katy winced when her brother's blaring voice nearly blasted out her eardrum. "Nice to hear from you, James. Apparently you are still in your zombie state after jet-setting from one side of the continent to the other."

"Damn right I am," James fumed. "I just got the most disturbing call from a concerned citizen who informed me that my daughter went out on a date with one of the local thugs! And worse, she went out with the same hoodlum last night with *your* permission and approval! What the hell are you trying to do? Ruin Tammy's reputation?"

"An anonymous call?" Katy asked calmly.

"Well yes, how did you know?"

Lester Brown had struck again, Katy predicted.

Leaving Nate to rinse the dishes and stuff them in the dishwasher, Katy wandered into the living room to ensure privacy. "I suspect it is Lester Brown who is determined to stir up trouble," Katy informed him.

"Fine, let him. I don't give a rat's ass about Lester. I care about my daughter!"

"Really? Is that why you're never home and I'm raising your child?" Katy countered.

"What has gotten into you?" James demanded. "You have avoided every potential confrontation and backed away at the first sign of conflict the past few years. You don't sound like yourself."

"Well, you sound too much like Dad, and it's ticking me off," Katy replied.

"Ouch."

"For your information, Chad Parker is a good kid who hasn't had a lot of breaks in his life. He cares about Tammy, and she is fond of him. True, Chad wasn't born with a silver spoon, but he is striving for a better life. He would never hurt Tammy. I'd stake my inheritance on it."

"You sound just like you did in the old days when you defended Nate Channing. When you were in high school, Dad pitched a fit about your choice of boyfriends," James grumbled. "By the way, the anonymous caller informed me that Nate Channing is back in town and that he is at your house as we speak."

"Damn that Lester," Katy muttered. "He is hell-bent on making a nuisance of himself, isn't he. He can't tolerate the fact that while Nate made a success of his life, Sonny went down the tubes and is seeing the world from behind bars."

"Katy, you sound too involved in this fiasco," James cautioned. "God knows you have been hurt enough. If I had known what was going on with your marriage, if I hadn't been so wrapped up in my own misery—"

"It's past, James," she cut in. "What matters is that you have enough sense not to get caught up in Lester's manipulative gossip. For each and every one of Nate's good deeds in this community, Lester has twisted the truth and cast shadows of doubt on Nate's motivation. I would like to sue Loudmouth Lester for slander. Will you take the case?''

"With my workload, are you kidding, sis? I'm scheduled to be in China all of next week and back in Washington, D.C., the week after.''

"But if it comes to that, will you back me up, James? Will you throw your legal weight around for me? This is important to me.''

He sighed heavily into the phone. "Okay, Katy, but how can you be so certain that you aren't the one being manipulated? Lester said Nate was after your money and that—''

"Hang Lester!'' she erupted. "You can't trust anything that man says. As for you, you trusted me to raise Tammy, and I love that kid as if she were my own. I want the very best for her, you have to know that, James. She is above prejudice, and she has been taught to look past fashionable clothes and flashy cars to see into the heart and soul of people. That's where I look when I want to know the real Nate Channing. He's good and decent and kind and caring—''

"And you never got over him, did you, Katy?'' James interrupted.

"Maybe not. I certainly never found any of those genuine qualities in the man Dad made me marry. Did you find them in the woman Dad handpicked for you?''

"Ouch again,'' James mumbled.

"The truth pinches, James,'' Katy told him. "What I need is your support and your trust in my judgment. As for Tammy, she has learned good judgment. And while I'm bossing you around—''

"No kidding! Are you on something?''

"Certainly not, but I want you to tune in to your daughter, starting now, this very minute. You've drifted apart. Get to know Tammy, even if it's only for two days twice a month. She needs to know you're interested in what's going on in her life, that she can come to you when she has a problem to resolve. She needs to know you care, James.''

James chuckled. ''And here I was the one who called to offer you a little brotherly advice.''

''Sorry I stole your thunder.''

''You know what? I really don't mind all that much. You sound good, Katy, really good. Tell Nate hello for me, though I doubt he remembers me. I haven't seen the notorious bad boy of Coyote Flats in years.''

''I'll do that, James.''

Katy clicked off the portable phone, then pivoted to see Nate leaning leisurely against the doorjamb, his arms crossed over his chest, his feet crossed at the ankles. His dark brows were lifted in amusement as he appraised her.

''Funny, I could have sworn James was the older brother, not the baby brother. Can he deal with having *you* tell *him* what's what?''

''He took it just fine, thank you for asking.'' Head held high, Katy limped toward the kitchen to hang up the phone. ''Sometimes even big brothers need straightening out.... James said to tell you hello.'' She frowned, perturbed. ''Lester has been spreading propaganda, and James hasn't been around enough the last few years to know what a menace he is. James needed to know the truth—''

Nate snagged her hands as she strode past. Her learned reaction was to pull away, but she stopped herself, then allowed Nate to draw her gently into his embrace.

''Katy, it worries me that you're being sucked into the middle of this ongoing feud. I never, ever want you to get hurt. I'll pack up and leave town before I'll let—''

She pressed her fingertips to his lips, shushing him. The thought of never seeing Nate again turned her heart wrong side out and squeezed the spirit from her soul. She had dealt with losing Nate before, and she didn't want to think about going through that torment again. Even if they couldn't share a future, even if she couldn't…well, share the intimate stuff…she couldn't *not* have him in her life.

James was right, Katy realized. She had never gotten over loving Nate. He had been the forbidden light and love of her youth. Quite possibly, he was the one great love of her adulthood—sex or no sex included.

Nate's attempt to improve conditions in the community touched her heart. His determination to make a difference in the lives of those five boys who had no parental guidance and encouragement stirred her soul. The way he tried to protect her, to revive her lost spirit made her adore him all the more.

Maybe it was time to find out if she could respond to a man again. If she couldn't respond to Nate, then she couldn't respond to anyone. Maybe it was better to know from the onset what kind of relationship they could share.

Would Nate be offended if she came right out and asked him to make love to her? Did men ever get offended by that kind of proposition? But heavens, she didn't want to leave him with the impression that she was using him as a sexual guinea pig, either! Never that.

Uncertain what approach to take, Katy stood in the circle of Nate's arms, arguing with herself, second-guessing herself.

"Katy, there's something on your mind. What is it?" Nate asked. He tipped her chin up to stare deeply into her eyes. "You know you can tell me anything. I'm your confidant, your friend. What's wrong?"

Hoo-kay, here goes, thought Katy. Just step out on that spindly limb and see if it breaks off behind you. "Nate, if I asked you to do something for me, would you do it?" she asked nervously.

"Name it and consider it done," he said without hesitation.

"You don't know what I'm about to ask," she pointed out.

"Doesn't matter," he insisted.

She managed a grin, though she was as jittery as all getout. "I…um…want your…um…body."

That got his immediate attention. Nate's jaw dropped on its hinges. His eyebrows shot up like exclamation marks. "What'd you say?" he chirped.

Katy forced herself to make direct eye contact. "You heard me, Channing."

He shifted from one foot to the other. "You think that's a good idea? We never discussed what happened during your marriage."

"No, we didn't, but I suspect Fuzz filled you in on all his suspicions." Katy swallowed nervously and toyed with the buttons on the placket of Nate's bright-yellow knit shirt. Her courage was fizzling, and she was having serious misgivings about taking their relationship to new levels when she was uncertain about the outcome. "Look, Nate, if you don't want—"

"Oh, I want, all right, like hell blazing," he quickly assured her. "But I don't want to spoil our relationship by moving too fast or expecting more than you're prepared to give. It's true that there is…a lot of…um…history between us. But there is also this terrific friendship that I don't want to lose. I refuse to pressure you, and I can tell that you're a little apprehensive about…well, you know.

"Regardless of what you might think, there haven't been that many…er…women between now and the first time we…er… Well, hell, Katy. Don Juan I'm not." He drew in a deep breath, raked his fingers through his hair until it stood on end, then sighed. "I don't want to frighten you in any way. I want it to be good for both of us."

"Good?" She felt better knowing he was as uncertain as she was.

"Okay, great, sensational, off the charts," he said, grinning rakishly.

She peered up at him from beneath a fringe of feathery lashes. "And if it's not?" The nervousness came rolling in like the high tide. "If I react…" She cleared her throat when the words clogged up, then her face flushed rose-red. "Nate, I was..." She just couldn't say the word. It was too humiliating to tell him how Brad had gotten his kicks by taking her against her will, the same way he forced himself on that poor coed at college.

Nate held his breath, waiting for her to confide in him. He thought Katy needed to get the nightmare out in the open, to deal with it and then get past it. Was that the right way to handle the situation? he wondered. Was he making this more difficult for her? Well hell, he didn't know.

"Katy, there is nothing you can't tell me," he said as he drew her deeper into his embrace, hoping she would find it easier to communicate with him if her face was resting against his chest, while being held comfortingly. "What did he do to you, Katy? I'm here. I'm listening and I care."

The softly uttered words, spoken with such gentle sincerity while his strength surrounded her, was her undoing. The dam of emotion burst and Katy sobbed against his chest.

"He...raped me...." she said on a gush of breath. "He delighted in it. I hated him, but there was nowhere to run. He didn't want me or the baby. He was trying to punish me. He didn't accidentally drive into that electric pole. He steered my side of the car directly toward it! But the joke was on him, wasn't it."

When Katy all but fell to pieces, Nate scooped her up in his arms and headed toward the staircase, to her room, to the place that had been her childhood haven. He let her cry. He thought she needed a good cry, deserved it, though he bled with every hot, gut-wrenching tear that soaked the front of his shirt.

Nate eased down on Katy's bed, cradled her possessively in his arms. For the longest time he just held her, let her cry until there were no tears left and the bitter emotions had drained out. He didn't speak, just waited until she lay limp and spent in his arms. Then he curled his index finger under her quivering chin and tipped her flushed face to his.

"It's over, Kat. It's past," he whispered, then grazed his lips across her mouth. "My miserable, hellish childhood is behind me. Your nightmarish young adulthood is gone. We survived, you and I."

She nodded jerkily, then sniffed.

Nate tucked her head against his shoulder and laid back on the pillow. "But now we have a chance to start fresh. We're not a couple of innocent kids in the back seat of a car, hanging on to each other, seizing a moment in an uncertain world. I suppose the world will always be a little on the uncertain side, but we know how to weather the storms, Katy. We've lived through the worst, following a ray of hope."

Katy smiled against his sturdy shoulder. "When did you get so philosophical?"

"During those long days of riding the range with nothing between me and the blue sky but open space and cattle. And during those days when I was sitting in a trashy mobile home on an oil-well site all by my lonesome.

"Everybody needs to be alone with his own thoughts on occasion, to sort things out, to appreciate the best part of himself and to change the rest of it."

"What parts did you keep?" she asked, peering up at him.

Nate stared intently at her. "I kept holding on to the things you taught me, Katy. To care about others, to take pride in my talents, to strive to improve myself."

"You're going to make me cry again," she said, her breath hitching. "I look awful when I cry."

"Do you?" he smiled. "I hadn't noticed."

It was that quiet statement that gave her the courage to kiss him with the intent of pushing past her inhibitions, to ignore the ugly scars that crisscrossed her hip and thigh. She touched him the way she wanted to be touched, with reverence and tenderness. Her hand glided beneath his shirt to feel the washboard muscles of his belly, the powerful width of his chest, knowing he wouldn't use his strength against her, only his gentleness.

As before, he let her set her own pace, let her discover him by touch, by response. His rumbling groan encouraged her to caress him. And she did, with hands and lips and the soft stirring of breath.

"Oh, woman," Nate said raggedly. "If this isn't heaven, it's as close as I'll ever need to be."

Chapter Nine

Katy smiled, overcome by an unfamiliar sense of feminine power. She was eager to please him, eager to erase all the bad memories and replace them with wondrous new sensations. She pulled away Nate's shirt and drew lazy circles around his male nipples, then skimmed her moist lips over the dark furring of hair that disappeared into the waistband of his jeans.

Nate took her hand in his and placed it over the zipper of his jeans, showing her what she was doing to him, just in case she thought she wasn't having an ardent effect on him. She heard him moan when she dipped her hand beneath his waistband to touch the ridge of his fierce arousal. For the first time Katy wanted to experience the full spectrum of lovemaking. She wanted to feel a man's hands on her—this man's gentle hands. Hands that held the power to heal past pain, the power to pleasure and satisfy.

Katy rose to her knees, pulled her blouse over her head, then watched him watch her with hunger in his eyes. She saw him move slowly toward her, accepting the silent invitation.

Flashbacks momentarily assailed her, but at the first tender touch of his lips, the world spun out of control and the ugliness of the past was forgotten. Katy wasn't accustomed to unhurried lovemaking that allowed her to enjoy each tantalizing sensation, but Nate seemed to have no intention of satisfying himself in a heated rush. He acted as if he had all the time in the world to devote to her, to share mutual passion.

Katy knew that she had overcome the first hurdle of apprehension when warm, tingling sensations spilled through her. She was responding eagerly, because Nate's caresses were like the whisper of summer wind, like the languid stroke of a feather grazing her skin. She melted into the mattress, giving herself up to him willingly, trusting him completely.

His hand swept down her jeans-clad legs in an erotic massage that paused on her thigh, then swirled around her calf. Katy's breath faltered and her ribs threatened to shatter beneath the fierce thud of her heartbeat. Nate touched her tenderly, letting the eager anticipation build on itself, letting her experience each pleasurable sensation before she was assailed by another, then another. She felt herself arching toward his wandering hand, waiting as if she were the parched earth hungering for a sip of slow, gentle rain. She savored each raindrop of sensation he instilled in her, marveled at his unlimited patience and leisurely pace.

His lips skimmed over the slope of her shoulder, nuzzling against the sensitive point at the base of her neck. Katy shivered helplessly, then held her breath as his moist kisses glided deliberately over the swells of her breasts. His tongue grazed one rigid crest, then the other. Katy's arms instinctively moved to encircle his neck, holding his head against her sensitized flesh as he suckled lightly, then playfully tugged at her aching nipple with his teeth.

Indescribable sensations rippled through her as Nate dedicated the same unhurried attention to the other taut nipple. She whispered his name on a broken sigh as pleasure intensified and channeled through every inch of her body, leaving her to burn from the inside out.

"Mmm," Nate murmured against her supple flesh. He brushed the palm of his hand over the beaded peaks of her breasts, then swirled his fingertips across the silky terrain of her belly. "Definitely heaven to touch. But I'm feeling greedy, Kat. I want all of you. But only if you want that, too. If you don't, all you have to do is tell me to back off and I will. No matter how difficult it is, I promise you I will."

She arched helplessly against his hand and moaned in sensual torment. That was all the answer he needed. Although Nate felt desire rushing through him like floodwater, urging him to take what he needed, he clenched his teeth and vowed to set a snail's pace.

He was used to that pace, wasn't he? He had coaxed Katy from her self-imposed shell an inch at a time. No way was he going to turn this moment into a flashback from her tortured past. He wanted Katy to want him with every part of her being. He wanted her hot and aching and pleading for him to glide over her, to possess her at the same moment that she possessed him.

To that dedicated end, Nate gently pushed away her jeans, little by little, holding her in sexual suspense. He trailed his hand over the elastic waistband of her panties, then stroked the sensitive flesh of her inner thigh. He felt her tense when his hand skittered over the scars on her hip, but he reassured her by pressing his lips to the slick, reddened skin, kissing away her remembered pain.

When his hand glided back to the satiny flesh of her inner thigh, he tugged at her panties, letting the scrap of fabric become another kind of erotic caress. He groaned when he felt the moist heat of her desire luring him closer, tempting him to take what she freely offered. He nudged her legs apart to stroke the secret petals of her femininity. He felt the dewy softness of her desire bathing his fingertip, and he savored the scent and feel of the woman he longed to arouse until she came completely undone in his arms. He wanted Katy to remember nothing but his touch, his caress, his gentle kiss.

Though her wild responses nearly got the best of him, Nate reminded himself to take his time with her. He wanted this night to go on forever and ever, and he refused to deny himself the pleasure of enjoying each ardent response he called from her. He stroked her over and over again, teased her, aroused her until she gasped aloud.

"Nate?" she wheezed between panted breaths. "Come here."

"I'm here," he said, a smile in his voice. "There's no place else I'd rather be."

"You're not close enough," she whispered achingly.

"Soon," he promised.

He bent his head to touch his lips to the most secret part of her, tugged at her until her body wept for him, caressed him in return. Sizzling pleasure pulsated through him when he probed deeper with tongue and fingertip, and she caressed him in the most intimate ways imaginable.

It only seemed right and fitting that the taste of her desire was the only taste he had known, for that's as he wanted it, and he would treasure the secrets of her passion forever.

"Nate, please!" Katy clutched at his shoulders, drawing him above her. Her eyes glittered with such intense desire that Nate found himself hypnotized by the aching need he had summoned from her.

When her lashes fluttered down, as if she was embarrassed that he still held the very essence of her in his hand, Nate smiled tenderly.

"Look at me, Katy," he whispered. "Never be ashamed of the magic between us. I want to watch you come alive in my arms when we're one. I want you to see what making love with you does to me."

Katy was unaccustomed to such openness in lovemaking. It

required courage to meet those dark eyes that stared intently at her while her body shimmered uncontrollably in response to the intimate caress of his hand.

He smiled at her tentative expression, then bent his head to kiss her, letting her taste her desire for him. With each languid stroke of his fingertip Katy felt need coming uncoiled inside her, expanding, burning, bursting with immeasurable pleasure.

"Oh…oh…" Katy gasped when another wave of phenomenal sensations swamped and buffeted her. "Nate—"

His mouth came down on hers, silencing her cry of urgency. She needed him now, this very instant, and he was still wearing his jeans!

Nate felt her trembling with need, felt her feminine body crying out to fill the aching emptiness…. And hell! Here he was, still wearing his boots and jeans. Not to mention that he was flat out of protection. Double damn it!

Swearing at himself, he kicked off his boots and jerked down his jeans. He held himself above her, just barely—so close to going over the edge that he wanted to scream in torment.

"Nate?" she whispered. Her questioning gaze searched his face.

"No protection," he muttered in frustration. "I wasn't expecting this to happen. And damnation, here we are, acting as irresponsibly as we did as kids."

"Doesn't matter," she murmured shakily. "All that matters is that I've never felt like this before. I want you so bad it hurts, Nate."

She drew his head steadily to hers, then kissed the breath right out of him. When she arched toward him, he moved instinctively, burying himself inside her, feeling her holding him so sweetly, so gently that he cried out when the blinding rush of ungovernable passion slammed through him.

Nate didn't know what happened next, because intense pleasure bombarded him, scattering conscious thought. Vaguely, he was aware that Katy's nails were digging into his shoulders while she chanted his name.

And then, wham! He was driving against her, and she was answering him thrust for frantic thrust. He felt her convulse around him, and suddenly he was free-falling through space. Incredible pleasure expanded, surged through every cell of his body. Nate swore it couldn't get any better than this…and then a tidal wave of passion swamped him, and he realized it *could* get even better—because it just had.

Was he grinning like a Cheshire cat? Yup, he must've been, because he swore the muscles in his face were about to snap. Oh, yeah, he had been Mr. Gentle and Sensitive, hadn't he? Not hardly! He'd just driven himself into Katy until he could go no deeper, no harder, no faster…and then he'd lost it.

What the hell's the matter with you? Nate scowled at himself. He had intended to make certain that Katy had been thoroughly satisfied, but he'd become overwhelmed by the fantastic sensations of pleasure and plunged headlong into oblivion.

"I'm sorry," he mumbled against that soft, sensitive spot he'd discovered beneath her left ear. "Guess I got a little carried away back there."

She chortled as she trailed her hand down his spine. "Guess I did, too. Forgot to feel threatened. Must've been that Channing magic at work. It was nice."

"Nice?" Nate lifted his head, grinned at the smile that curved her lips upward, then decided she was pretty okay with how things turned out. Maybe he hadn't disappointed her too badly. "Nice? Just…nice?"

"You looking for spectacular, Tex?" she teased, blue eyes dancing with mischief.

"Well, yeah. At least it was spectacular from up here."

"Yeah?" she said hopefully.

"Absolutely spectacular. Fireworks, bells clanging, and all that," he said convincingly. "You?"

She looked very thoughtful, though he thought he detected

another twinkle of mischief in her eyes. He wanted to shout to high heaven. Here was the Katy he remembered so well. Sweet and playful, a dozen indefinable pleasures radiating around her.

"Well, I'm not sure," she said. "I sort of lost track of time and sanity there for a few minutes." She peeked up at him through that fan of long, curly lashes. "But maybe if we do it again I'll remember to pay more attention next time."

He cocked a brow in response to her provocative grin. "And maybe you also forgot that I went skydiving without a parachute. That's pretty risky business, Kat. So much for being responsible adults."

Nate's reference to a lack of protection made Katy burst out laughing. The sound went all through him like charges racing through an electrical circuit. God, he loved the sound of her laughter. He basked in the sunlight of her smile. He adored that cute dimple that creased her cheek.

No matter what happened in his effort to win over this town, Nate had rediscovered the younger version of the Katy he'd known in the past. The world could go to hell in a handbasket, but Nate would savor this treasured moment. No one could take this precious memory away from him. He felt young again, as if in this bright, glorious instant of time he had revisited the past and recaptured the best part of his youth.

Then his cell phone rang, and Nate cursed Alexander Graham Bell's disruptive invention. Nate considered not answering, just letting the moment glide past the interruption. But Katy glanced down at his tangled jeans where he'd tucked his phone.

"Are you going to answer it?"

"I'd rather not," he mumbled. "If I was packing a pistol I'd just shoot the damn thing."

"It might be important," she told him.

"As important as this? No way."

In Katy's opinion, Nate couldn't have said anything that

could make her feel better at that moment than what he'd just said. *As important as this? No way.* For that, and so much more, she adored him. His poignant words had gotten Katy past any uncomfortable moments that might have arisen in the aftermath of shared passion.

Reluctantly, but knowing it was necessary, she reached for the phone that shrilled from beneath the pile of discarded clothes.

Nate grumbled when Katy leaned over the edge of the bed and handed the damned phone to him. "Hello? Channing here," he said begrudgingly.

"Nate? Sorry to bother you, but there's something I thought you should know."

It was Chad Parker. There was an urgency in his shaky voice that sent up a red flag in Nate's mind. Nate eased away, then sat up on the side of the bed. "What's wrong, kid?"

"It's Jake," Chad said quickly. "He went off half-cocked."

So join the club, thought Nate. He wasn't the model of restraint tonight, either.

"He's really pissed off at Lester Brown because the old bastard harassed him earlier tonight. Jake borrowed his kid sister's bicycle and rode out to Lester's place. He's all heated up about telling Lester that you aren't any of those things the old coot says you are."

"Damn. I'm on my way. Are you with Tammy?"

"Yes, sir. I'm calling from the Coyote Grill," Chad reported.

"I don't want you or Tammy anywhere near Lester's place. Understood?"

"Yes, sir."

Katy bolted up in bed. "What happened?"

Nate clicked off the phone. "Jake thinks he needs to give Lester his version of a character reference on my behalf. I thought I had that knot-headed kid convinced that fists don't solve problems, they only create new ones."

Nate tried to scramble into his clothes as quickly as he had jerked them off. He muttered when he got his jeans on backward and had to start all over again.

"I'm coming with you," Katy announced.

"No, you aren't" he said very insistently. "I don't want you to get involved in this mess."

"Not *involved?*" she sputtered, offended.

"*We* are involved," he was quick to assure her. "I'm crazy about you, in case you haven't figured that out. And because I am, I'm probably overprotective. But I'd rather take a bullet in the chest than see you hurt in any way." He stared at her as he zipped his jeans. "Stay here, Kat. Please. You want me to beg? I'm begging. I'll call you the first chance I get."

"Promise."

"Cross my heart."

"Sure you won't let me follow through with my dastardly murder plot? It's a humdinger," Katy insisted, forcing a smile, though he could see the apprehension and concern in her expression.

Nate relaxed a bit. Knowing Katy wasn't going to fight him on this made him feel a smidgen better. He didn't want to hightail it out to Lester's place to intercept Jake, knowing he had annoyed Katy so soon after he'd made love to her and then was forced to leave her in a flaming rush. He'd like to deal with one crisis at a time in his life, thank you very much!

"If I can't resolve the potential problem, I'll call you, and you can relay the details of your humdinger plot," Nate said before he bent to give her a swift kiss.

"Nate?"

"Yeah?" he said over his shoulder, on his way out the door.

"I'm pretty crazy about you, too," she told him. "I want you back in one piece, so don't do anything that falls in the valiantly heroic category. Okay?"

"Deal." He winked at her. "I'll be the perfect coward, if that makes you happy."

When he disappeared into the hall, Katy slumped back on the bed. She didn't believe him about that coward business, she was sorry to say. Nate Channing didn't have a cowardly bone in his big, brawny body. If Jake Randolph got himself in harm's way, Nate would go the distance to protect the kid. That, Katy could count on, because she was convinced that Nate Channing was the kind of man you could always count on, no matter what the risk to himself.

Katy hurriedly donned her clothes and battled the fierce impulse to follow Nate, just in case he needed backup. Twice, she headed for the front door, then cursed mightily. She had made a promise to Nate, and she couldn't go back on her word, as much as she would have liked to in this instance.

If Lester Brown harmed one single hair on Nate Channing's head, she would personally dedicate her life to making Lester's existence on Earth a living hell. And that, Katy told herself as she paced the floorboards, was one promise she would definitely keep!

Nate spotted the bicycle reflectors when he turned into the gravel driveway that led to Lester's farmhouse. The place was a junkyard, Nate noted. Two old-model pickups were sitting on concrete blocks—the tires were missing. The lawn was thick enough to bale. The storm door sagged on its hinges, and the miniblinds had yawning gaps between the slats. Nate was granted an unhindered view of Lester, who was dressed in a sleeveless undershirt. He was lounging in his chair, sipping from a longneck.

The man was a slob, and he had a mouth the size of Texas. For a second, Nate toyed with the temptation of just clobbering the cantankerous son of a bitch until his lips swelled shut. Too bad Nate couldn't follow through with that plan without bringing more trouble down around his ears.

Before Jake Randolph could climb off the bicycle and stalk to Lester's front door, Nate honked the horn. The kid halted in his tracks, then whirled around. Nate studied Jake in the bright beams of the headlights, seeing the clenched fists, the hostile thrust of chin, the swelling around his eye. The kid had worked himself into a fine lather. Nate wondered if the kid had gotten knocked around at home by his old man, and then decided to pass along a punch to a deserving target.

"Whoa, Jake," Nate called as he bounded from his car. "Wait up."

"How'd you know where I was?" Jake growled.

"Lucky guess. It's Saturday night. Knew you'd be anxious to visit with your favorite friend in the whole wide world."

Jake scoffed at Nate's attempt at humor. "Yeah, right."

At close range Nate could see the purplish bruise and swelling around Jake's right eye. He swore under his breath, wishing he could return the favor to whoever had taken his frustration out on this kid.

Before Nate could say another word, the porch light flicked on and Lester appeared behind the sagging storm door. The look on Lester's face was priceless. He assumed he was about to be pulverized.

Nate sorely wished he could accommodate.

"'Evening, Lester," Nate said cordially.

"...addya want?" Lester sneered, then flipped the empty longneck in his hand, holding it like a weapon. "You hoodlums better get out of here or I'll call the sheriff."

"Call the sheriff what?" Nate asked flippantly.

Lester bared his yellowish teeth. "Watch that smart mouth of yours, Channing."

"Oh, sorry. Don't know what came over me," Nate replied, his tone nowhere near apologetic.

Suddenly, inspiration struck Jake. He decided to turn Lester's devious tactics of twisting the truth on him and see how he liked it.

Nate hitched his thumb toward Jake. "My young friend tells me that you popped him in the eye. That true, Lester?"

Lester reared back as if he had been sucker-punched. "'Course not!"

"His word against yours, Lester," Nate pointed out. "I know for a fact that you've been spreading lies about me, so it stands to reason that you would lie about this, too. The kid's gonna have a real shiner. You wanna go ahead and put your autograph on it, so we can show it to the sheriff when he gets here?"

"I'm not calling the sheriff," Lester muttered, then scowled.

"But you said—"

"Forget what the hell I said!" Lester spouted. "Just get off my property!"

"Okay, but the crowd down at the Coyote Café sure is gonna be disappointed to hear that you assaulted a minor."

"More 'n likely his drunken daddy did it," Lester jeered. "Kid probably deserved what he got, too."

Nate stared deliberately at the bottle in Lester's fist. "On second thought, maybe we better get the sheriff out here to give you a sobriety test. That was real mean-spirited of you to knock around this kid who's half your size, Lester. And here he was, coming out to tell you that we've decided to paint and spiffy up this dump you call a house."

"What?" Lester stared owl-eyed at Nate.

"Yup, we scheduled you for next Saturday. This place is a real eyesore. You'd probably have time to fix it up yourself if you didn't camp out at the café most of the day."

"Get out of here!" Lester bellowed.

"Sure, whatever you say, Les." Nate held up his hand in mock surrender. "Just take it easy. Don't blacken Jake's other eye in one of your fits of temper. He won't be able to read from the Bible at church tomorrow."

With extreme satisfaction, Nate watched Lester slam the door. Dust fell from the woodwork. The porch light flickered.

Jake dropped his head and kicked a rock across the driveway. "Guess I just about screwed up, didn't I?"

"Yup," Nate confirmed as he laid his arm around Jake's slumped shoulders and turned him toward the car. "If you had landed a blow in Lester's big mouth, he would have used the incident against you, against me. I learned the hard way that throwing punches only makes a situation that much worse. You have to learn to channel your anger and frustration into a positive outlet. Otherwise, you do nothing but confirm people's low opinion of you.... Come on, kid, let's put your bicycle in the trunk of my car and I'll drive you home."

"Don't wanna go home. The old man probably hasn't passed out yet," Jake mumbled.

Nate winced, remembering instances when he hightailed it to his hiding place near the pond, then slept in the barn when his dear old daddy went on a rampage. Jake didn't have a barn to hide out in. He barely had a house.

"How'd you avoid getting clipped by your old man?" Jake asked as he plopped on the bucket seat.

"I learned to recognize the signs and count the beer and whiskey containers in the trash. My dad got real mean and nasty after a six-pack. When he had the eighth bottle of beer under his belt he came up swinging, and I knew it was time to hightail it out of the house," Nate said, without an ounce of emotion in his voice. He had gotten past the hurt, anger and confusion, and could recite the unpleasant incidents as if he were a news reporter. "You can press charges against him, call the Department of Health and Human Services, or stick it out until you turn eighteen."

"I got nowhere to go," Jake murmured as he brushed his hand over his swollen cheek. "And there's my kid sister. Can't leave her to defend herself."

Nate's heart went out to the kid. He knew Jake felt trapped in an intolerable situation, and every day was another exercise in torment.

When Nate had returned to Coyote Flats, he never imagined that he would find himself involved in so many lives. He had planned to win acceptance and earn a little respect, then sit back and enjoy his financial success. Instead, he had taken on five young charges, a former sheriff who could talk a man's ear off, a feisty cook and an elderly aunt he didn't even know he had. Furthermore, he had dragged Katy into the thick of what had become constant turmoil with Lester Brown and John Jessup.

Nate sighed tiredly. At what point, he wondered, had he lost control of his life?

He fished out the cell phone to inform Katy that he had defused the situation—temporarily, at least. The sound of her voice had a calming effect on him. But it didn't do a blessed thing for the King Kong-size headache pounding at his brain. Nate knew what would relieve that, but he wasn't going to be able to make a repeat performance at Katy's house tonight. Nate had an angry, hurting kid to take home, and he had to ensure the boy wasn't in further danger from being pounded flat by his old man's doubled fists.

Katy's mouth dropped open when a troop of men, carrying armloads of boxes, filed into the library at midmorning on Monday. The foreman of the crew smiled cordially at her, then gave her the once-over. For the first time in years Katy didn't cringe when a man showed interest. Amazing what the Nate Channing School of Confidence had done for her. She no longer tried to downplay her femininity, no longer felt threatened by no more than a masculine glance. It was grand to be okay with herself as a woman, as a person, again.

"Ma'am, where do you want us to set up these computers?" the foreman asked.

"Computers?" Katy repeated stupidly. "But I didn't order any computers."

"No, ma'am, the electronic equipment is being donated to

the library by the Sunrise Oil Company." He glanced at the picnic tables and grinned. "Oops, I guess we better bring in the conference tables and chairs first. While we replace your picnic tables, you can decide where to set up the computers."

"New tables and chairs?" Katy tweeted, bewildered.

The good-natured foreman, who looked to be hovering around the age of forty, grinned at her dumbstruck expression. "I'm told this is part of Sunrise Oil's public relations program. Our next stop is the school to deliver the other computers."

Katy sat down before she fell down. Nate had arranged all this? He was donating the electronic equipment and furniture to the library and school, even when the citizens of Coyote Flats still treated him like an unwanted case of the plague?

Katy was incensed at how unappreciative folks around here had been while Nate carried on his community service and beautification crusade. Everybody was suspicious of Nate's hidden agenda, thanks to Lester's motor mouth. But did that stop Nate? Goodness no. The generous, community-minded man, who was treated like public enemy number one, continued doing his good deeds, despite public criticism and suspicion.

Blast it, if folks around here didn't appreciate Nate's efforts pretty damn quick, she was going to knock their collective heads together!

Katy watched the foreman motion for his crew to stack the boxes in an out-of-the-way corner, then he wheeled around to haul off the picnic tables. Katy beamed in satisfaction when the men carried in four expensive oak tables and matching chairs. Suddenly this Podunk library looked classy. With a fresh coat of paint this place would take on a cheery, inviting atmosphere.

"Oh, before I forget, the boss asked me to inform you that his paint brigade would be here about four o'clock, if that's okay with you, ma'am."

"Okay? Okay! That will be wonderful," Katy said enthusiastically.

"The Sunrise computer guru should arrive about two o'clock to get your systems up and running and tie you into the Internet," the foreman reported as he positioned the last computer on the table. "Have a nice day, ma'am."

Katy flashed him a grateful smile. "Thank you so much! I'm going to order a plaque that credits Sunrise Oil with these wonderful donations. I can't begin to express my gratitude, but please relay my deepest thanks to your boss."

The foreman and his crew stood there staring at her. Katy couldn't figure out why she had left them so stunned, until the foreman said, "Ma'am, that smile of yours is appreciation enough. I swear you have the kind of smile that lights up a room."

She did? Still grinning with excitement, Katy watched the men troop out. Well then, she decided, she would have to flash a smile more often. Her expression must have displayed the extreme pleasure that was rolling through her...

All because of Nate...

Katy wanted to track him down and kiss him breathless for his donations, for...well, just for being him! The man had turned her life completely around, and she couldn't thank him enough for that. If only she could find a way to express the full extent of her appreciation, to repay him for his unending kindness. Katy promised herself that she would reciprocate, somehow or another.

Chapter Ten

Katy's elation remained with her throughout the day. It must have showed, too, because folks stopped and stared when she strode into the Coyote Café at high noon. Even Lester Brown shut his big trap long enough to appraise her colorful sky-blue business suit with its hiked-up hem, her curly 'do and her delighted smile.

For once, Katy didn't withdraw from the attention she received and slink to the corner booth. She parked herself in the middle of the crowded café without a second thought. She considered herself living proof of the magic Nate Channing could work on her and the other folks around here, if they would respond rather than crawling into their shells like leery turtles.

Forty-five minutes later, Katy exited the café, unaware of her limp. She didn't feel less than whole or handicapped because of it. She felt…fabulous, rejuvenated, ready to take on the world.

She was pretty sure the wattage of her smile was still generating on high power when Nate and his teenage charges showed up at four o'clock, because Nate skidded to a halt and drank in the sight of her. Without the slightest hesitation, Katy marched right up to him, flung her arms around his neck and kissed the breath out of him, despite the audience of attentive teenagers. She decided she was right in thinking these boys needed to witness positive affection, a healthy man-woman relationship, because the examples seen in their homes were distorted.

"Thank you a thousand, gazillion times for the tables, computers and the soon-to-be paint!" Katy told him.

Tired though Nate was—what with working double days without taking time to rest—he smiled in return. It was impossible not to. Katy's dazzling smile, which cut an adorable dimple in one cheek and made her azure-blue eyes glisten with inner spirit, was contagious. Her metamorphosis was nearly complete, Nate mused in satisfaction. This was the Katy he remembered, the one whose image had been floating around his mind for sixteen years.

"If I tell you that you look absolutely breathtaking and that killer smile puts my head in a tailspin, you won't think I'm shallow or superficial, will you?" Nate asked while she hugged him a second time. "Truth is that I'm as crazy about your dazzling good looks as I am about your sharp mind."

"There is nothing shallow or superficial about you, Nate," Katy quickly assured him. "And thank you for the compliment."

"And you're welcome for the donation," Nate replied, then glanced sideways. "Are the computers functioning properly? Is your Internet service working?"

Katy nodded excitedly. Curlicue curls bounced around her bewitching face. Nate wanted to return her hug, to draw her shapely body against his, and to assure her that one look at her was equivalent to a feast of aphrodisiacs. But he held the handle to a can of glossy white paint in each fist. If he dropped them, they would probably land on her feet.

Nate forgot about the irritation of exiting from the bank a few minutes earlier to see that someone—as if he couldn't guess who—had written Get Out of Town in white shoe polish on the windows of his car. Drug Lord had been printed on the hood and trunk. Apparently, Lester had aggressively accelerated his crusade to run Nate out of town before Nate spread the word that the old coot had blackened Jake Randolph's eye—not that Nate would have actually stooped to Lester's level and spread an outright lie. But obviously Lester wasn't taking any chances.

Lester didn't know how to handle counterpropaganda, except to heap more suspicion on Nate's head. But Nate's ongoing problems with Brown and Jessup seemed tolerable when Nate found himself basking in Katy's radiant smile. In fact, he swore the new Katy was more electrifying and endearing than the one he'd known sixteen years ago. She truly looked as if she had regained interest in living, in herself. She had reconstructed her life and was making giant strides with each passing day. The changes Nate saw in her bordered on phenomenal.

"I have one request, though it's short notice," Nate said after he put the boys to work placing protective covers over the furniture.

"Name it," Katy insisted.

"I wondered if you and Tammy would drive to Odessa with me for a shopping spree. I talked to Tammy earlier and she told me she doesn't have homework tonight. Since she is fashion-conscious, I would like her to select some clothes for my crew. Sort of as a bonus for their cooperation and hard work. You know, a couple of pair of trendy jeans and shirts for each of the boys."

"Oh, Nate, how considerate of you! What a wonderful idea. I'll be happy to go with you, but you have to let me pay for half the purchases," she bartered, then flashed another knock-you-to-your-knees-and-keep-you-there smile. "Can't let you have all the fun and satisfaction, Channing."

"I wasn't trying to maneuver you into—" he tried to object, only to be cut off in midsentence.

"I know you weren't. You should know that I'm not the least bit influenced by Lester's ridiculing propaganda. I'm simply irritated with myself for not thinking of it first."

Nate glanced over the top of her shiny blond head to see the boys working industriously. "Yo, guys, I need to make a run to Odessa. Can I count on you to finish this job and clean up? Fuzz said he would stop in later with sandwiches and colas, then close up the library. Katy and Tammy are coming with me."

The boys nodded simultaneously and continued working.

"Thanks, fellas. I appreciate it."

"And I appreciate *you*," Katy told the boys. "This dreary old place is going to look terrific when you're finished."

Katy barely got the words out of her mouth when Millie Kendrick, wearing a new straw hat with shiny new plastic birds and greenery attached to the brim, came up the handicapped ramp and pushed her way through the double doors with her shopping cart.

"You aren't putting my boys to work without their after-school snacks," she said with her usual gruffness. "Boys! Get over here and take these cookies and colas off my hands before I'm tempted to eat them all myself." She tilted her head back, and there was a playful sparkle in her eyes. "Gotta watch my figure, ya know."

The boys converged on Millie like a pack of starved coyotes. "Thank-you-ma'ams" filled the room.

"And I've had just about enough of that 'ma'am' stuff," Millie harrumphed. "You call me Aunt Millie, ya hear?"

Nate stood aside, watching Millie dole out three varieties of homemade cookies and a selection of soft drinks from her shopping cart. Instinctively, Nate reached for Katy's hand, giving it a gentle squeeze. For the first time in his life Nate thought he understood what a real family bond felt like. These neglected kids, this tenderhearted old woman who put up a gruff front, and Katy, who had regained her vibrant spirit, were as important to him as Fuzz Havern. Together, they had given Nate something this community hadn't—a feeling of appreciation and acceptance. This community might never welcome him, but this unlikely family of his made him feel as if he had come home.

Although it hurt to know that he might always be rejected by his hometown, Nate tried to tell himself it didn't matter. He was still giving something back to his birthplace because he felt obliged and inspired to do it. If he was putting forth the effort selfishly hoping to be offered the key to the city and to be crowned King of Coyote Flats, then his motivation was entirely too self-serving, anyway, he reminded himself. But still...

Nate cast aside the whim and followed Katy through the front door. She gasped in outrage at the sight of shoe polish and hate messages printed on his car.

Nate shrugged. "It'll wash."

"Damn that Lester Brown," Katy huffed as she stamped down the steps. "He is really asking for it."

"Yeah," Nate agreed. "And if you let him have it, the same way Jake tried to do, I'll have to defuse another volatile situation."

Reluctantly, Katy settled her ruffled feathers. "Fine, I won't pound the jerk flat and mail him to Antarctica, but I want you to know that I've had it up to my eyeballs with him."

Wheeling around, Katy dashed back to the library and returned a moment later with wet paper towels to remove the shoe polish from the windows.

Nate slid beneath the steering wheel, then watched Katy plunk down, still steaming like a clam after witnessing Lester's

latest prank. "You really do look gorgeous," he complimented her, marveling at her animated features, the spirited
sparkle in her eyes.

"Thank you, but don't think you can flatter me out of my
fit of temper," she warned, despite her pleased smile. "Maybe
you have developed the patience of a saint, but Lester makes
me feel like the devil!"

"I'm nowhere near saint status," Nate contended as he
backed from the parking space.

"In my eyes, you are. In the eyes of those boys, and of
Millie and Fuzz, you are. Apparently, the rest of the folks in
this town are legally blind and terminally stupid!"

Nate smiled in amusement. "Is there any chance of you
calming down before we reach Odessa?"

"Maybe." Katy crossed her arms over her chest and tipped
up her chin. "And maybe not. I may decide to blow the lid
off this town if folks don't wise up. The mousy little Katy
Bates is gone, vanished."

"Whatever you say, Dr. Jekyll. When you and Mr. Hyde
get your act together, let me know."

Katy slumped back in the plush seat when Nate pulled into
her driveway and honked the horn to notify Tammy they had
arrived. "I called Fuzz this afternoon and asked for advice on
the best way to handle the situation with Jake and the abuse
he's taking from his father," she said solemnly. "Fuzz told
me you had discussed the matter with him yesterday and that
he was already making contact with the proper authorities."

Nate nodded. "Fuzz would like to handle that situation. He
has the experience and professional connections and contacts.
Jake is afraid to leave home because of his kid sister. I get
the impression that Jake runs interference for her, and he
would rather be his dad's whipping boy than let his sister
endure what he's been through."

Katy clasped her hands tightly in her lap, her head downcast. It wasn't difficult for Nate to tell that the conversation had unearthed memories from her hellish marriage. "I wish I would have had the gumption to sneak out of the house and contact Fuzz when...I had to deal with Brad," she said quietly. "But it's difficult when you've been convinced that you deserve the abuse, when you've given up the battle and tiptoe around for fear of inviting more violence."

Nate took her hand and brushed his lips over her whitened knuckles. "I would have borne your pain if I could, Katy. If I'd had any inkling—"

"Finding a way to help Jake and Chad and the other boys will heal my pain and erase the bad memories," Katy interrupted. "I told Fuzz that I want to donate to the cause, in whatever manner he feels will be most effective. But no matter what, I want those kids as far away from the bad situations at home as they can get."

When Tammy bounded off the porch and jogged to the car, her ponytail bouncing, Nate grinned. Tammy was bubbling with excitement about her duty as expert fashion consultant. Nate found himself caught up in her enthusiasm. For a few hours he was going to enjoy getting away from the hustle and bustle of overseeing the building construction, conducting business for the main office over the phone, and forgetting the frustration Lester Brown launched at him.

As it turned out, Tammy was a power shopper. Nate could barely keep up with Tammy and Katy as they zipped in and out of shops in the mall, chatting excitedly about their bargains and how the boys were going to become the trendsetters at Coyote Flats High School. Because of the Bates women's superior skills in shopping, the boys ended up with twice as many articles of clothing as Nate originally intended. All at rock-bottom bargain prices, Katy insisted. But Nate wondered if Katy hadn't paid more than half the cost and kept the fact to herself. He wouldn't have put it past her.

During the drive back to Coyote Flats, Nate found it difficult to keep his eyes on the highway. His gaze and attention kept shifting to Katy. He wanted to top off this productive evening by cuddling up in Katy's bed and rediscovering the pleasure they had shared. However, with Tammy underfoot Nate knew that was a bad plan.

Wanting Katy had become a constant, tangible thing. Nate told himself he should have been satisfied that their first intimate encounter in sixteen years had been mutually satisfying. But hell! Now that he knew exactly what he'd been missing, he wanted to invent even more ways to pleasure her. Once every couple of weeks just wasn't going to cut it with Nate.

For damn sure, he was going to have to keep the proper protection on hand. He had been irresponsible that first time, and he wasn't sure how Katy felt about having a child....

The thought sent a warm splinter of pleasure through Nate. His child. Although he was the first to admit that he didn't know anything about raising a child, he knew the wrong way to do it. He had lived that nightmare. Nate made a pact with himself, there and then. If he ever brought a child into this world, that precious child would know he was loved, wanted, accepted and respected—all those things he had never known in his youth.

Whoa, back up the baby carriage, he told himself. *You haven't even considered marriage before. You never asked Katy how she felt about marriage after the hell she has been through. There is a huge difference between occasional love-making and married with children, pal. You can't even consider the prospect until you have earned respect and credibility in this town. You can't ask Katy to tie herself to a social outcast. You've already dragged her into the simmering cauldron of gossip Lester cooked up. Until you have this town's respect you can't have Katy and don't you let yourself forget that.*

Nate took his silent lecture to heart. He had an office to construct, a staff to hire, a ton of community service projects in the works, and a group of teenagers to guide and protect.

If he failed to make a fresh start in town, he couldn't link Katy to adverse gossip. She was just beginning to get her life together. She deserved the second chance he'd never had, because folks around here were convinced that he could never overcome his bad breeding, that he was up to something evil and illegal.

Deep down, Nate knew the turmoil caused by Lester Brown and John Jessup was working on his self-esteem. With each new incident, another corner of his confidence cracked. For the sake of Chad, Jake and the other boys, he had to keep trying…at least until he faced utter defeat in this community.

God, why did people have to continue judging him with the yardstick of the troubled kid he had been sixteen years ago? Why couldn't folks measure him by the merits of the man he had become?

Because, he realized bleakly, that was what they knew, what they remembered. Lester Brown wasn't about to let anyone forget the unruly, insolent, bitter teenager who had struck out against a rotten home life, against his frustration with the world. Lester refused to allow Nate to rise above Sonny's level. In Lester's mind that would cast a bad reflection on him, and Lester would have to admit that he had been a failure as a father.

Nate mulled over that thought after he dropped off Katy and Tammy. His high hopes of making a new life for himself in his hometown hinged on winning the respect of this community. And he'd better win folks over pretty damn quick, because it was becoming increasingly difficult by the day to ignore all the cold shoulders he encountered. Especially when he could return to Odessa and be accepted for the success he had made of his life. How long could a man stay where he wasn't wanted without giving up the battle? Nate asked himself on his way home.

For the past two weeks Katy's contact with Nate had been sporadic. He'd made fleeting pit stops at the library, and they'd shared hurried conversations over the phone. Although Katy practiced self-improvement daily, it seemed the reason— namely Nate—that she had changed her attitude toward life and altered her physical appearance didn't have time for her. It was as if Nate were on a frantic, time-consuming crusade, and she couldn't understand the sense of urgency driving him.

There were times when Katy wanted to come right out and ask Nate if she was as important to him as his juggling act of dozens of missions in life. Yet, she couldn't work up the nerve to confront him with her feelings of neglect. Even when she mentally rehearsed the conversation several times a day, it came off sounding as if she were selfish and demanding.

No, Katy had decided, Nate's community service, his work with the boys and the need to get Sunrise Oil's branch office in full operation were more important. Nate was meeting himself coming and going. He was the walking cliché of a man who had entirely too many irons in his campfire.

Still, Nate was getting no respect or recognition from the citizens in Coyote Flats. Signs had been posted beside Nate's driveway, ordering him to pack up and leave—or else. Garbage had been dumped in the middle of the road leading to his home, implying that he belonged with the discarded trash.

It infuriated Katy to the extreme. She hated the fact that Nate was treated like a menace, that he was ostracized and ignored. Even Alice Phelps had expressed concern to Katy that her son might become the innocent young victim of drug infiltration and that Nate was responsible.

Katy had lost her cool, right there on the sidewalk outside the pharmacy. She told Ali to pull her head out of wherever she'd stuck it and wise up to the fact that Lester Brown and John Jessup were carrying on a personal vendetta to make Nate look bad. Katy had recited every good deed Nate had done for this ungrateful town, and she'd asked Ali who had provided more community service, Lester or Nate.

Ali responded with the kind of mind-controlled thinking that did Lester proud. "Well, Nate could simply be trying to cover up his illegal drug activities behind smoke and mirrors, you know."

That comment really got Katy's dander up. "Lester has done a job on you and everyone else in this town," she muttered at Ali. "Do me a favor and put a date to the last day you used your college-educated brain to do your own thinking and make reasonable decisions, rather than relying on the slanted version of propaganda that's come from Lester's flapping jaws."

The comment got Ali's attention, thank goodness. She frowned pensively and said, "I guess I have been relying on gossip and hearsay. The rumors I've heard have been passed by several upstanding families in town, too. But I suppose it was Lester who initiated the talk."

"Darn right he did, and people haven't shown good sense by listening to his yammering. I would dearly like to know why you and everybody else consider Lester such an authority on the life and times of Nate Channing."

Ali shrugged. "I guess it's because Sonny Brown and Nate used to hang around together. Lester probably knows Nate better than the rest of us."

That logic incensed Katy. "Nate has been away from this town for sixteen years," she reminded Ali. "People can change in that length of time. Look how the incidents of the past ten years changed me. But thank God I got my act together, with the help of Nate's kindness and encouragement."

Ali stared pensively at Katy. "You do look and act more like your old self," she agreed.

"And you are nothing like the bashful, timid, self-conscious young girl I went to high school with," Katy quickly pointed out, then drove home her point. "You have changed for the better, Ali, and so has Nate Channing. I shudder to think that I will continue to be judged as the woman I became during my disastrous marriage to Brad. And I certainly don't regard you in the same light as I did when you were in high school.

"Folks in this town, you included, are being unfair to Nate by judging him as if he were the same kid who left town years ago. The reason people aren't being sensible about the positive changes in Nate is because of Lester Brown's continuous, harsh criticism."

"I guess you're right," Ali murmured thoughtfully. "I let Lester convince me that Nate is guilty of the accusations until he proves himself innocent."

"Which is the exact opposite of the way our justice system is supposed to work," Katy replied. "The truth is that I am surprised at Nate's patience with this unforgiving town. If he throws up his hands and gives up on all of us, we are going to be thoroughly ashamed of the way we have treated a man who returned to give something positive to this community.

"We are being manipulated by a man who went bankrupt because he was too lazy to work. Now Lester spends his free time running off at the mouth, trying to drag Nate down to his level. Lester has done nothing except raise a son who turned hard-core criminal. Our taxes are paying Lester's welfare pensions, and we are housing his son in a penitentiary. If we don't involve ourselves in this community, it is going to dry up and blow away."

Katy gave the same speech to several library patrons who wandered in from the street that afternoon. She pointed out the new tables and computers that had been generously donated by Nate. Slowly but surely, Katy hoped word would spread around town that Nate was making the kind of contributions that no one else had bothered with. Furthermore, it was Nate and his young charges who showed up at the charred remains of the grocery store to haul away the clutter and unload new building materials. Had anyone else taken time from their lives to lend a helping hand? No!

Of course, the patrons at the library had repeated Lester's

claim that Nate and his hoodlums had started that fire, so why shouldn't they be the ones to clean up?

Katy had fumed over those foolish comments while Nate continued working double days, then painted and repaired neglected homes in an effort to improve the looks of the town. But Katy knew this ongoing fiasco was getting to Nate, even while he plodded determinedly ahead. *Her* smiles might have become brighter this past month, but *Nate's* were flickering on dim wattage. The man needed a morale boost as badly as she once had.

There was a time, Katy recalled, that she had encouraged Nate to be the best he could be, urged him to ignore the condemning gossip swirling around town. It seemed the time had come once again for her to encourage him, to remind him of his special qualities and good deeds.

On that determined thought, Katy dressed carefully for the evening she had planned, then sent Tammy off for her Saturday night date with Chad. Katy checked all her restrictive inhibitions at her front door and drove off into the night. It was definitely time to return a little of that Nate Channing magic, she decided. Tonight was the night.

Nate channel-surfed through one-hundred-fifty stations, but none of the television programs appealed to his present mood—which was damn lousy. A real bitch of a mood, in case anybody cared to ask. Which no one in this deadbeat town did. And here he was trying to save this community before it disappeared from the map!

Waste of time, thought Nate. No one wanted to give this place an economical boost. No one wanted anything to do with him. When he walked down the street, heads turned in spectacular attempts to ignore him. Most recently, the post office clerk called to say that he needed to pick up his mail because the rural delivery driver couldn't leave mail, on account of

someone accidentally plowing over his mailbox. Sheesh!
Would he ever see an end to this harassment?

Yeah, when he cleared out of town, he thought dejectedly.

Tonight Nate was sitting here wishing Fuzz had been home
to provide companionship and distraction. Fuzz, however, had
invited Mary Jane Calloway to a movie in Odessa. The two-
some had become good friends. Nate was pleased about that,
of course. Still, he was sitting here feeling sorry for himself,
lonely as hell and frustrated that the construction crew hadn't
completed the finishing work at the branch office. Nate was
anxious to get the business in operation and hire a staff. Of
course, when the citizens realized *he* owned Sunrise Oil, they
would probably refuse to work for him. Nothing like shooting
themselves in the foot, Nate mused irritably.

When the doorbell buzzed, Nate expected to be greeted by
carolers spouting "So long, farewell, good riddance, and get
the hell out of town." Or maybe there was a lynch mob in
his driveway, ready to string him up to the nearest tree. He
wouldn't be surprised at that, either.

Nate's eyebrows jackknifed, and he almost choked when he
saw Katy leaning provocatively against the supporting beam
of the porch, wearing a body-hugging knit dress that displayed
about a mile of shapely, silk-clad legs. With the porch light
serving as her spotlight, she struck a seductive pose and rested
her hand on her cocked hip. When she smiled invitingly at
him, his male body came to immediate attention.

"Hi there, handsome," she purred playfully. "I'm a rep-
resentative for the Katy Bates Feel Good Escort Service. Got
time for a demonstration?"

Nate, his bad mood forgotten, burst out laughing when Katy
batted her baby blues at him with grand exaggeration, then
gave her best Mae West impression—puckered lips, swinging
hips and all.

"By all means, come in, ma'am." When he held open the

door for her, she presented him with a rear view of her drum-roll walk. Nate's eyes nearly popped out of his head.

"You home alone, sugar?" she drawled, tossing one of those come-hither glances over her practically bare shoulder.

Desire hit Nate like a runaway locomotive. Katy's transformation was absolutely and totally complete, he realized. She had gained enough confidence in herself, and faith in him, to portray the role of vamp and seductress without feeling threatened.

At first glance, Nate's male hormones had come to rigid attention. But with each hypnotic sway of her hips, each teasing smile and suggestive wink, Nate felt his temperature rising to full boil.

It was just that, he realized. Katy walked in, somehow knowing that he was desperately in need of being cheered up, and poof! She rocked his world.

"I brought along a bottle of wine," she drawled as she reached into her oversize bag. The knit top to a two-piece swimsuit plunked to the floor. Katy bent over to pick it up, presenting Nate with an unobstructed view of cleavage.

Nate groaned. He was hard and aching and he hadn't even touched her. "I don't drink," he reminded her.

"Neither do I, sugar."

That exaggerated wink and knock-'em-for-a-loop smile came again.

Nate was a goner.

"But hey, sweetums," she cooed, striking a Cleopatra pose. "What say we break all the rules tonight? Hmm? A relaxing swim, a glass of wine, a thorough massage, yadda, yadda."

Nate's rioting male hormones applauded the yadda, yadda.

"Now then." She slinked toward him, her hips swaying like a porch swing. "Let's get you into something more comfortable. You are way too overdressed, sugarplum."

Chapter Eleven

Nate stood there, mesmerized by Katy's impish grin, while she unbuttoned his shirt and tossed it over the back of the nearest chair. When her hands coasted over his chest, his pulse leapfrogged. Muscles tightened in sensual anticipation. When her glossy lips grazed his male nipples, Nate swore his legs were about to fold up like lawn chairs.

"You do this sort of thing often, ma'am?" he wheezed as her hand tripped down his ribs, lingering to caress and sensitize.

"My first time, actually. How am I doing so far, handsome? I have to return my report card with your signature to Miss Katy. I'm hoping for straight As."

"I'd have to say you're a Rhodes scholar in the school of seduction," Nate chirped when her adventurous hand skimmed the band of his jeans.

"Gosh, that should bump me up to the head of the class. I'll be the highest-paid escort at Feel Good Services."

When she kissed him, Nate definitely felt good all over. When she melted into him, as if he were the missing half of her soul, his arms banded around her. He savored the intoxicating taste of her kiss, absorbed the feel of her lush body gliding provocatively against his, burned with a fire that defied restraint.

Nate breathed her in, savored her, drew strength from her. She had become everything he needed tonight, because he did need her and she had somehow known it. For that, and so much more, he adored her.

Time spun backward, halting on one of those nights he remembered as a frustrated teenager. He'd gone to meet Katy, deciding to call it off because her father had ordered him to keep his distance, insisting that he wasn't fit to associate with her. Katy had told him that he was the only boy she wanted to be with, needed to be with. She had built his confidence, held him and convinced him that he mattered to her, that he was somebody special....

Suddenly, Katy was touching him intimately, and Nate lost himself in the magic Katy spun around him. He felt like a swimmer going down for the third time, and he didn't care if he ever came up for a breath of air. Katy's arousing touch was more than enough to sustain him.

When Nate reached for her, Katy stilled his hands. "Tonight I intend to seduce you and return the pleasure you gave me when we first made love. But when you touch me I forget how to think, so don't distract me, sugar."

"Katy, you don't—"

"Ah, but I do," she contradicted as her lips coasted down the column of his neck. "I have to, because pleasuring you gives me pleasure, too."

Nate's body constricted with need when her petal-soft lips drifted over the padded muscles of his chest. Sensual lightning speared through him, intensifying his ravenous hunger for her. When her hand trailed around the band of his jeans to ease down his zipper, Nate forgot to breathe, couldn't think of one good reason why he needed to.

His legs wobbled unsteadily when she pushed down his jeans and left him standing in a pool of denim—and bubbling with desire.

When Katy gently cupped him through the fabric of his briefs, stroking the hard length of him, Nate felt the floor shift beneath his feet. He was trembling in an effort to maintain his balance, shaking with profound need.

A tormented groan rumbled around in his throat when Katy trailed tantalizing kisses along the wedge of hair on his chest. Nate clenched his teeth to keep from moaning when she knelt before him to slowly, evocatively remove the fabric that separated his aching flesh from her moist lips.

Her butterfly kisses fluttered over him while her hands drifted from thigh to ankle. Nate quivered helplessly when she measured him from base to tip with her tongue. With each erotic kiss and caress, pleasure burgeoned inside him. When she took him into her mouth, nipping gently with her teeth and teasing him with that wicked tongue, sharp talons of desire raked over him.

Nate wheezed as he braced his hand against the wall for support. "You trying to kill me or something?"

"Or something," she teased impishly. "Is it working?"

"Mmm," Nate rasped hoarsely. "I—"

His voice shattered when she nuzzled her cheek against the sensitive skin of his thigh, then stroked him until he gasped in barely controlled restraint.

A silvery drop of need betrayed his attempt to hold himself in check. He reached out with his free hand to cup her chin, trying to discourage her from plying him with more exquisitely tender torture, but Katy refused to be restrained. Her lips and fingertips brushed over his rigid length again and again. She tasted his need for her, suckled him gently, caressed him until his lungs shuddered in an attempt to draw air. Maddening pleasure buffeted him, threatening to knock him to his knees.

"Katy...stop," he groaned in unholy torment.

She ignored him. She drew his hand along with hers as she touched him intimately. Nate nearly went out of his mind. The gentle pressure of her warm lips, the brush of her tongue and fingertips sent white-hot flames racing through him. She was melting him down to liquid fire, and he swore he was going to erupt like a volcano if she didn't stop what she was doing to him.

"Katy..." Nate wheezed when bulletlike sensations overwhelmed him. He needed her now—a minute earlier would have been even better! "Katy...!"

He didn't remember how he'd gotten Katy's clothes off so quickly—didn't really care. All he knew was that they were on the sofa, naked in each other's arms, panting to draw breath while a multitude of hungry sensations descended on them. Lights from the big-screen TV flashed across their joined bodies as he buried himself deeper and deeper with each desperate thrust that sent him into wild, reckless abandon. He knew he was moving too fast, must have deprived Katy of the pleasure he wanted to offer her, but she had taken him too far past the point of self-control. With a tormented cry of ineffable pleasure, Nate clutched Katy to him and felt his need for her explode...then burn down the night in a holocaust of fiery flames....

"Well, darn it," Katy muttered a long while later, when she could finally think straight. "I remembered to bring protection, and then I forgot to use it."

"Katy, we need to talk about that," Nate said huskily, easing down beside her on the sofa.

Katy didn't want to discuss it because she was prepared to accept responsibility if consequences arose. Furthermore, she wasn't sure this was the night to look too far into the future.

Tonight, Nate needed to regain confidence in himself. This wasn't about tomorrow or nine months from tomorrow. It was here and now.

"You want to sit around chitchatting while my expensive new bathing suit goes to waste? No way, buster. The thing makes me look like Dolly Parton. You wanna pass up something like that?"

"Well no, not if you've fussed," Nate said, chuckling. "You win, Boom-Boom Bates. I'll meet you at the pool in a few minutes."

She winked saucily. "Okay, tiger, but don't bother dragging out a swimsuit on my account. I wasn't planning on either of us wearing a suit for too long, anyway."

Nate came to his feet, profiled by the strobelike lights from the TV. Lord, he was magnificent. He had a body like an Olympic athlete and a smile that beguiled.

"I'll bring the wine," Katy said, rising to her feet.

"I'll bring the glasses," Nate volunteered, then let his gaze glide possessively over her. "I'll be back in five minutes."

"Make it four or you'll miss the Dolly Parton look-alike fashion show."

He grinned at her. "I'm definitely *there,* darlin'. Four minutes flat."

Katy scurried into the bathroom to don her suit. She surveyed her reflection in the mirror, assured that the push-'em-up-so-he-won't-fail-to-notice halter top displayed her feminine assets to their best advantage.

The thong didn't cover much skin and revealed the unsightly scars, but Katy had gotten over feeling self-conscious about it. Nate had assured her that the patches of slick, discolored skin on her hip and thigh didn't bother him. Because of Nate, she was okay with it. Because of him, she was finally content with herself. She was no longer a victim of her hellish past. She was alive and free and unrestrained in her emotions.

She was never going back to that self-imposed shell where she'd hidden out for a dozen years.

Katy sauntered to the indoor pool and struck a provocative pose in a cushioned lawn chair. When Nate arrived, wearing a skin-tight black suit that indicated he was still eager, willing and aroused, Katy grinned mischievously. She came to her feet, strutted her stuff, then struck another eye-catching pose.

"Well, hello, Dolly." Nate leered outrageously at her. "That suit is everything you claimed it would be. Your future clients will definitely get their money's worth with you."

Katy preened playfully, as if posing for a photo session for the swimsuit issue of *Sports Illustrated*. Nate threw back his head and howled at the moon.

Giggling like a couple of silly teenagers, Nate and Katy made out in the lawn chairs, then skinny-dipped in the pool.

Katy couldn't remember spending a more carefree, enjoyable evening. There were just the two of them wrapped in the gentle rush of water, the echo of murmured voices, the sensual glide of their bodies.

Nate made love to her in the water, as if he had all the time in the world. He discovered each place she liked to be touched, brought her to the brink of mindless abandon, then drew her back from the edge to arouse her again…and again. And when he came to her, standing four feet deep in water, wrapping her legs around his hips and setting the rhythmic cadence of passion, Katy cried out in shimmering pleasure—and he answered as they tumbled into ecstasy together.

A pack of coyotes yipped as they loped across the pasture, then the sounds died into silence. Nestled in Nate's arms, Katy pressed a feathery kiss to his lips.

"You know I've always loved you, Nate," she whispered. "It was the one thing that kept me sane all those years. I'll go on loving you until I breathe my last breath. You are everything I've conjured up as the perfect man. You're considerate, generous, dedicated to your causes, an unsung hero."

She cupped his face in her hands and stared deeply into his obsidian eyes. "Unconditional love, Nate, the kind without boundaries and limitations. I will always be here for you, just as you have been here to bring me back to life. Don't ever give up on yourself," she implored him. "Don't ever give up the fight, because goodness is on your side. No one around here is half the man you are. Believe that. I do, because it's true."

And then she kissed him with all her heart and soul, with all that she was. She offered him her encouragement, her strength and her support. Then she untangled herself from his arms, kissed him good-night and glided away to retrieve her clothes. She left him there with the assurance that even when his spirits hit rock bottom there was someone who believed in him, someone who cared about him—for who and what he was.

Nate watched Katy evaporate into the shadows like a fading fantasy. Silence descended, but this time it wasn't the lonely kind of silence that had hounded him most of the evening. The night was filled with the promise that he would never truly be alone, that he was wanted and appreciated, and that his efforts weren't in vain.

Because Katy inspired Nate not to break stride, he drove off the following morning, intent on his destination. While Lester Brown was sprawled in his favorite booth at the Coyote Café, sipping coffee and shooting off his mouth, Nate was at the trashy farmhouse, armed with paint, garbage bags and a crew of teenagers who assisted him. Nate had decided to defy Lester's cruel taunts and follow Katy's suggestion of plotting a humdinger murder.

And that is exactly what Nate did. He *killed* Lester Brown with kindness.

He cleaned up the lawn, and painted and repaired the house

so thoroughly that Lester barely recognized the place when he got home.

To Katy's amusement, she heard about Nate's good deed, right from the old coot's mouth. Lester was ranting and raving at the café when Katy arrived for lunch Monday morning. Lester was carrying on about how Nate and his hoodlums had sneaked out to whitewash his house and spiff up the yard without permission. Lester was threatening to call Sheriff Peterson to arrest Nate for trespassing.

"You mean to say the very man you have bad-mouthed did what you are too lazy to do?" Katy asked him, right to his face. "Nate cleaned up that eyesore by the highway? My goodness, what a wonderfully generous thing for Nate to do." Katy glanced at the patrons in the restaurant. "It kind of makes me ashamed that none of the rest of us thought to make that generous gesture. How about y'all?"

The patrons hesitated, then nodded their heads.

"None of us pitched in to paint the other seven houses Nate and his crew tidied up, either, did we?"

Another round of bobbing heads.

"We haven't reached out to our fellow men as we should have, have we?" Katy continued. "There are underprivileged children in town who live a hand-to-mouth existence, and we have looked right past them. We shake our heads and say, 'Gee, that's too bad.' But Nate Channing is doing something about the problems we face here. He dipped into his personal funds to beautify this town and make it a better place to live and raise children. I think he should be applauded, not condemned for it."

On that parting remark Katy sailed out the door. Let Loudmouth Lester refute what she'd said. If he tried, he would come off sounding exactly like the jerk he was.

Katy was still operating on an adrenaline high when she returned to the library. Throughout the day she continued her campaign to see Nate elected Citizen of the Year. Each time someone entered the library she sang Nate's praises for the computers, tables and fresh coat of paint. She was determined to counter every word of Lester's bad publicity, notifying everyone she came in contact with of the truth about Nate's civic-minded efforts.

If nothing else, the folks in Coyote Flats were going to hear both sides of the story. Given the facts, maybe people would realize they hadn't treated Nate fairly.

Shortly before five o'clock, Chad Parker burst into the library, his eyes wide with alarm, his face white as yogurt. "Katy, come quick!" he said, panting for breath. "Nate had an accident!"

"Oh, God!" Katy was on her feet in a single bound. She grabbed her purse and shot toward the door with fiendish haste. "Tammy, close up for me. I'll call you as soon as I can."

Katy took the steps two at a time to reach her car. Chad flounced on the passenger seat, cursing under his breath.

"What the blazes happened? Where's Nate?" she asked anxiously.

"He's at Jake Randolph's house," Chad muttered. "We got permission from Jake's mom to paint the house. She picked sunshine yellow. Then Jake's dad came staggering out the door, bellowing like a moose, ordering all us boys off the property. Nate was on the ladder—"

Visualizing the worst, Katy's heart dropped to her ankles.

"—because he volunteered to paint the high peak so none of us guys would have to risk falling. Nate said his life insurance and health insurance were all paid up so he was the most likely candidate for the job," Chad continued shakily. "When Jake's old man started cursing at us, Nate tried to explain that we were donating our time and supplies for the project. But Jake's dad was drunk out of his gourd, and there

was no reasoning with him. He let out a roar, then shoved the
ladder sideways.''

Katy clamped her fists on the steering wheel and accelerated. If Nate had been permanently paralyzed, she was going
to take that crazy drunk apart like a jigsaw puzzle.

"Nate fell into a tree, then catapulted to the ground. He's
hurt pretty bad,'' Chad diagnosed. "He just laid there gasping
for breath. Then Jake went berserk. He lowered his head and
plowed into his old man's belly and knocked him to the
ground. Jake was throwing punches and yelling about how the
old man wasn't going to hurt anybody else ever again. We
pulled Jake off when his old man passed out.

"But that stupid Lester Brown was standing across the
street, carrying on about how the whole lot of white trash on
the wrong side of the tracks was getting what we deserved.''

"Chad, do you think your mother would let Jake spend the
night with you?'' Katy asked. "I don't think Jake should be
near his dad until things simmer down.''

"Sure,'' Chad said with a shrug. "It's not like my mother
will be around. She hasn't been home in two days.''

Katy gaped at him. "And you didn't report her missing?''

Chad glanced out the side window. "She's shacked up with
her latest boyfriend. Happens all the time.''

Katy wheeled into the driveway at Jake's house to see the
boys hovering around Nate. Jake's dad lay spread-eagled in
the grass, sleeping off his latest binge.

Vaulting from the car, Katy raced toward Nate. There
wasn't a speck of color in his face, and he was holding his
ribs, sucking in labored gasps of air. His leg was bent at an
awkward angle. Katy's inexperienced diagnosis was that Nate
had broken his leg—or at the very least, suffered a serious
sprain. She wasn't sure about the condition of his ribs, but if
he had punctured a lung... The frightening thought put her
into immediate action.

"Help me get him into my car,'' Katy ordered hurriedly.

"Gently, boys. Let's not make things worse than they already are."

"I'm so sorry, Nate," Jake said through broken sobs. Tears rolled down his cheeks. "I wish my old man was like you! You give a damn and look how you get paid for caring!"

Grimacing, Nate reached up to ruffle Jake's coal-black hair. "You give a damn, too, Jake," he whispered through clenched teeth. "That's what makes you the better man. Don't let anybody tell you different…. Oh, geez!" He sucked in his breath as Katy and the boys lifted him off the ground. "I don't have time for this, damn it."

"You don't have to worry about a thing," Katy insisted, backing carefully toward the car. "The boys will finish this project. No sweat, right, guys?"

Heads bobbed rapidly in agreement.

"Tammy and I are volunteering to help in whatever capacity we're needed. Your crew knows the drill at the construction site, so they can continue doing their jobs."

Through his pained gaze, Nate stared at Katy. She thought he was trying to smile, but the expression wobbled on his ashen lips. "Thanks," he wheezed.

When the boys loaded Nate into the back seat, Katy scurried into the driver's seat. She dearly wanted to back over Lester Brown, who was still standing on the curb, a smug smirk plastered on his doughy face.

"Jerk," she muttered at him.

"Katy," Nate said in a pained hiss, "maybe it would be best—"

"Save your breath," she interrupted. "Let's find out what's broken and what's not, then we'll talk."

Katy drove to Dr. Wilson's small clinic and pulled up beside the rear exit. The physician was on his way out when Katy hailed him. He gave Nate a quick examination, then unlocked the door to retrieve a wheelchair.

Nate hissed in pain as he struggled to situate himself in the wheelchair. God, he felt awful. Every breath was the equivalent of inhaling darts. His knee felt as if it had been twisted from its socket. If getting his knee back into place hurt as badly as knocking it out, Nate would just as soon leave it where it was. The intense pressure in his chest was nauseating, but since he'd skipped lunch he figured he wouldn't embarrass himself by upchucking.

"Now, then," Doc Wilson said, easing Nate onto the examination table. "Let's check your chest first."

Katy prayed nonstop while the physician examined Nate's ribs. She thanked the Lord that Nate wasn't paralyzed, but she asked for no broken ribs.

"Two broken ribs," the doctor confirmed.

She supposed that particular prayer had come too late.

While the doctor wrapped up Nate's ribs, Katy stepped from the room so Nate could be de-pantsed. She knew undressing was bound to hurt, what with his leg swelling by the minute. Sure enough, she heard Nate yelp a moment later.

Finally, the doctor wheeled Nate into the hall. "Severe strain," he told Katy. "I've given him pain medication, and it'll probably make him dopey. He's going to be extremely uncomfortable for a few days, whether he's sitting up or lying down. I want him off his feet for the rest of the week."

"Done," Katy affirmed.

"I don't have a week to lie around," Nate grumbled, jaws clenched against the pain.

"Of course you do," Doc Wilson assured him. "The tendons and ligaments around your knee need time to heal. I'll call the pharmacy and tell them you're on your way over to pick up a prescription and a wheelchair. They won't close up until you have your medication."

"Thanks, Doc Wilson," Katy said gratefully.

The physician stared pensively at Nate. "You say you fell while painting a house?"

"The eighth house in his community goodwill program,"

Katy interjected quickly. "Not to mention the donations to the school and library. With our Good Samaritan out of commission, I guess the rest of us will have to take up the slack."

Doc Wilson's gray brows shot up, then he glanced speculatively at Nate. "I didn't realize—"

"Most folks haven't a clue how much Nate has done for this community," Katy interrupted. Might as well campaign every chance she got. "Some folks around here are spreading negative gossip about Nate, but I have seen him in action. We need more Nate Channings in this town."

Doc Wilson pursed his lips and regarded Katy as she eased Nate into the back seat. "You're looking well, young lady. Glad to see it."

"Thanks, Doc. I'm happy you noticed. More of the Nate Channing magic at work. He gave me back my misplaced confidence."

"So I noticed."

When Katy drove off, Nate shifted on the seat. "Am I running for public office or something? You sounded like a campaign manager singing my praises."

"Did I?" she said innocently. "I guess I have a tendency to yammer when I'm nervous. Seeing you banged up makes me excessively nervous."

Katy glanced in the rearview mirror to see that Nate had his eyes closed. There was noticeable tension in the lines bracketing his flattened lips. Apparently, the sample tablets of pain medication the doctor crammed down Nate's throat had yet to take effect.

Five minutes later, Katy glanced back to check on Nate. He had slumped against the seat, his head lolled back. Good, she hoped he didn't remember being jarred while she drove. She hoped he slept through the rest of the trip and didn't feel all the bumps on the gravel road that led to his house.

After Katy picked up the prescription and wheelchair, she headed out of town. Nate didn't make a peep, just lay there with his arm wedged protectively against his side, his breathing shallow. Katy slid off the seat and hurried to the door to notify Fuzz and Mary Jane. With Fuzz's assistance, they propped Nate in the wheelchair and rolled him up the sidewalk. His head rolled against his shoulder, his eyelids drooped at half-mast.

He looked like hell, Katy was sorry to say.

"I've got his bed turned down," Mary Jane said while she held open the door. "Maybe I should stay overnight."

"I'll be here with him," Katy insisted. "You'll have to listen to him grouse and complain about being bedridden all day tomorrow. Might as well start your combat duty in the war zone on a good night's sleep."

"This should be loads of fun," Fuzz said, shaking his head. "The man doesn't know the meaning of inactivity. I think this might be a good time for me to take a long road trip to California or Florida. Nate is going to be hell to live with until he's back on his feet."

"You'd leave him in this condition?" Katy asked as she wheeled Nate into his room.

"Of course not, I was just yakety-yakking." Fuzz smiled fondly at the invalid. "I've gotten pretty attached to this man. Wouldn't think of bailing out on him after all he's done for me."

A true and loyal friend, Katy mused. At least there were several folks around here who cared about Nate.

As soon as she and Fuzz maneuvered Nate into bed, Katy grabbed the phone to check in with Tammy. "Can you manage staying by yourself tonight?" Katy asked. "Normally I wouldn't leave you home alone, but I need to stay with Nate."

"I'll be fine," Tammy insisted. "I'm sixteen, you know."

"That's what worries me. Wild parties, boys ransacking the house, and Lord knows what all," she teased.

"Right, we'll party all night, soon as I finish studying for the mid-semester biology test."

Assured that Tammy had plenty to keep her occupied, Katy called Chad Parker.

"Is Nate going to be okay?" Chad asked without preamble.

"Nothing broken that won't mend," Katy reported. "But Nate will be out of commission for at least a week."

"Jake is taking this badly," Chad confided quietly. "He's been sitting here, staring at the wall. He feels responsible. He's ashamed of his father, but this is the real kicker. Jake really looks up to Nate, ya know?"

"I know, Chad. Put Jake on the phone."

"'Lo."

"Jake, Nate is going to be fine after a week of R and R," Katy announced. "But he asked if you would be in charge of making certain all the jobs at the construction site are completed each evening after the work crews leave."

"He wants me to be in charge after what my old man did?" His voice cracked.

Katy crossed her fingers and lied. At the moment, Nate didn't know where he was, but she was certain he would allow Katy to speak for him and ensure that Jake knew Nate didn't hold the kid responsible. "Yes, he did, Jake," Katy confirmed. "Nate is confident that you can handle the responsibility. When he's feeling better, you and the other guys can stop in to see him. I'll call tomorrow night so you can report on the progress."

"Tell him that I'm really sorry," Jake murmured. "I won't let Nate down, none of us will. Whatever Nate wants done, we'll do it."

"He appreciates that, Jake. Now, get to your homework. You know Nate wants to see an improvement in those grades."

"I'll do the best I can," Jake promised.

Katy smiled. "That's all Nate will ask of anyone. He expects nothing more, but he doesn't want you to settle for less."

When Katy contacted Millie Kendrick, the old woman

howled in dismay. Clearly, Millie was fond of her nephew, though she delighted in pretending to be a tough old bird. Nate was right about her. Millie was a tenderhearted softy. She insisted on visiting Nate the following day, and Katy promised to drive her out during lunch hour.

Emotionally exhausted, Katy plopped into the chair and stared at Nate's wan face. He looked as vulnerable as she had ever seen him. She knew Nate hated vulnerability and hid it as best he could as a teenager. Now he was trying to hide the fact that he was disappointed in this stubborn town that refused to accept him.

Folks had written him off as No-Account Nate years earlier and refused to alter an opinion formed years ago. Nate had desperately needed guidance back then, and he desperately needed acceptance now. He offered the kind of encouragement to his young charges that he hadn't received. He was the positive influence in the boys' lives, an influence he hadn't had. Katy knew that Nate was giving the boys what he had needed but never received.

Katy wished with all her heart that Nate would see *her* as *his* salvation, his much-needed moral support, because she was compelled to help him however she could.

Tears clouded Katy's eyes as she impulsively reached over to take Nate's hand. "Maybe you never tried to be my hero, Nate, but you always were," she whispered. "You most definitely are now.... Please let me be yours, too."

Chapter Twelve

Nate groaned drowsily as he drifted to a higher level of consciousness. God, he felt crummy. Somebody had sneaked in to stuff his mouth full of cotton. His skull was pinging like a tuning fork. His vision was blurry, and he was hopelessly disoriented in the surrounding darkness.

Was he in a hospital? He blinked, then squinted to see if light glistened off metal safety bars at the end of the bed. No bars on the bed, he realized. Glancing sideways he recognized the familiar shape of the armoire that held his bedroom television. Home. That was a relief. He didn't know how he had gotten here. Those drugs that Doc Wilson had stuffed in his mouth were worse than a knockout punch.

Katy must have driven him home and called on Fuzz to lug him into bed. Katy... Nate smiled faintly, remembering how she had charged over from the library like a one-woman cavalry to handle the situation. She had taken command better than a field general during the crisis. She may have all but shriveled up for a few years, but she was back in top form now. When the chips were down, Katy Bates came through, damning torpedoes and sailing full-steam ahead.

Nate wondered if she knew he'd always wanted to be her hero and felt he had never quite measured up. He certainly didn't now, because he was flat on his back, unable to get up and every square inch of his body hurt like hell.

All Nate had going for him as a kid was his good looks, but his father had a way of screwing that up for him with a few skin-splitting blows. Things hadn't improved until the old man got hauled off to jail for drug possession, assault and battery, resisting arrest and... Jake couldn't recall what other charges had been piled on. Whatever they were, his old man had committed them at least once or twice in his life.

Nate tried to shift position and felt as if someone had thrust a dagger into his rib cage. Must be Lester Brown's voodoo, Nate thought sourly. The old cuss was probably lounging in his recently painted house, sipping suds and poking pins in a doll that had Nate's name attached to it. Well, phooey on Lester. Nate was going to get better, just to spite the bastard.

The first thing Nate needed to do was wash the cotton from his mouth so he could swallow. He clutched his throbbing ribs and tried to sit up. Excruciating pain forced him back down. The painkillers had worn off and every movement was torture.

"Nate?" Katy's voice whispered across the dark room. "Are you awake?"

"Either that or I'm dead. I can't tell which. Why are you here?"

She appeared above him like an angel bending down from heaven. "Because you need me. Where else would I be?"

"I needed you to catch the ladder before it crashed into the tree," he grumbled.

"Hmm. Are we a little cranky?" she teased softly.

"We really need a drink and some of those pain pills. I've

decided to be a weakling and take all the pills the doctor will allow.''

"Hurting?" she asked worriedly.

"That's one way to put it," Nate grumped.

Katy limped into the bathroom to fill a glass, and Nate cursed under his breath. *She* had survived a serious car crash that left her in the hospital for surgery and months of physical therapy. *He* had plowed into a tree and he was whining about it. He was being a big baby, but damn it, he hurt all over, and he had a trillion duties to perform this week. He had never been incapacitated in his life—except for those few days when a lightning bolt nearly fried him to the metal spire of an oil rig in New Mexico. He'd dropped twelve feet to the ground, just in the nick of time.

"Here you go," Katy said, handing him the glass of water.

"Thanks," he murmured.

"You're welcome...Nate? Before you drift off to sleep, I have to tell you something."

"I hope it isn't more bad news. I'm not my charming self at the moment."

"You are always your charming self, even at your worst," she insisted.

Katy squatted down beside his bed, careful not to jar him and inflict more pain. "I've wanted to tell you what I learned the year after you left town sixteen years ago. I've tried to find the right moment, but there isn't one."

Nate frowned when her thick lashes fluttered down, and she stared at her hands. "So tell me before those pills kick in and I drift into never-never land," he requested.

She glanced up to meet his gaze. "You were set up that night, Nate. It was my father who paid Sonny Brown to plant drugs in the pocket of your jacket."

The news stole the breath clean out of his lungs. Nate had never questioned what had happened, just figured Sonny had gotten scared and stuffed his stash of illegal substances in

Nate's pocket before Sheriff Havern pulled them over for an unannounced vehicle safety inspection. Nate had waited for Sonny to speak up, but the kid had let Nate take the rap, and Fuzz Havern had whisked him out of town before Nate could defend himself....

Nate suddenly remembered something Millie Kendrick had said to him the first day he returned to town. She had made a remark he hadn't understood, and he hadn't pressed her because he was in a flaming rush to speak to Katy at the library.

What he did to you wasn't fair, not fair at all. Tried to tell him so, I did. But the old fool wouldn't listen to me, Millie had told Nate.

Obviously, Millie knew that Dave Bates had framed Nate, all because of his interest in Katy. And Fuzz must have suspected the judge had resorted to underhanded tactics to remove Nate from Katy's life. Fuzz had implied that he had decided to use an alternative plan of dealing with Nate without sending him in front of the judge. Fuzz knew he couldn't fight the all-powerful Judge Bates and win, but Fuzz could depend on Bud Thurston to take Nate under his wing. Nate wondered if Fuzz had promised Judge Bates that Nate would have no further communication with Katy. Probably.

That was why Fuzz had insisted that Nate break all ties with his hometown, for fear Judge Bates would find a way to put Nate in prison.

"Nate." Katy sniffed and swiped at the tears dribbling down her cheeks. "What happened to you was my fault. It was all because of me, Nate. I didn't learn the truth until I overheard my father talking to Sonny Brown on the back steps late one night a year later. Sonny had been paid to set you up, and then he blackmailed my father to keep silent. But Dad bided his time until Sonny screwed up, then he handed down a stiff sentence.

"If I had known where you were, how to contact you back then—"

Nate pressed his forefinger to her trembling lips to shush her. Emotion tumbled through Nate. Learning of the betrayal, combined with his frustration, the pain caused by his injuries and his futile attempts to win over this town, sent his spirits nose-diving to rock bottom. Why the hell had he even tried to come back? Why had he tried to win the respect of these people? Talk about hopeless causes!

Damn it, he hadn't wanted to *buy* respect and friendship in his hometown by announcing that he owned Sunrise Oil and had returned to provide better job opportunities and increased salaries. He had wanted to earn acceptance by making positive contributions to the community. That's why he kept his donations to the town a secret.

Well, he needn't have bothered. He was never going to earn credibility here. His arrest sixteen years ago had sealed his fate in the eyes of the folks in Coyote Flats.

The high-and-mighty Judge Bates had seen to it that Nate was labeled as a worthless hoodlum. Damn the man! Because of Dave Bates, Nate had been whisked out of town, and Katy's life had become a living hell. Nate wasn't sure he would ever forget what the judge had done to him, but Nate would never, ever forgive the man for what he had done to Katy. If not for that incident Nate would have been around to protect Katy, even if the judge refused to let the bad boy of Coyote Flats near her.

God, he had been at the mercy of a snobbish, corrupt man who was determined that his will would be done! Nate despised everything Dave Bates stood for, despised him for making it impossible to change the past!

"I guess I have your dear old daddy to thank for my inability to make a new start in my hometown," Nate said, his voice rumbling with bitterness, anger and pain. "In the eyes of folks here, I'll never be anything except the belligerent kid with bad breeding, the kid who wasn't good enough for sweet Katy Bates. Once a loser, always a loser."

"That's not true," Katy insisted.

Nate laid his head against the headboard and stared grimly into the darkness. "Not true? Try to convince people around here of that. But then, you've already tried, haven't you? I know because I've heard you defending me, for all the good it does."

"Given time, they'll come around," she tried to assure him.

"Let's face it, honey, folks around here are never going to see me for what I have *become,* only what I *was.* That's why my community service projects meet with suspicion. People are waiting for the other shoe to drop, waiting for Lester's predictions to come true. He's got the whole damned town convinced that I'm dealing drugs because, thanks to your father's manipulation and Sonny's betrayal, I was pegged as a drug dealer when I was spirited out of town. And worse, Lester is accusing the boys of being part of my gang, and he claims Millie's house is a drop-off and pickup point for drug trafficking.

"Damn," Nate muttered bitterly. "I've really got to hand it to your dad. He sure as hell knew how to ruin my life and never give me a chance to live down past mistakes, didn't he?"

"Nate, stop it," Katy cried. "That's all in the past. I'm dreadfully sorry about what my dad did, but you can't let him win. Just stop—"

"No, *you* stop it, Katy," Nate cut in harshly. Pain throbbed through his weary body and anger took hold of his tongue. Nate did the unforgivable, he lashed out at Katy—something he swore he would never do. "It's time for a reality check here. I'm never going to be good enough for you, so why kid myself. I am sure as hell not going to drag you down into the slums with me. I'm not going to let this damned town think I've cast some evil spell on you in order to take control of your money and set up the American version of the drug cartel in Colombia, right here in Coyote Flats!"

"Nate, you're talking out of your head!" she said frantically.

"Am I? Maybe I finally got the in-your-face reality check I needed. You try crashing into a tree and lying there in the grass, listening to Lester laugh his head off from across the street and shout that he hoped I broke my good-for-nothing neck. If it isn't Lester condemning me, it will be somebody else whispering that I'm nothing but a hoodlum, that I'll never be good enough for you, that I don't belong in this self-righteous damn town! Ouch!" Nate grated his teeth when pain slammed through his ribs and robbed him of breath.

"Nate, calm down. You're only making your injuries worse by working yourself into—"

"Go home, Katy," he interrupted with a growl. "And don't bother coming back. I'll be fine. In fact, I'd be better off back in Odessa. I'll send someone else to manage the new offices. I don't want anyone around here to know who really owns and operates Sunrise Oil. I'm sure the folks in town would only find another way to twist the truth and turn it against me."

"You can't leave," Katy whispered, reaching for his hand, only to have him withdraw from her physically and emotionally. "You've done so much for this community—"

"And all the thanks I've gotten are repeated slaps in the face," Nate broke in angrily. "How many times do you expect me to turn the other cheek? How many times am I supposed to wash the graffiti off my car and ignore my hate mail?"

With pained effort, he turned his back on her and squeezed his eyes shut against the agony, frustration and undeniable defeat. "Just go home and leave me alone."

"I love you," she whispered raggedly.

"Yeah well, you shouldn't. All that loving me has ever done is bring you down and allow your father to take absolute control of your life. He didn't do me any favors, either. He gave me a reputation that I'll never be able to live down around here, no matter what I say or I do. You know as well as I do that small towns are notorious when it comes to knowing every last thing about a person's background. Trying to redeem myself after a sixteen-year absence has proved impossible. I tried to come home again. I failed and I quit!''

"Now, you listen to me, Nate Channing," Katy snapped as she surged to her feet. "You are not quitting. We can fight this together."

"I'm through fighting," Nate said dejectedly. "This town can have its fondest wish and so can your father. I'm leaving, and I don't plan to come back again."

"Don't you trust me?" she asked suddenly.

"Trust you?" Befuddled, Nate glanced over his shoulder. "What has that got to do with anything?"

"Plenty!" she said in a huff. "It's fine and dandy for you to blow back into town and turn my life around, but when you have trouble, you don't trust me enough to be the shoulder *you* lean on! How do you think it makes me feel, knowing you don't think I've got what it takes to lend you a helping hand?"

"It's not—" he tried to protest, but Katy railed on.

"It is obvious to me that you don't think I'm strong enough or competent enough to handle the job. But of course, Mr. Tough Guy doesn't think he needs or deserves to ask for help from anyone else. You can't bring yourself to ask for support. That would be too humiliating, wouldn't it? If you can't go it on your own, just as you did when you were a kid, then you're outta here. Well, let me tell you something, Nathan Daniel—" Katy plowed on "—you aren't going to turn my life around and then quit on me! I won't let you. Do you hear me?"

"Who can't?" he said, then grimaced. "Go yell somewhere else. My body is screaming in pain. No need for you to make it worse than it is. Just get out of here. Now!"

He heard her mutter a few curses that he didn't ask her to repeat, heard her rush from his room, and he told himself it was for the best. He was damned sick and tired of fighting for the respect he would never get, tired of busting his ass to please and never being accepted and appreciated. At least not here, not in this town.

Nate was always going to be looked upon as the bad breed from the bad seed. All the money and generous donations in the world weren't going to change anyone's opinion of him. Thanks to Judge Bates, Nate's fate had been sealed the night that stash of dope was planted in his pocket.

It was time that Nate stopped believing in unattainable dreams and accepted reality. Reality was that you couldn't go home again, not when you left as a good-for-nothing kid who had been framed for a crime by the one man in town powerful and influential enough to control the direction of your life!

Furthermore, Nate couldn't bring himself to ask for Katy's help. It wasn't just because he'd grown accustomed to going it alone, either, but he couldn't explain that to her. It would upset her more than she already was.

"Aunt Katy? Are you okay?" Tammy asked as she halted at the kitchen door.

Katy slammed the skillet down on the stove and whipped the scrambled eggs until they begged for mercy. "I'm fine. Swell. Couldn't be better." She dumped the eggs in the hot skillet and heard them sizzle and pop.

They had nothing on Katy Bates.

"I studied really hard for my biology test last night," Tammy ventured.

"Good."

"Are you upset about something?"

"Upset?" Katy all but shouted in frustration. "If I were upset I'd be yelling! I am not upset, okay? Here, butter your toast."

"You and Nate had a fight," Tammy guessed as she caught the tray of butter Katy shoved across the counter.

"No, he had a fight, I listened," Katy muttered sourly, then dumped the eggs on the plate and drowned them in ketchup.

"Whoa!" Tammy squawked. "I like eggs splattered with a little ketchup, not ketchup *drowning* the eggs."

Katy blew out her breath, braced her hands on the counter and stared at the mess she had made of Tammy's breakfast. Struggling mightily, Katy battled to get herself under control. She had been beating herself black and blue since she had confided what she knew about her father's betrayal to Nate. She never should have told Nate, especially last night. What was she thinking? Talk about terrible timing!

Why, the poor man couldn't even sit up, and she had sent him reeling with the emotional blow of discovering that her father had altered the course of Nate's life, all because God Almighty Judge Bates didn't think Katy's boyfriend measured up to the Bates standards of excellence and prestige.

Damn it, Katy knew it would upset Nate to learn the truth. She hadn't wanted to tell him, kept putting it off. But when she and Nate became so deeply involved, keeping silent felt like another form of betrayal.

And worse, Nate had thrown up his hands and given up on the two of them, on this town, on himself. He didn't have faith in Katy to help him when he was down. That really stung!

"Um...I'll be at the library as soon as school is out," Tammy said as she picked at her ruined breakfast.

"No need." Katy turned around, leaned against the counter and tilted her chin to a determined angle. Okay, she thought. She had screwed up by telling Nate the truth while he was down and out. It wasn't the first mistake she'd ever made and probably wouldn't be the last. She would find a way to talk sense into Nate. She refused to let him give up on himself, on *them*.

Nate hadn't allowed her to wallow in self-pity and crawl back into her shell. He had drawn her out, built up her confidence. And by damned, she was going to do the same for him, whether he wanted her to or not!

"The library will be closed today," Katy announced. "I'm declaring a holiday. In fact, I'm closing the place down for a couple of days. I'll be home to fix our supper around six o'clock."

"Okay." Tammy grinned impishly. "We aren't having ketchup soup for supper tonight, too, are we?"

Katy chuckled. "No."

"Er...what's the holiday?"

"Get Nate Channing's Head Back on Straight Day," Katy declared.

"Did he suffer a concussion when he fell?" Tammy asked.

"No, but there's a possibility that he might if he doesn't come around to my way of thinking," Katy vowed.

Tammy took a few more bites of her soupy scrambled eyes, then appraised her aunt. "I really like the new you."

"So does Nate," Katy muttered. "He just doesn't know it yet."

Tammy frowned, bemused. "What does that mean?"

"Get going," Katy said, scooping up the textbooks. "Ace that test, kid. Do your auntie proud."

When Tammy left for school, Katy cleaned up the kitchen. Nate thought he was going to quit? Give it up? Throw in the towel? Like hell, Katy fumed. Let Lester Brown win this battle? That would be a frosty day in hell!

For once, justice was going to prevail, even if justice fell short of the mark when it came to political scandals that were ignored and murderers who walked scot-free because of legal technicalities. Well, maybe the rest of the world had a different set of ethics and values, but here in Coyote Flats, there was going to be some justice, and Katy Bates was going to dispense it!

Katy put on her tennis shoes and marched out the front door. Her first order of business was to indirectly let Nate Channing know that he couldn't get rid of her easily. She loved that idiotic man. And she thought he loved her, too. Of course, since he had convinced himself that he would never be good enough for her, he wouldn't say the words.

Furthermore, Katy had an inkling that Nate believed he was protecting her from damaging gossip by leaving Coyote Flats as soon as he was back on his feet. That sounded like something he'd do. Didn't he think she could withstand gossip? Did he honestly believe that she gave a flip what Lester Brown and the rest of the nonthinkers around here thought?

There were a select few in this town whose opinion truly mattered to Katy. She cared what the people she loved thought, the ones she respected. Nate was at the top of the list, and he better give her some credit for her capabilities. She was going to take over for him until he recovered from his injuries, and she was going to whip this town into shape in her spare time!

Nate was on a first-name basis with pain for two endless days. It hurt to breathe, to eat, to sit up and lie down. It hurt worse to realize that he had come down on Katy like a ton of falling rock. That was the last thing he had ever wanted to do, and damned if he hadn't done it.

Yet, he knew that if the anger, pain and sense of betrayal hadn't been bearing down on him, he probably wouldn't have done the sensible thing and sent her on her way.

It was for the best, Nate kept telling himself. Even if his methods left a lot to be desired.

Like clockwork, meals were being delivered to Nate's room, along with the medication that allowed him to sleep off his misery. Fuzz and Mary Jane trod lightly around him. Must have been his menacing growls that scared them off. They came and went without much chitchat, not that Nate was in the mood to be social. He sure as hell wasn't. He'd nearly bit off Fuzz's buzzed head when he asked how Nate was feeling.

Then Nate jumped down Mary Jane's throat when she asked the same question.

Nate felt like hell warmed over a dim flame. He cursed himself a dozen times a day for the way he had treated Katy, then he invented a few more oaths to hurl at himself when the old curses lost their sting. He knew it was best if Katy got out of his life, but it hurt to lose her. Yet, what was the use of trying to make a place for himself in this town? Waste of time. Waste of Katy's time. She needed to get on with her life...without him in it.

Inching sideways, Nate tried to reach the phone so he could make some business calls, before he drifted off into la-la land with the help of the sedatives. Might as well do something constructive, he told himself.

He frowned when he realized the phone had been unplugged and removed from his room. "Fuzz!" Nate winced when his barking voice ricocheted around his head and vibrated all the way down to his tender ribs.

Fuzz poked his head around the partially opened door. "You rang, Your Snippiness? If you want to chew on me, may I suggest some of Millie's chocolate chip cookies instead."

"I want the damn phone," Nate muttered crossly.

"No can do."

"Why the hell not?"

"I've been instructed to see that you have absolute rest."

Nate frowned darkly. "By whom?"

When Fuzz didn't respond immediately, Nate tossed him a glare. "Well?"

"The orders came from Madam Attila."

"Who? Millie Kendrick?"

"Nope," Fuzz replied.

"Mary Jane Calloway?"

"Wrong. Guess again."

"I'm not in the mood for guessing games," Nate said, then scowled.

"I have been instructed to inform you that your business is under control, and there is nothing for you to worry about. The contractors are being carefully supervised at the construction site, and the cleanup crew is keeping the grounds looking like a showplace. All of your business-related calls are being handled promptly and efficiently."

"By *whom?*" Nate repeated impatiently. "And don't give me that Madam Attila baloney again. Who took over my life? And it better not be Katy because I told her to go away and not come back."

"Stupid thing to do," Fuzz muttered. "Why'd you do it?"

"Because," Nate growled obstinately. "You wouldn't understand and neither would she."

"Obviously not, since you won't explain yourself."

"Which I won't," Nate snapped.

Fuzz threw up his hands, clearly frustrated with Nate, who refused to confide where he was coming from. Fuzz didn't have a clue. "Okay, fine. Be that way. I won't tell you that Katy has taken charge of your business, if that makes you happy."

"Fuzz!" Nate called when the retired sheriff wheeled around and headed for the door.

"Now what?" Fuzz muttered.

"Katy told me it was the judge who set me up the night you whizzed me out of town and told me I couldn't come back."

Fuzz sighed audibly, then ambled across the bedroom to drop into a chair. "So it was true, was it? I had my suspicions, but I didn't have evidence."

"That's why you took me to Bud Thurston's ranch and kept track of my progress," Nate presumed.

Fuzz nodded somberly. "I thought you'd gotten the rotten end of the deal, and I believed you when you told me Sonny had stuffed the dope in your pocket to save himself from arrest. But it was difficult to go up against the judge, because he had a very personal interest in wanting you as far away from Katy as you could get. When I returned to town I tried to get Sonny to own up to drug possession, but he kept insisting it was your stash, not his.''

Rehashing the past put Nate's emotions in turmoil. It hurt to realize that Sonny had not only been a sneaky coward who'd been looking to protect his own hide, but that he had also conspired to betray Nate and sold him down the river for a price. Yet, Nate felt the need to discuss the incident, to assure Fuzz that he hadn't lied all those years ago. ''According to Katy, Sonny was paid to stash the drugs in my pocket, then he blackmailed Judge Bates in exchange for silence.''

Fuzz's eyes widened. ''No kidding?'' When Nate nodded, Fuzz shook his head in disgust. ''So that's why the judge ordered me to keep a close eye on Sonny's activities. As soon as that rascal broke another law, the judge put him away with a stiff sentence. Damn it, I really hate it when a man puts himself above the law to see his will done. What little respect I had for Dave Bates is gone for good.''

So was Nate's. Dave Bates had manipulated and destroyed too many lives.

''Now, bring me the phone, Fuzz,'' Nate said in a no-nonsense tone. ''I have to check in with my secretary and one of my field supervisors in New Mexico.''

''Nope,'' Fuzz maintained stubbornly, rising from the chair. ''Katy wants you to rest and so do I.''

''Well, I don't want to rest, damn it!'' Nate roared.

''Too damn bad. In bed is where you're going to stay, and I'm not letting you near a telephone.''

''Fuzz!'' Nate grumbled when the ornery retired sheriff walked off and refused to return.

Nate glanced down to see Taz sprawled in the corner. Even the mutt had been lying low since Nate had been injured.

Furthermore, it seemed to Nate that everybody was enjoying the fact that he was laid up in bed. No one would bring him a phone or the wheelchair so he could contact his office or leave his room. For crying out loud, he had things to do and places to go. He even had to drag himself into the bathroom when nature called, and he wore himself out when he tried to ease back into bed. He hated this feeling of vulnerability. He'd suffered from it too much as a kid.

Nate figured he had pissed off Katy royally when he unloaded on her two nights earlier. Surely she hadn't gotten so irritated with him that she intended to ruin his business dealings just to punish him for doing what he knew was the right thing for the two of them.

No, Nate assured himself. Katy wasn't that vindictive. If he could count on nothing else he could count on that. She went around doing good deeds for the unappreciative folks in this crummy town. Well, she was a better sport than he was. Must have been all her good breeding, he supposed. He and Taz were the outcast mongrels in this world. Two of a kind. A couple of mutts.

So, what was Katy doing to his oil business? he wondered. She was a librarian, not an oil executive. She'd have his business orders so screwed up it would take weeks to sort things out. He didn't want to see her fail, wanted to prevent her from putting herself in a situation where she might fail and he would feel…Nate chopped off that tormenting thought and scowled. He wished he wasn't tortured by that old hang-up from his childhood, but he was, damn it.

Nate sighed heavily and reminded himself that it wouldn't be the first time an attempt to do good deeds went bad. He was living proof of that, wasn't he? But still…

Well hell, what did he care? He would be back in Odessa, and the new branch manager would have to deal with all the headaches. Fuzz would have this entire house to himself to putter around in…and Nate's young charges would slip back into their rut.

Nate winced at that depressing thought. This town could go to hell with his blessing, but those boys weren't going down with it. He would have to make some sort of arrangements—whatever necessary—to see that the boys had a chance in life.

That was the last sensible train of thought Nate could manage. The sedative was taking effect, and the pressure in his chest eased up. He would have welcomed the hiatus from pain if the bluest eyes in West Texas hadn't followed him into his disjointed dreams.

Chapter Thirteen

Katy's brows puckered as she watched one of the contractors at the construction site flip a smoldering cigarette butt onto the concrete floor. She'd had it with these rascals who never picked up after themselves. They were worse than two-year-olds!

She tramped over to grind the heel of her shoe on the smoldering butt. "Put the cigarette out, pal," she snapped. "The grocery store burned down last month because of an incident like this one. I want to see this building completed, not burned to cinders."

The rail-thin worker pulled a face at her. "When is Channing coming back?"

What the contractor really wanted to know, Katy decided, was when could he get her off his back. The answer was, Only when he started cleaning up after himself.

"Nate won't be back for at least a week," Katy announced. "In the meantime I will be in charge."

"Yeah, so we noticed," one of the crew mumbled, then scowled.

"You are hereby informed that I am making a list and checking it twice. Anyone who isn't pulling his weight around here can take a hike." She hitched her thumb toward the exit of the warehouse. "I've got five teenagers outside picking up the trash you and the other crews tossed around. All of those boys are working circles around you, so get back to work."

"Look, lady—"

"No, *you* look, buster," Katy broke in forcefully. "I caught one of your men in an office this morning, sprawled on the floor, sleeping off a hangover, resting his head on a blasted hammer! This afternoon, one of your helpers was standing around the corner, out of sight, tapping his hammer against the wall to make everybody think that he was actually accomplishing something. I'm sick and tired of this slow pace you're setting.

"According to the contract on file in the main office, you are two weeks behind schedule. Sunrise Oil does not pay for what it doesn't get. Are we clear on that?"

"Yeah." The bearded foreman with an attitude glared at her.

Not to be outdone, Katy glared right back. "Shift into first gear, and get the office doors hung before you shove off for the evening."

Katy was pretty sure the four men saluted her with their middle fingers when she wheeled around and limped off. But she didn't care what they thought of her. She had watched those jokers waste time with long, unscheduled breaks too often the past few days.

Digging the cell phone from her pocket, Katy punched in Nate's home number. Fuzz answered on the second ring.

"Fuzz? It's Katy. Did you hear back from the Department of Health and Human Services?"

"Yes, about twenty minutes ago," he confirmed.

"Did they cut through the red tape?"

"I think so. The caseworker is supposed to be here tomorrow. The wheels are in motion. Millie and Mary Jane approve of your idea and all systems are go."

"Glad to hear it."

"How are things going at the construction site?" Fuzz asked.

"Slowly," Katy grumbled. "These clowns spend more time finding ways to avoid work than actually doing it."

"Good help is hard to find."

"Amen to that." Katy spun around to ensure Tweedledum and his Tweedledee crew were still working. "How's Nate?"

"Irritable as a wounded rhinoceros. He demanded his phone to make business calls again this morning. I told him he couldn't have it. That didn't go over too well."

"Tough cookies," Katy said. "Nate was totally exhausted from working double shifts before he suffered those injuries. He needs to rest."

"You can't sell *him* on the idea," Fuzz grumbled.

"You're a retired sheriff. You know how to handle contrary inmates," Katy encouraged him.

Fuzz chuckled. "Yeah, but the only crime Nate committed was caring enough to get involved in this community."

"Then he just gave up," Katy murmured.

"Is that what happened? I wondered why his attitude turned so lousy."

"That's it in a nutshell. I made the stupid mistake of telling him what my father had done to him sixteen years ago. It wasn't a good time to tell him, but I thought he deserved to know the truth. That, combined with his pain and frustration, made him throw up his hands in defeat."

"Nate mentioned the incident to me yesterday. I was as hesitant to confide my suspicions about what really happened as you were. I never could find the right time to bring it up, either."

"He took it pretty hard," Katy reported. "Not that I blame him. I feel responsible for what happened to him way back when, and now. Having given up once myself, I know it takes several nudges and a lot of prodding to get back on track. I'm not about to let Nate give up."

Fuzz chuckled. "Then he doesn't have a prayer. Go get 'em, tiger."

"I fully intend to."

"I gotta go, Katy. The tyrant is yelling again. No telling what His Snippiness wants this time."

Katy switched off the phone. A faint smile pursed her lips as she imagined how difficult Nate was to deal with in his present mood. She had only caught a glimpse of his frustration the night he had ordered her out of his life and given up his attempt to win over this bullheaded town.

Nate's admirable strengths could also be his most notable faults, especially when he was confined to quarters, Katy mused. Undoubtedly, he was getting restless. He was probably wondering if her leadership would destroy his business. He probably doubted that she knew what the devil she was doing.

Well, she might not be an oil tycoon, but librarians who operated on the Dewey decimal system knew something about precise organizational skills. She had also pinched pennies on a limited budget at the library, and she knew how to get around, over and under obstacles standing in her path. She had applied those skills to the oil industry when she acted in Nate's stead.

Thanks to Nate she had regained self-esteem and had become assertive. She was gradually gaining self-confidence by handling confrontations with Lester and the hotshot crew foreman at the construction site. The additional experience assured her that she could handle Nate's duties until he recovered.

Come hell, high water—or both—the finishing crew was going to have the offices ready for occupancy by the time Nate was back on his feet, she vowed. Then she would hand the reins of command to Nate, and he would realize that he *could* trust her with his business, with his life, with his love.

As for the hidebound citizens of Coyote Flats, Katy wasn't sure how she was going to cure them of blind stupidity, but she was going to do it, sure as shootin'.

Retrieving the phone, Katy put in a call to Tammy to bring hamburgers and fries for the boys, who had been working extra hard all week to ensure Nate's projects weren't neglected.

"Sure, I'll be glad to bring out a picnic supper," Tammy assured her. "Anything else, Aunt Katy?"

"As a matter of fact, there is. The Spring Festival of the Coyote is coming up this weekend, and we need to get some baked goods prepared to serve at the food booths. I am also in charge of hauling folding chairs from the church to set up seating in the town square for the audience of the bands and vocal groups that are providing live entertainment. Do you think the boys would help you with that chore after they get off work? I have another matter I need to attend to this evening."

"I'm sure Chad and the other guys would be glad to help," Tammy confirmed.

"Sheriff Peterson informed me that he would rope off the entertainment area on Main Street this evening so we could set up the chairs, and the arts and crafts and food booths tonight."

"Not to worry, Aunt Katy. We'll take care of everything."

"Thanks, kiddo, I appreciate it."

Katy crammed the phone in her purse and strode off to double-check on the construction crew. She couldn't leave them alone for fifteen minutes for fear they would give themselves another break. As for the cleanup crew of teenagers, Katy didn't have to look over their shoulders. They were working their little hearts out for Nate.

No one offered Nate respect, he'd said. Bull, thought Katy.

There were five teenagers outside who worshiped the ground
Nate walked on. Someday those boys would become decent,
responsible, hardworking men who had been taught morals
and ethics by a positive role model. Even if Nate had convinced himself that he was fighting a hopeless battle, he had
built on the foundation for the future. It was the *youth* of
Coyote Flats who would eventually replace the lug-headed
Lester Browns of this community.

Nate didn't understand that he was winning the battle for
acceptance one teenager at a time. As for Lester, Katy planned
to have a long talk with him this evening. It was time to do
something about that pain in the patoot!

Katy frowned curiously when she cruised over the hill to
see two farm trucks pulling away from Lester Brown's barn,
which sat a quarter of a mile from his house. Alarm bells went
off in Katy's head when the truck drivers failed to turn on
their headlights as they headed north on the gravel road. Katy
drove past the house, then turned around near a grove of mes-
quite trees.

Hopping from the car, Katy hiked through the ditch and
noticed the silhouette of a man walking toward the house. Katy
had the unmistakable feeling that Lester was up to something
sneaky. She knew for a fact that Lester had declared bank-
ruptcy years earlier. She had often wondered how he could
live on the rent payments he received from what little farm
ground and pastureland he had left to his name. She assumed
Lester had applied for welfare or unemployment benefits to
support him, but she was beginning to wonder if Lester had
made arrangements for a more lucrative income.

Katy silently fumed when she recalled how Lester had ac-
cused Nate of dealing drugs and spiffing up Millie's house
for pickups and drop-offs. Interesting, wasn't it, that Lester
was hell-bent on casting suspicion on Nate. Maybe the fact

was that Lester wanted to distract the folks of Coyote Flats so no one would suspect *him* of wrongdoing.

Determined, Katy eased between the barbed wire strands of the fence, then cut diagonally across the pasture to reach the barn. She stepped inside to see a gigantic stack of square hay bales.

Hmm. Now why would someone deliver hay—in the cover of darkness—to Lester's farm when he no longer kept a herd of cattle or flock of sheep that needed feed?

Good question. Katy wanted a logical answer to go with it. She dug the cell phone from her pocket and dialed quickly. "Fuzz?"

"What's up, Katy?"

"I know it's late, but I just happened onto something very interesting when I drove out to speak to Lester Brown about the way he has been harassing Nate. Could you come out here and meet me in Lester's barn?"

"What's going on out there?" Fuzz questioned warily.

"I'm hoping you can figure that out, being a retired sheriff and all. I suggest you be discreet, Fuzz. I don't want Lester to know either one of us are snooping around in his barn."

"Sounds intriguing," Fuzz said. "I'll be there as soon as I can. Just be careful, girl."

"I will," she promised. "I'll just tuck myself behind all these bales of hay that were delivered to Lester's barn a few minutes ago."

"In the dark? Hay bales?" Fuzz hooted. "Lester doesn't run livestock."

"Like you said, Fuzz, it sounds intriguing."

"I'm on my way."

The phone clicked, then hummed. Katy disconnected, then limped to the far corner of the barn to position herself between the tall stacks of straw. Remembering how Lester had tormented Nate to no end with negative gossip, graffiti, and hate mail made Katy fume in outrage. Unless Katy missed her guess—and she seriously doubted that she had—Lester had been covering up illegal activities, while casting shadows of doubt and condemnation on Nate.

Just wait until Fuzz got here to dig into this pile of straw! Fuzz would know how to handle this situation, and Lester was going to be dreadfully sorry he had tangled with her!

Nate's brows shot up in surprise when Fuzz barreled into the bedroom, pulling the wheelchair. "Does this mean I'm finally allowed out of solitary confinement?"

"I've got someplace I have to be in a hurry," Fuzz said as he positioned the wheelchair beside the bed. "You can watch TV in the living room while I'm gone. The boys called a while ago and said they were coming to visit you."

Nate flinched when Fuzz grabbed hold of his arm to situate him in the chair. Nate barely had time to find a comfortable position before Fuzz wheeled him out the door and down the hall.

"What's the all-fired rush?" Nate demanded crankily. "Slow this thing down! I'm not in good-enough shape for racing."

Fuzz slowed his urgent pace. "Sorry. I'm working on a short clock. If you need anything, the boys can take care of you while I'm gone. Mary Jane already left for the night."

"Fine, but—"

Bemused, Nate watched Fuzz grab his baseball cap and fly out the door without so much as a goodbye. Nate's curious gaze drifted from Fuzz's departing back to the cordless phone. Painful though it was, Nate pushed himself toward the end table, then picked up the receiver. For two days he had debated about calling Katy and apologizing for being so terse with her the night he'd sent her away.

Of course, he hadn't changed his mind about getting out of her life, getting out of this sorry-ass town, but he did feel the need to apologize for hurting her. Damn it, she was the last person on this planet he wanted to hurt.

Impulsively, Nate dialed the number, disappointed that Tammy was the one who answered the phone. "Hi, Tammy. May I talk to Katy?"

"Sorry, Nate, but she isn't here. How are you feeling?"

"Lousy, but thanks for asking. Do you happen to know where I can reach Katy?"

"No, she said she had something to take care of this evening, but she didn't say where she was going or when she'd be back," Tammy reported. "Do you want me to tell her you called?"

Nate debated about that, wondering if fate had intervened to prevent him from hearing the sound of her voice, which would probably cause his resolve to crack. Yet, the thought of leaving town without talking to her didn't set well with him. It seemed like the coward's way out, and in no way did he want his departure to resemble the night he was forced from town sixteen years earlier. No way could he leave without telling Katy where she could reach him if she needed him.

"Ask Katy to give me a call when she gets home," Nate requested. "No matter what time it is, I want to talk to her."

"Sure thing, Nate."

Nate barely got the phone hung up when the doorbell chimed. "It's open. Come in."

Five fashionably dressed boys, their hair neatly clipped, filed into the living room. Taz came immediately to his feet to greet the guests and beg a few pats. The boys, who received very little affection from their families, gave the mongrel all the attention he wanted. Taz was happy as a clam when he received so many pats on the head and scratches behind his ears.

A pang of sadness stabbed at Nate while he watched the teenagers fawn over the mutt. He had gotten used to having these kids underfoot. Damn, it was going to be lonely as hell in Odessa without these boys, without Katy....

"How are you feeling, sir?" Chad asked as he sank onto the sofa, then glanced around the room. "Man, this is really a fancy place you've got here."

"Yeah," the other boys chimed in. "Really cool."

While four of the boys made themselves at home and carried on about the big-screen TV, Jake Randolph hung back, his head downcast, his hands stuffed in the pockets of his jeans. The kid refused to meet Nate's gaze. Nate suspected Jake was tormenting himself because of the incident that took place at his house.

"Chad, why don't you and the guys bring Jake and me a cola from the kitchen," Nate suggested. "Some of Millie's fresh-baked cookies are on the counter. Help yourselves to them, or any other snack you want."

When the boys strode off, Nate motioned for Jake to take a seat. The kid shook his head, refusing to budge from the spot.

"Just when things were starting to get better, it all went to hell," Jake grumbled bitterly. "I was starting to have a little pride in myself at school, because my grades are getting better. The new clothes you and Katy gave me made me feel like I fit in. It felt good to have other kids compliment my clothes, to admire something *I* had, ya know?"

Jake's head dropped lower, his shoulders slumped. "Then you got hurt while you were at my place. Now I don't feel like I belong here, don't deserve the job you gave me," Jake mumbled. "Not after what my old man did to you."

"That wasn't your fault," Nate told him.

Jake glanced up, his eyes filled with torment and regret. "Wasn't it? I know how my old man operates. I should have been counting the bottles of booze, just like you said. Because I didn't notice the signs in time, you're stuck in a wheelchair, and Katy had to close down the library so she could take care of things for you.''

''Did she?'' Nate had wondered how she managed to juggle her professional duties, as well as his. Now he knew. She had placed his needs and obligations above her own. That was just like Katy, wasn't it?

Nate made a mental note not only to apologize to Katy, but to thank her for her assistance, even if she did leave his business in a tangle and he had to deal with the deep-seated emotion that came with it. She was trying, he reminded himself. That was more than he could say for the rest of the folks in this town.

''How are things at home, Jake?'' Nate asked, motioning for the kid to park himself in a nearby chair.

Reluctantly, Jake moved forward, then slouched in the chair. ''Things aren't too good,'' he admitted. ''My old man got boozed up again last night. This time I counted the empty beer cans, then I left with my kid sister before the fireworks started. Mom must have decided she'd had enough because she hasn't been around in a couple of days.''

''I know it's tough, Jake,'' Nate murmured compassionately. ''You keep thinking your dad will change his ways, that this time will be the last time he gets tanked up and throws punches. But reality is that your dad needs professional help.''

''Not according to him,'' Jake muttered. ''He doesn't think he has a problem.''

Nate wasn't allowed to continue the conversation because the other boys returned with snacks and colas. He did admit that watching the intercollegiate basketball playoffs with the boys improved his disposition. Yet, even though Nate was pleased to have the boys' company, something was missing. There was still this aching loneliness that couldn't be filled.

Damn, it was going to be hell without Katy in his life. But he couldn't ask her to pull up stakes and move away with him. For better or worse, this town was her home, and she had committed herself to this community. She had poured her time, energy and money into the library. She was the first one in town to offer sympathy, food or whatever was needed when a family faced a crisis. Furthermore, there was Tammy to take into consideration.

Just give it up, Nate told himself. There was only one reasonable course of action to take. He would move to Odessa and give this town what it wanted—his permanent absence. As soon as the boys graduated high school Nate would encourage them to come to Odessa so they could work for him and take night classes at the college. Having them around would make his life seem complete.

"Yeah, right, Channing," Nate muttered under his breath. "That will never be enough to satisfy you and you damn well know it. You better accept the fact that you're going to leave here with a hole the size of Texas in your heart."

"Where have you been so long?" Nate asked when Fuzz finally returned shortly before midnight.

"Here and there," Fuzz said evasively. "Did you have a good visit with the boys?"

Nate nodded as Fuzz wheeled him to the bedroom. "I'm still worried about Jake. He and his sister need to get away from that bad situation at home. Then there's Chad, whose mother is hardly ever around. And Tyler, Richie and Will—"

"I'm working on the arrangements," Fuzz interrupted. "A social worker from the Department of Health and Human Services will be here tomorrow afternoon to appraise the cases."

Nate glanced up, surprised. "When did you have time to set that up?"

"In between jumping and running every time you called me," Fuzz teased good-naturedly.

"Sorry about that. I guess I've been hard to live with this week," Nate said as Fuzz maneuvered him beside the bed.

"Hard to live with?" Fuzz snickered. "That's putting it mildly, son. You've been hell to live with."

"Well, you won't have to put up with me much longer. I'm moving back to Odessa and appointing an office manager to handle the branch office."

"What?" Fuzz howled in disbelief.

Nate flinched uncomfortably as he struggled to sit down on the edge of his bed. "Let's face it, Fuzz. I'm never going to be accepted here. And worse, I'm causing you, Katy, Millie, Mary Jane and the boys grief by association. The best thing for me to do is leave," he said, defeated.

"Katy is right. You have given up." Fuzz let loose with a disgusted snort. "I never thought I'd see this day."

"Well, it has arrived," Nate insisted. "A man has to be a fool to keep beating his head against a locked door. Thanks to Judge Bates my fate was sealed permanently. No one in town has any intention of forgetting who and what I was, and no one will believe the *honorable* Judge Bates framed me."

Fuzz braced one hand on the headboard and the other on his hip. "Now, you listen to me, buster. Nobody ever said life was easy. From what I've seen, it's nothing but complicated and messy. Take you, for instance. You battled your way through a difficult childhood, then you got your act together with Bud Thurston's help. Then you got in on the ground floor during the oil boom, worked your butt off, made some wise investments and found the success you deserve. If you had told folks around here that you own Sunrise Oil, you would have gotten instant respect."

"Would I?" Nate begged to differ. "I would have been using my influence as owner of the company and my money to buy friends in this town. That's not the same thing, and it certainly isn't the way I want to acquire acceptance."

Fuzz frowned pensively. "I guess I see your point."

"Then you should also realize that I can still boost the economy of this town while I'm in Odessa. I can have my staff buy leases to drill wells, and the local landowners will profit from them. There will be plenty of jobs available when the office opens. Money will pour back into town when the oil wells are in production. I don't need to be here in person to hand out royalty checks and payroll checks.''

"But you need to be here for Katy," Fuzz said quietly. "That woman really cares about you. You'd have to be blind in both eyes not to see that."

"It just won't work," Nate muttered fatalistically.

"Then make it work!"

Nate shook his head dismally. "I'm damned tired of *making* things work. I did what I came here to do and it's time I left."

Fuzz walked away, muttering contradictions to Nate's logic, but Nate had had plenty of time to lie in bed and sort out his thoughts. When he could stand on both feet, then he was as good as gone.... And most folks in Coyote Flats would stand up and cheer about it.

Chapter Fourteen

Katy was bone-weary by the time she returned home shortly after midnight. She found the note Tammy left in the kitchen, informing her that Nate wanted to talk to her.

A phone call just wasn't going to cut it, Katy realized. It had been almost a week since Nate had sent her away. Too many lonely, frustrating days—and nights. Well, enough was enough. Nate may have decided to walk away from this town, from *them,* but he wasn't physically able to leave *yet.*

After a quick shower, Katy drove off, intent on seeing Nate in person. Using the key Nate kept inside the storm door, Katy let herself into the house and moved silently down the hall. The moment she saw Nate lying in bed—the night-light in the bathroom casting shadows across the bedroom—the tension of the day melted away.

Nate had dozed off, she noted. He lay on his back, the white bandages around his ribs in stark contrast to his bronzed skin. The sheet was draped across his hips, and his hands were resting on the sculpted muscles of his belly.

Katy smiled ruefully as she approached the bed. Her dreams of a future with Nate had shattered around her, but she just kept clinging to the hope that he would change his mind about leaving. Yet, she understood why he wanted to go back to a place where he was respected, accepted. The past two months hadn't been easy on him.

Carefully, Katy eased down beside Nate, finding the contentment that had eluded her for days. She cuddled up as close as she could without disturbing Nate's sleep. Whatever he had wanted to say would have to wait, because Katy didn't want to spoil the feelings of satisfaction that stole through her.

This was where she had always belonged—by Nate's side, for better or worse, in sickness and in health. And this is where she would stay as long as he let her. She could only pray that he would realize they could weather any storm, as long as they were together. They were soul mates, she was certain of it.

On that wishful thought, Katy drifted off to sleep.

Nate awoke, feeling the strangest, unaccountable feeling of contentment. He didn't know what prompted it, just knew that he had enjoyed the best night's sleep he'd had in days. The scent of Katy's perfume clung to him as he eased onto his side. Damn, his forbidden dreams were really becoming vivid, weren't they? Nate could almost swear he could feel an aura of warmth beside him, as if Katy had actually been there with him all through the night.

Groggily, Nate opened his eyes to stare at the empty space beside him. A muddled frown beetled his brow when he saw the note lying on the extra pillow. Nate picked it up and held it to the light that streamed through the window.

I still love you. Nothing will ever change that.

                                                                    Katy

Nate closed his eyes against the riptide of emotion tumbling through him. Katy had been there beside him during the night, despite the fact that he'd hurt her, had sent her away and told her not to come back. True, loyal, forgiving, unfaltering, that was his Katy. When all the rest of the world went to hell she would always be there…if he let her.

But he couldn't let her do that. He couldn't let his own selfish desire bring her more trouble and heartache, Nate told himself resolutely. Her place was here in Coyote Flats.

His wasn't.

"Well, glad to see you're awake, especially since your breakfast is hot off the stove," Mary Jane Calloway said as she buzzed through the door. "Hungry?"

"Not particularly," Nate mumbled at the energetic, red-haired widow who breezed into his room.

"Too bad. Eat it and like it. Then we'll get you into the shower."

Nate frowned darkly. "Why this sudden burst of interest in me? You've taken a wide berth around me all week."

"Darn right I did." Mary Jane set the tray of eggs, bacon, toast and coffee on his lap. "You turned mean and nasty. I'm not getting paid to get my head bit off, just to cook and clean."

"Thanks, Mary Jane. I'll eat because you fussed," Nate said, offering her a peace-treaty smile.

The older woman grinned at him. "That's better. Keep that smile handy, handsome. You'll want to wear it while we're attending the Spring Festival of the Coyote."

Nate's smile turned upside down. "I am not going into town. I don't care what kind of festivities are scheduled."

"Of course you're going. Didn't I just say so? Fuzz also says so. Millie and I are here to help you get dressed after you have your shower."

Nate was not going to be bullied by two old women and a retired sheriff, even if he did happen to be physically chal-

lenged at the moment. He'd had his fill of the folks in Coyote
Flats, and he was not going to be humiliated by letting people
smirk and look down their noses at him while he was rolled
down the street in that blasted wheelchair.

"I'm not going and that's final—"

When Mary Jane crammed a slice of toast in his mouth,
Nate nearly choked.

"Don't mess with me, buster," she said, giving him the
evil eye. "Just eat and keep your trap shut, or I'll call in
reinforcements. Millie and I aren't putting up with your nonsense this morning."

"I'll eat," Nate growled as he snatched up his fork, then
stabbed the sunny-side-up eggs until they wept all over his
plate. "But I sure as hell am not going into town. You wanna
join the festivities? Fine. Go. Take Millie and Fuzz with you.
I'm staying here."

"Fuzz has already left for town," Mary Jane informed him.

"Why? Is he the master of ceremonies or something?"

"Nope, the mayor is, same as every year," she told him.
"Now, eat your bacon. It's cooked exactly the way you like
it."

Grudgingly, Nate sampled the bacon. It was perfect, but so
was everything Mary Jane cooked up. He was going to miss
her mouthwatering meals and her to-die-for desserts when he
moved back to Odessa. Nate considered asking Mary Jane to
go with him, but he refused to deprive Fuzz of Mary Jane's
fabulous cooking. Besides, the two had become good friends.

Millie appeared in the doorway. "Is that boy behaving himself?"

"More or less," Mary Jane replied. "He's eating. That's a
start."

"I'm staying here," Nate told his aunt in no uncertain
terms.

"Are not," she said in her customary gruff voice. "Nobody

is missing the social event of the season. We only have two a year, and it's a long time till the Christmas parade.''

Nate set aside his fork and stared pointedly at Millie, then at Mary Jane. ''Look, I appreciate the fact that you have decided it's time I got out of the house to breathe some fresh air. I'd like nothing better myself. But I'm not going farther than the front porch, where I plan to make a few business calls. I am *not* going to town and that is that... Hey, cut that out!''

Nate's eyeballs nearly popped out of his head when the two women descended on him. He found himself playing tug-of-war with the sheet, because these two banshees were trying to pull it off of him. He was wearing nothing but briefs and bandages!

Despite his attempt to hang on to the sheet without ripping another tender rib loose, Millie and Mary Jane won the battle. Embarrassed, exasperated, Nate glowered at them, but neither woman backed down.

''You gonna get off your duff and shower or do I have to bathe you?'' Millie asked gruffly.

''All right, damn it,'' Nate said, and scowled. ''I'll shower, but I'm not leaving the house!''

Millie crossed her arms beneath her ample bosom and glowered at him. ''After all I did for you when you were a kid? This is the thanks I get? Now, you listen to me, you ungrateful whippersnapper, all's I'm asking is for you to attend the festivities for a few hours. The way you're carrying on you'd think I asked you to walk barefoot over hot coals. Now, get up and get into this blasted wheelchair, 'fore me and Mary Jane are forced to drag you into the bathroom by your heels.''

''Fine, I'm going!'' Nate shouted.

''Good!'' the women shouted back, then marched from the room.

Mumbling and grumbling, Nate inched off the bed and struggled into the wheelchair. Muscles screamed. Pain shot through his chest. Those old hens thought they could boss him around now that he was laid up, did they? If this was how it felt to have parents lording over him, maybe he was glad he hadn't had any to speak of.

Slowly but surely, Nate rolled himself into the bathroom, then removed the bandages. He switched on the faucets, then maneuvered onto the shower bench. The warm mist sprayed down on him, rejuvenating him. He asked himself why he hadn't made the effort to shower days earlier, rather than settling for those spit baths in bed.

Suddenly he felt ten times better, much to his surprise. He also stayed in the shower as long as possible, pretty certain those banshees wouldn't come in after him while he was stark naked.

Nate was forced to switch off the faucets when the water ran cold. When he had toweled dry, he made his way back to the bedroom to dress.

It wasn't easy to dress, if anybody cared to know. Pulling up his briefs and jeans, while suffering from cracked ribs and a strained knee, was sheer hell. Nate gave up trying to tug the T-shirt over his head, just left it draped around his neck. It was the best he could do.

"You decent, boy?" Millie called from the hall.

"Since when did you let that bother you?" he shot back.

Millie and Mary Jane came through the door, looking all smug and gloating. Nate fired them a glare hot enough to scorch the iron off a skillet.

"You aren't wearing that shirt," Millie declared, then jerked it over his head. "Looks like something that belongs in a ragbag. Mary Jane, hand me one of those high-dollar polo shirts from the closet. The red one will be fine."

Nate swore under his breath when the two women finished dressing him. When they had crammed his socks and shoes on his feet and slicked back his wet hair, they proclaimed him suitably dressed to attend the festivities.

Spring Festival of the Coyote, Nate thought with another snort. Here was yet another glaring example of this town's lack of originality. Some communities celebrated Frontier Days, Cowtown Days, Antique Tractor Shows and Hee-Haw Mania.

But not in this neck of the woods. It was coyote this and coyote that.

Furthermore, Nate didn't have to dress up and go all the way into town to be insulted, rejected and harassed. He was receiving plenty of hate mail, thank you very much.

Regardless of his distaste in attending the Festival of the Coyote to view hand-painted ceramic coyotes and wood-carved coyotes, listen to coyote-calling contests and eat coyote-shaped cupcakes, Millie and Mary Jane loaded him in his car and drove him into town.

The festival hadn't changed much in sixteen years, Nate noted as Mary Jane wheeled him down the sidewalk. Main Street was still roped off with yellow crime-scene tape. Pictures of howling coyotes were still painted on shop windows to commemorate the festivities. Tent booths still lined both sides of the street. An upraised stage still occupied the town square, and folding chairs sat in a semicircle near Coyote Fountain.

Nope, nothing had changed. Nate was still unwanted baggage with a reputation that he couldn't overcome, no matter how hard he tried.

"Good, you made it."

Nate's heart fluttered when he heard Katy's cheerful voice behind him. His breath stalled in his chest when she circled around his wheelchair to smile at him. She looked absolutely radiant in her sunny yellow halter dress and sandals. If he had expected this encounter to be uncomfortable, he was mistaken. You would have thought he had never spoken harshly, then ordered her out of his house, his life. It was as if the incident hadn't happened. Katy treated him as if she was delighted to see him.

"You're looking much better, more rested," Katy said as she leaned down to brush a kiss against his cheek.

"Do I? It must be because I've been forced into doing absolutely nothing but rest for a week," he replied grumpily.

"R and R agrees with you," she said, ignoring the grumble in his voice. She turned to Millie, her cheery smile still intact. "I bought you a new shopping cart. One with a padded handle. I think you've gotten your fifty thousand miles out of the wheels on the old one." She gestured toward the hardware store. "It's over there, Millie, all charged up and ready to go."

Nate blinked in amazement when he saw the expensive motorized cart with its cushioned seat and metal basket attached to the padded handlebars. Judging from the astonished look on Millie's face, she was delighted with the unexpected gift.

Nate wished he had thought of it.

"Oh, my gawd!" Millie wheezed. "That's for me?"

"Yes," Katy affirmed. "You can tool around town and turn on a dime. No more pushing a cart. It's time you started riding in one."

"I don't know what to say," Millie whispered, tears spilling from her eyes.

"A thank-you will do just fine, Millie. And my thanks to you for being Nate's guardian angel all those years. I'm grateful that you were there to keep an eye on him."

Once Katy showed Millie how to operate her newfangled cart, the old woman zigged and zagged through the crowd, giggling in delight while Mary Jane galumphed alongside her.

"That was really nice of you," Nate murmured, then squirmed uncomfortably. "Er...the reason I called last night—"

"Well, look who showed up to spoil the day. It's No-Account Nate, the cripple."

Nate gripped the armrests of his chair, willfully restraining his temper. But it was damn hard when Lester Brown and his shadow, John Jessup, strode up to smirk down at him.

To Nate, it seemed the world had screeched to a halt, and then time spun backward. Sitting in this wheelchair represented all the seething frustration and vulnerability Nate had experienced as a teenager. Suddenly, he was right back where he started.

"When are you going to catch a clue, Channing?" Lester taunted in a loud voice, calling plenty of attention to himself. "Nobody wants you here. Go crawl back to whichever rock you slithered out from under."

Folks stopped what they were doing and turned to stare at Nate. Those suspicious, unwelcoming glances that eroded his pride and confidence came again. Nate hated being the center of condemnation. He was damn sick of this. Sick of this unforgiving town. He should never have let Millie and Mary Jane drag him here.

"Let's go, Katy," Nate muttered.

When she tried to push the wheelchair past Brown and Jessup, the men blocked her path.

"This is your last warning, Mr. Drug Lord," Lester jeered hatefully. "Turn your wheelchair around and roll out of town."

"That's it!" Katy burst out. "I have had it with the two of you!"

When she stamped around the side of his chair, Nate clamped hold of her arm. This was exactly what he was afraid would happen eventually. Katy was trying to come to bat for him in front of a crowd. Her name would be forever linked and dragged down with his bad reputation, his bad breeding. She would become as much an outcast as he was.

"Katy, don't—" Nate winced in pain when she jerked loose from his grasp.

"Sorry, Nate," she apologized, but her attention was riveted on Lester, John and the crowd that was closing in around them. "It's time this nonsense stopped, and I intend to put a stop to it."

To Nate's astounded disbelief, Katy elbowed her way between Lester and John, then stamped toward the stage. She jerked the microphone from the stand and held it in her hand. Electrical equipment squealed and squawked, drawing undivided attention to the plywood stage that had been erected in front of Coyote Fountain.

"I have something to say to everyone in Coyote Flats," Katy announced huffily. "I have watched the whole blessed bunch of you let Lester Brown and his sidekick speak for you, think for you. Since when do good and decent folks take the word of a man who has done absolutely nothing for this community?"

"Katy, stop!" Nate shouted at her. He had a very bad feeling about this. She was going to have gossipers tongue-wagging from both ends if she continued this public outburst in his defense. Damn it, if he could walk he would have stormed onto the stage, dragged her off of it and spirited her away.

"Stop?" She laughed bitterly. "No way, Nate. I'm not going to stop until I've had my say. This festival isn't going to proceed until I'm finished, either."

Katy's gaze swept over the crowd. "For two months Nate Channing has done one good deed after another to improve this community. He has donated his time, labor and money to repairing homes, tidying up empty lots and helping those who need a helping hand. In return, he has been treated like an outcast. But the plain and simple fact is that Nate Channing came back to town to offer this community the economical boost it desperately needs."

Nate knew what was coming next. Katy planned to spill the beans about who owned Sunrise Oil. "Katy, wait!" he called out as he rolled himself toward the stage.

"You have seen the signs posted at the construction site

outside of town," she continued. "The property belongs to Sunrise Oil Company. What you don't know is that Nate Channing owns and operates Sunrise Oil."

Murmurs rippled through the crowd. Nate felt a sea of gazes roll toward him. Well, hell!

"That's right," Katy confirmed. "It was Nate Channing who donated the computers to the school for your children. He also donated tables, chairs and computers to the library. I recently learned from his secretary that he has purchased permanent flag holders and plaques to be placed in the cemetery, honoring our war veterans. He also purchased Christmas decorations and hundreds of strings of lights so we can celebrate the holiday season in style by setting up spectacular light displays in the park and the town square. All these generous contributions were offered to bring pride in the community and economic growth to people who have looked upon Nate with suspicion and mistrust.

"If any one of you would have encountered the same obstacles Nate Channing faced, when he tried to give something back to his hometown, you would have thrown up your hands and left town weeks ago," Katy thundered. "But did Nate quit on you? No, he kept working to better this community. He has already put five young boys to work and taught them to give of their time and effort to improving their community. He has become the stand-up role model who has taught his young charges to take pride in themselves, to live up to their potential."

Hundreds of gazes swung to Nate, then bounced back to Katy.

"He plans to open the branch office for his oil company here and staff it with people from his hometown. He could have constructed those offices anywhere. But he chose to do it here. God knows why, since this town hasn't given him the slightest respect or encouragement. Yet, Nate is determined to increase family incomes and see that this town prospers. There will be more opportunity for job advancement and more money in our pockets because of Nate Channing's generosity."

Nate sat there in his wheelchair, staring at Katy with a sense of amazement. It suddenly dawned on him that she had come an incredibly long way these past two months. The first time he'd seen her she couldn't make eye contact with him. She barely spoke above a whisper for fear of calling attention to herself, and she downplayed her femininity. Yet, here she was, a microphone in one hand, waving wildly with the other, and reading the citizens of Coyote Flats every last paragraph of the riot act.

Whew! She was blasting away at folks with both barrels—on his behalf. She scolded folks as if they were naughty children for doubting his acts of kindness and generosity, for believing Lester's propaganda about Nate's drug activities.

"And you, Lester Brown, you have deceived us by blackening Nate Channing's name and reputation," Katy blustered. "Actually, you are the one who has been trafficking drugs and stashing the illegal substances in your barn and then dispensing them throughout Texas!"

A tidal wave of gasps swept through the crowd.

Nate's mouth dropped open as he swiveled in his chair to see the color drain from Lester's ruddy face.

Silence descended when Sheriff Peterson, retired Sheriff Fuzz Havern and three special agents from the Drug Enforcement Agency strode forward to read Lester his rights. He was cuffed and led away, while John Jessup received his Miranda warning for being an accomplice in drug trafficking. Nate was still trying to shut his sagging mouth when Jessup was bustled away and stuffed into a patrol car.

All eyes, Nate's included, swung back to the stage where Katy stood in all her oratorical splendor and glory.

"It is time Nate Channing had his day," Katy declared. "It is time we opened our hearts and our minds to this kind, generous man. We, the citizens of this community, let ourselves be taken in by scheming criminals. We allowed the worst elements in society to do our thinking and to turn us against the one man who came here to make a difference, to help us improve our lives. Incomes generated from Sunrise Oil promise the dawn of a new day for this town. We have a chance to make a new beginning and look to a progressive future.''

Katy paused, then stared at the crowd for a long moment. ''And do you know why Nate Channing has worked tirelessly for this community? Well, I'll be happy to tell you why. Because he wanted to give every last person in Coyote Flats something you weren't willing to give him. *A second chance.*''

Nate swore a feather could have dropped on the street and it would have sounded like a nuclear bomb. The crowd gathered in a semicircle around him. He could feel them inching closer, feel their gazes zero in on him. But Nate's absolute attention was transfixed on the woman standing at center stage in that yellow dress that complimented her complexion and her shapely figure. All the love and pride and affection Katy felt for him was radiating from her face, from her eyes.

''Don't you think a man who has given so much, who has dedicated himself to giving even more to this community, deserves a second chance? Nate Channing gave me a second chance in life. I had all but given up on myself until he showed up. I owe him the greatest of favors, and so do the rest of you. If Nate Channing isn't the Citizen of the Year, maybe of the *decade,* then I don't know who is!''

Then suddenly, Nate couldn't see Katy, because the citizens of Coyote Flats swarmed around him. Hands thrust forward in greeting. Heartfelt apologies flowed like a roaring river bursting through a dam. Thank-yous flooded from smiling lips. People patted him on the shoulder and inquired about the extent of his injuries.

They came in droves, young and old alike.

When Alice Phelps approached, she flung her arms around

Nate's neck and hugged the stuffing out of him, apologizing profusely for not being neighborly. Alice set a precedent and Nate found himself hugged and kissed on the cheek about a hundred times the next half hour.

People lined up on the sidewalk, waiting their turn to express appreciation for his generosity. For the first time in Nate's life he actually felt as if he belonged in this town. He was being treated with the kind of respect and friendship he thought he'd never get.

And all because Katy had stood up for him, refused to let the misinformed citizens defeat him. No one had ever stood up for him like that. Oh, certainly, Fuzz and Bud had instructed and guided him, but Katy Bates had taken on the entire town for him!

Nate received so many dinner invitations that he wouldn't have to eat at home until Thanksgiving. And damned if Nate didn't think it was a grand idea to name every festivity and business establishment after the town's namesake. In fact, he was feeling so good he wanted to throw back his head and howl with the coyotes.

When the receiving line dwindled down and folks wandered off to enjoy the food and craft booths, Nate saw Fuzz Havern ambling toward him.

"My, my, aren't you the celebrity around here," Fuzz said, chuckling.

"Thanks to Katy." Nate craned his neck in an effort to locate Katy. He knew he was still wearing a stupid smile that was a combination of pride, relief and immeasurable pleasure. "Where is Katy, anyway?"

"Aw, you know Katy," Fuzz said, then shrugged. "She's always working behind the scenes during events like this. While everybody else is wandering around, enjoying themselves, she is serving the community in whatever capacity she's needed."

Nate frowned curiously as Fuzz rolled him down the sidewalk to purchase lemonade from one of the food booths. "How did you find out that Lester was storing and distributing drugs?"

"I didn't," Fuzz replied. "Katy did."

Nate's eyebrows jackknifed. "Katy?"

"Yup. The superhero herself. Still blows my mind to think she is the same reclusive woman who slunk around here the past few years. You worked a miracle on her." Fuzz stopped to buy Nate and himself a drink, then he took a long sip. "Mmm, nothing better than fresh-squeezed lemonade."

"Nothing better," Nate agreed. "Now, you were about to tell me how Katy got involved in a drug bust."

"She drove out to talk to Lester last night," Fuzz reported. "She noticed some suspicious activity going on in Lester's barn. Hay bales were being delivered and unloaded, then the trucks drove off without flicking on the headlights. It made her suspicious, so she hiked across the pasture to investigate. Then she gave me a call to come take a look at what she had stumbled onto."

"So that's where you rushed off to last night," Nate guessed.

Fuzz nodded his buzzed head. "When I got to the barn, Katy and I clipped open a couple of hay bales. We found plastic sacks filled with all sorts of illegal substances. I called Sheriff Peterson, who contacted the DEA. This morning, while Lester made his usual trip to the café, we took a search warrant with us and seized possession of the stash. We also searched Lester's house and found smaller sacks of the drugs that he was preparing for distribution. Then we searched Jessup's home and vehicle and we found another stash of illegal substances."

"I'm surprised Lester didn't claim I had set him up to take the fall," Nate muttered, then sipped his lemonade.

"Yeah, Katy was worried about that, so she decided to kill two birds with one stone by socking it to the folks of Coyote

Flats to let them know how badly they had misjudged you and simultaneously lowering the boom on Lester. The poor bastard was so shocked to learn that his illegal activities had been discovered that he didn't have time to protest and hurl accusations at you.''

Fuzz grinned in supreme satisfaction. ''Ole Lester was too busy listening to the reading of his rights and watching me cuff him to think straight. I think it's fitting that Lester and his worthless son are going to be reunited…in prison. Good place for the both of them, in my opinion.''

Nate decided it was very fitting that the son who set him up sixteen years ago, and the father who had been giving Nate grief since he returned, got exactly what they deserved. Maybe there was justice somewhere in this world. For a while there, Nate had just about given up on truth, justice and the good old American way.

He had also given up on himself and this town.

But Katy, like a fairy princess, had waved her magic wand and made everything turn out right.…

And she claimed that Nate didn't trust her enough to take command of a difficult situation.…

Nate winced uneasily when he realized Katy had been right about him. For years he had depended solely upon himself and expected nothing from no one. He was afraid to put complete faith in Katy, didn't think she could assume command of his business dealings without botching up. He had been so busy trying to protect her that he hadn't stopped to realize that she had become the epitome of capability and reliability—his equal in every arena.

Damn, thought Nate, he had some serious apologizing to do. He glanced around, but still he saw neither hide nor hair of Katy. Apparently, Wonder Woman's mission was finished here, so she had sailed off on her next crusade.

''Fuzz, I have a favor to ask,'' Nate said abruptly.

''Ask away,'' Fuzz replied.

When Nate pointed to one of the stores on Main Street, Fuzz chuckled in amusement. ''Fasten your seat belt, son,'' he said as he took control of the wheelchair. ''We're going to see how fast this chair can fly without mowing down half the citizens in Coyote Flats. Hot damn, this is turning out to be one hell of a day!''

Chapter Fifteen

Katy was totally exhausted by the time she came down from her adrenaline high and completed all her duties for the spring festival. After a week of nonstop activity, she wanted nothing more than to soak in a bubble bath, then fall into bed and wake up a week from Saturday. She had accomplished her purpose at the Festival of the Coyote. She had given her rousing speech to restore Nate's reputation, and she had seen to it that Lester and John had received their just desserts.

Of course, next week was going to be every bit as busy and hectic, she reminded herself. She still had several duties to attend, more arrangements to make. She was also going to have to squeeze in time to pack up her belongings and move out of this house—her father's monument to propriety, wealth and prestige. But it was right and fitting, Katy mused as she peeled off her clothes and sank into the steamy bath.

Katy had only enjoyed five minutes of peaceful solitude when someone rapped soundly on the door.

"Aunt Katy?"

Ah, would the day ever come when she could take a relaxing bath without interruption? "What is it, Tammy?"

"I talked to Daddy a while ago, and he said your idea sounded super to him. He said all systems are go. We can move whenever we want, and he'll be back next weekend to help."

"How are things going for James in China?" Katy called out.

"Daddy says things are going so well that he can leave a day early and fly to Washington, D.C., to wrap up the negotiations, then be back here for a few days of vacation. He wants to take me to Dallas on a shopping spree if we can fit it into our moving schedule. Can I go?"

Katy smiled in satisfaction. Her brother must have taken part of her lecture to heart. James was making an effort to spend quality time with Tammy.

"We'll work around your Dallas trip," Katy assured her niece.

"Thanks, Aunt Katy! You're the best…and is it okay if Chad and I borrow your car? We want to cruise down to Coyote Grill for an hour or so."

"The keys are on the kitchen table. Don't lay rubber. I prefer to keep it on my tires."

When Tammy bounded off, Katy sank into the tub. Alone at last! She was going to vegetate until every ache and pain caused from standing on her feet, serving sloppy joes, chili dogs and hamburgers at the church food booth, eased off. Her gimpy leg was killing her, and it had been for hours on end.

A faint smile pursed her lips, recalling the stunned expression on Nate's face when she stamped onto the stage and grabbed the microphone. The truth was that she had been nervous as all get-out. She had planned that entire scene and had been waiting for Lester to open his big mouth. Even though she had rehearsed what she wanted to say, her heart had pounded ninety miles a minute while she stared at the crowd that focused full attention on her.

After so many years of skulking around, making very little social contact and doing no public speaking whatsoever, Katy figured her legs would fold up and her voice would crack in mid-speech. But all it had taken was one glance at Nate sitting there in his wheelchair, and her courage was fortified instantly. The words she wanted to say came pouring out.

That moment had been worth all her preliminary apprehension. When she saw the citizens of Coyote Flats gather around Nate, her heart nearly burst from her chest. She had succeeded in her campaign to put Nate's bad reputation behind him. At long last, he had earned respect and had been recognized as the honorable, generous man he had become. People had extended their hands in acceptance—the one thing Nate desperately needed.

Right about now, if she knew Nate—and she had come to know and understand him exceptionally well—he was feeling elated, yet disappointed in himself.

As well he should, thought Katy. After he turned her life around for her, he should have realized that she felt the need to come to his rescue at the lowest moment in his life. But he hadn't trusted her to handle his duties while he was laid up. He hadn't had faith in her to protect and provide for him, just as he protected and provided for her.

Until today, Nate had played the role of protector. He had provided strength, encouragement and inspiration for Katy. The moment Nate had been injured had become a turning point in their relationship. Katy needed to show her strength of character, and Nate needed to know that he could count on her when he was down and out. She wanted to be on equal footing with him, to prove to him, and to herself, that she was worthy of his love.

Katy suspected that Nate was feeling ashamed of himself for ordering her out of his life and giving up the fight. Of course, he wouldn't come crawling back, begging for forgiveness. He couldn't, not with his sprained knee and cracked ribs. That would be too painful. She did, however, expect to hear from him in a day or two. The man loved her, after all. It was in the sound of his voice, his deeds and actions, his incomparable gentleness. Katy had suspected it when Nate showed up in town and began spending his time trying to reconstruct her self-confidence and enthusiasm.

Yet, until today, Katy hadn't felt she was equal to the remarkable man he had become. Now she could stand beside him as his partner…provided she hadn't become overly optimistic about his feelings for her. In which case, she was going to feel like a complete idiot if she had misjudged Nate.

The negative thought made Katy squirm in her bath. Nate did love her…didn't he?

With Tammy, Chad and Fuzz's help, Nate was situated at the foot of the steps that led to Katy's upstairs bedroom. The engagement ring that he and Fuzz had purchased at the jewelry store that morning was burning a hole in Nate's pocket. All day, Nate had tried to single out Katy, but she had been busy serving food and drinks to festival-goers and dashing off to replenish supplies.

Although Fuzz had suggested that Nate put his plans on hold until tomorrow, he refused to wait. Tired though he was, he needed to get things settled between Katy and him. His guilty conscience was gnawing at him, and he couldn't tolerate much more of it.

When Tammy, Chad and Fuzz filed out the door, Nate stared at the staircase. He couldn't walk up the steps, but he was determined to catch Katy's attention. Nate threw back his head and howled at the top of his lungs.

                              * * *

Katy sat straight up in the bathtub when a strange howling
noise floated toward her, then faded into silence. She waited
a moment, then resumed bathing.

The howling sound erupted again.

"Now, what?" Katy grumbled as she came to her feet, then
grabbed a towel.

The unidentified sound grew louder and louder. Muttering
about the interruption of her long-awaited bath, Katy donned
her bathrobe and strode down the hall. She stumbled to a halt
and stared down at Nate, who was positioned at the foot of
the steps. His head was tipped back and he was howling like
a dying coyote.

"You could have rung the doorbell," she yelled over his
howls.

Nate grinned at her. "Yeah, but this is more appropriate."
His gaze ran the full length of her. "I must have interrupted
your bath."

"Yes, but there will be other baths," Katy said as she descended the steps. She sank down in front of Nate to appraise
the broad grin that affected every handsome feature on his
face. "Did you come by to chew me out for exposing all your
carefully guarded secrets to the folks in Coyote Flats?"

"Nope. That was some speech you gave, Katy," Nate complimented her. "I wish I had it on tape."

Katy lounged on the staircase, grinning smugly. "I was
pretty darn good, wasn't I?"

"You were terrific. The best."

"Thank you." She beamed at him. "So…I assume you
came by to apologize."

Nate shifted awkwardly in his wheelchair. "I behaved like
an ass," he admitted. "If I had been able to stand up, I would
have been kicking myself repeatedly for sending you away,
for not having the kind of faith in you that you've had in me.
I guess I convinced myself years ago that I had to make it on
my own, that relying on someone else would end in disap-

pointment, because my parents disappointed me time and time again.''

''Oh, Nate...'' Katy's eyes clouded with tears when she realized what he was trying *not* to say. He was still trying to spare her feelings, still trying to protect her. He hadn't asked for her assistance, wouldn't let himself expect it, because he didn't want to be disappointed in *her,* in case she failed him the way his parents had. He hadn't wanted her to come to his rescue, because he refused to let her take a chance on letting him down. He'd cared enough to ensure that didn't happen by shooing her away, refusing to let her stand in his stead.

His heart was in the right place, she supposed. But because of his disappointments in childhood, his methods were distorted. God love him, he had only been trying to spare her, and him.

Nate stared at the air over her left shoulder, then shifted awkwardly. ''The truth is that I've always wanted to be your knight in shining armor. I wasn't there to rescue you from your hellish marriage. When I ended up flat on my back, defeated by a drunk, who was just like my own father, I figured I had failed miserably again.''

''You have always been my hero, Nate,'' Katy told him, ''even when you were flat on your back. Maybe you haven't realized it yet, but I needed you to rely on me when you were down and out. I need to be needed, too, Nate. We both do.''

He looked directly at her then. ''I'm so damn sorry that I sent you away, Katy, sorry that I didn't offer you the confidence and faith you needed. But never doubt that I want and need you. That's been the one constant in my life. Whether or not I thought I deserved you didn't matter. I still wanted you.

''Then, like a fool, I struck out at Lester and John and all the people in Coyote Flats who rejected me, and I ended up taking out my pain and frustration on you. You're the very last person on Earth that I wanted to hurt.''

"I know," she said simply.

He did a double take. "You do?"

"You said you were crazy about me, remember?"

"Well, that wasn't entirely correct," Nate amended, smiling. "It goes a lot deeper than that." He reached for her hand, bringing it to his lips. "It goes heart-deep, soul-deep. Maybe I did come from bad breeding and a bad background, but you taught me to have pride in myself, to live up to my potential, to make something of myself."

"You certainly did that," she assured him. "You are the best thing that ever happened to this town. And most certainly, you are the best thing that ever happened to me."

"I'm truly sorry about the other night," Nate apologized again. "If I could retract what I said, I would—a dozen times over."

She smiled adoringly at him. "It's already forgotten. People often say a lot of things they don't really mean when their spirits are deflated and they are in excruciating pain. I know, because I have been there and done that."

Nate knew she understood completely because she had suffered heartache and injuries far worse than his. She understood everything he had lived through because she loved him....

Suddenly, Nate realized that no matter how deep his anger, despair and pain, the knowledge that Katy loved him had been there with him all week. He had never doubted Katy's affection. She had proved it with her words and deeds. Even when he turned his back on her and stumbled in defeat, he had known that she still cared about him.

"Katy, there's something I need to tell you," Nate whispered as he held her hand in his. He met her gaze, hypnotized by that twinkle of spirit in her eyes, the way her smile cut a dimple in her left cheek. "I love you. I never stopped loving you, either. Will you give me a second chance to prove that you have all my faith, my trust and my love?"

"Oh, Nate!" Katy launched herself at him, her arms twining around his neck.

"Ouch!" Nate grimaced when she collided with his tender ribs. "Uh-oh…" He knew they were in trouble when he felt the wheelchair rear back. He shouldn't have set the brake when he positioned himself at the bottom of the stairs. Big mistake. Katy's forward momentum set the chair off balance and Nate was flat on his back before he could brace himself for the blow.

"Ow, that really hurts!" he squawked.

"Oh, God, I'm sorry!" Katy bounded off him before she caused further injury. "Are you okay?"

"No, I'm not okay," Nate wheezed as he rolled carefully to his side, then climbed from the overturned chair. "I'm not going to be okay until you accept this." He steadied himself on his good knee, reached into his pocket for the jewelry case, then presented it to Katy. "Marry me, sweetheart. I want the right to hold you, to love you for all the days of my life, because there is a place in my heart where you've always been, where you'll always be."

Tears streamed down her cheeks, and her hands trembled as she opened the velvet case to see diamonds winking up at her. "It's beautiful," she breathed raggedly.

He slipped the ring on her finger, watching the stones glitter with promises of their future—save one. Katy had yet to promise that she would marry him. He wondered if she was hesitant because her first marriage had been pure hell.

"Katy? You will marry me, won't you?"

Katy stared at him through a mist of tears, then broke into a dazzling smile. "Of course I'll marry you. I *have* to marry you."

His mouth dropped open. "Are you pregnant?"

"I don't know about that yet, but Fuzz and I made arrangements to convert this house into a combination of community foster home and safe house for abused and neglected children.

Millie agreed to be a part-time house mother and Mary Jane is going to do the cooking. I could live with my brother, but I was sort of hoping I could live with you instead.''

"You made all the arrangements while you were juggling my business dealings, working at the library and helping plan the Festival of the Coyote?'' Nate stared at her in astonishment. "When did you have time to do that?''

"I *made* time,'' Katy clarified. "The boys in your crew need a place that feels like home, a place where they are surrounded by people who care about them. As soon as I find a replacement at the library, I plan to manage the house.''

She smiled wryly. "It seemed only right that my father's home should become a haven for kids he considered beneath the Bates's social status, don't you agree?''

Nate nodded his head. "You are something else, woman.''

"No,'' she contradicted. "I'm someone much better because of you. And so are those boys who are going to have the chance in life they deserve.''

"I'm hoping there will be some boys and girls in our future. Our children,'' Nate murmured. "I may not know how to be the world's greatest father, but I promise you that I will be totally committed to you and our babies, Katy.''

When Katy pressed her lips to his and told Nate she would marry him any day of the week, Nate forgot about the dull pain in his ribs, the throbbing ache in his knee. And there, at the foot of the steps, on the plush carpet, he took Katy in his arms and communicated his love for her. In turn, she thoroughly expressed her love for him.

Nate had never experienced such tenderness, desire and completeness. It seemed he had waited all his life to know what it felt like to be well and truly loved, to be loved in return, to be wanted, needed and appreciated.

Katy convinced him that he made all her dreams come true with each heated kiss, each sizzling caress. And when they came together, one heart beating for another, he knew without question that all the heartache and pain of his past had taught him to recognize and appreciate the true gift of life. Every obstacle he had overcome had made him the kind of man who was worthy to receive Katy's unconditional love.

That bitter, defiant kid who had left Coyote Flats had returned as a man. It was his love for Katy that had caused him to be sent away, but it was that same enduring love that had brought him back to stay.

Nate was convinced that the right kind of love had come along at the wrong time in his life. He and Katy had been too young the first time around. But what they shared, what they felt for each other, refused to fade with the passage of time. If not for second chances, Nate wouldn't have known such pleasure, such incredible happiness.

He had become exceptionally fond of second chances and was convinced that everybody deserved them.

"Nate?" Katy murmured a long while later.

"Mmm" was about all he could get out, so sated and content was he.

"Tammy and Chad are going to be back soon. I don't think we would be setting a good example if they found us naked in the dining room."

Nate opened his eyes and stared up at the steps, then shifted his attention to the formal dining room suite to his left. "Probably not," he agreed.

"Do you think you can get up?"

He grinned at her concerned expression. "Because of you, Katy Marie, I'm pretty sure I could fly if I needed to."

She returned his grin, then reached for the pile of discarded clothes beside them. "I thought *we* just did."

He chuckled as she helped him back into his clothes. "You know, Katy Marie, I think we're going to be doing a lot of flying the next hundred years or so."

"You can count on it, Nathan Daniel." She glanced toward the window. "But you better get out of your holding pattern and put down your landing gear, because the kids just pulled into the driveway.''

"Well, hell," Nate grumbled as he hurriedly fastened his jeans, then wrestled with his shirt.

By the time Tammy and Chad, with Fuzz Havern on their heels, came through the front door, Nate and Katy managed to sit upright on the steps. The dreamy-eyed teenagers might not have realized what had occurred during their absence, but nothing escaped Fuzz's observant gaze. He grinned in wry amusement as he and Chad maneuvered Nate into the wheelchair he'd fallen from.

Fuzz glanced deliberately at the engagement ring that he had helped Nate select that morning. "Katy must've said yes to you more than once tonight," Fuzz murmured confidentially.

Nate flushed with embarrassment. "Er...she did agree to marry me. Will you be my best man, Fuzz?"

"I'll be proud to stand up with you, son," Fuzz replied. "But as far as I'm concerned, you are the best man I've ever met."

"I couldn't agree more." The smile that blossomed on Katy's face took Nate's breath away. "I'm going to spend the rest of my life loving the very best man *I* ever met. That's a given."

When Katy bent to brush her lips over his, Nate knew that the past was truly behind him. He and Katy had survived the worst, tested their strengths to the limits and proved to themselves, and to each other, that they had earned the right to happiness, earned the right to share this special kind of enduring love.

Epilogue

Fuzz Havern sat on the porch swing, holding a baby girl in one arm and cuddling a little boy on his lap. The mutt called Taz nudged his nose under the boy's arm, begging for attention. Taz was absolutely crazy about these two kids.

A wide grin spread across Fuzz's lips as he watched Katy and Nate stroll down the hill toward the spring-fed pond that glistened with the spectacular colors of sunset.

Damn but life was good, thought Fuzz. He had two babies who called him Grandpa and a young couple who called him Dad. Fuzz hadn't been blessed with children and grandchildren until Nate Channing made him a part of his family.

Yes siree, things had changed in this Podunk town, he mused. These days, Katy and Nate were the heart and soul of Coyote Flats. Katy's safe house for abused and neglected children was a godsend to the community. Nate's oil business provided better career opportunities and higher incomes for citizens who had been struggling to make ends meet. New businesses were springing up in town, and the place was jumping with optimism.

The boys Nate had taken under his wing had graduated from high school and were attending college in Odessa, while working part-time at Sunrise Oil's main office. Tammy and her father had grown exceptionally close these past few years, and she was also attending college in Odessa so she and Chad could spend their spare time together.

Everybody around town knew that if you were down and out, Katy and Nate would offer you a helping hand. The love they shared just kept bubbling up and overflowing on the folks in Coyote Flats.

Damn good thing Nate Channing had come back to town, thought Fuzz. If not for Nate, this place would've dried up and blown away a few years back. There would've been nothing here but the lonely, forlorn howls of coyotes.

Kinda made a man believe in miracles. Kinda made a man proud that he had taken time to touch the life of a wayward kid who'd run clean out of places to turn all those years ago.

"Look, Grandpa." Justin Channing pointed his pint-size finger at the couple silhouetted against the sunset. "Daddy's kissing Mommy again."

"Yup, he sure 'nuff is," Fuzz replied, chuckling. "He does that a lot, doesn't he?"

The small, dark head bobbed. "Lots."

"That's because your mommy and daddy love each other as much as they love you and your baby sister."

Justin reached out to pat Andrea Channing's tiny, delicate hand. "That's lots," the toddler confirmed.

Fuzz smiled as indescribable warmth filled his heart and soul. There wasn't anybody within a hundred miles of Coyote Flats who didn't know how much Nate loved his wife and kids. It was magical, inspiring. But then, that's the way true love should be, Fuzz thought as he stared down the hill. Katy